I0552360

REDEEMING THE PLAYBOY

S.L. SCOTT

Second Edition
Copyright © S.L. Scott, 2019

All Rights Reserved.

Except as permitted under the U.S. Copyright Act of 1976, no part of this publication may be reproduced, distributed or transmitted in any form or by any means, or stored in a database or retrieval system, without the written permission of the author.

This is a work of fiction. Names, characters, places, and incidents are either a product of the author's imagination or are used fictitiously. Any resemblance to actual people living or dead, events or locales is entirely coincidental.

Published in the United States of America

ISBN: 978-1-940071-86-2

Cover design by Kari March Designs

You're the sky.
I'm the Earth.

1

MALLORY

"You always look incredible, but more in a beach-laidback-natural-hottie kind of way," Sunny says, smiling. My childhood friend has always been a great confidence booster. She pushes my long brown hair behind my shoulders, appraising and approving. "You're going to knock your man's flip flops off when he sees you all dressed up at the party tonight."

I love my friends but the attention, although lovely, makes me feel self-conscious. I turn toward the mirror and pat the blush pink mini-dress fabric down over my stomach, which is noticeably flatter and toner under this fitted material. There's no hiding in something so tight, but this dress has a sweet charm of innocence about it as well. It's appropriate for meeting the parents and impressing the boyfriend equally.

Doing a turn to see the back of the dress, I realize I've been vacationing in paradise over a month now. Hawaii is more amazing than I expected and a bonus is that I'm much more active here than back at school, where I'm bogged down with schoolwork and part-time jobs. I've caught the Aloha spirit and I can already tell it's going to be hard to board that plane back to Colorado in August.

"You make that dress look amazing, Mallory." Evan's sister, Kate, stands behind me and our eyes connect in the mirror's reflection.

"No lie?" I say, needing to be reassured one more time.

"No lie," she responds softly and smiles. "Evan is gonna love it on you."

Feeling my cheeks heat, I look down, thinking of Evan. My boyfriend. *My sexy surfer*—the man I've fallen head over heels, hands, and common sense for since the moment I landed on the island. He's the hottest guy I've ever seen and all that's sexy—his hard, chiseled body, his sun-lightened messy hair, his brilliant mind, and his smooth-talking lines —yep, all mine. Although I shouldn't admit it, I'm in way too deep with him and too happy and in love to care. Looking into the mirror again, I smile. This time because Sunny and Kate are right. Evan is going to love this dress.

"A toast is in order," Kate says as she pours three glasses of champagne. "This is our only chance to look fancy in Hawaii." She raises her glass into the air and we follow suit. "Here's to Fourth of July parties, carefree summers, and our sexy men!"

We clink glasses and drink, downing more than half the champagne. Liquid courage is needed for me to show off this dress like it deserves.

As I put on my makeup, Kate sits next to me on the bed. Her bedroom at her parent's Hawaiian mansion is where we decided to get ready for their annual Fourth of July party. Her room is spacious, spotless, and very feminine. Each of us sets up in a corner and we spread our stuff out. "You know, Evan's told me how much he loves your eyes. He called them hopeful and infinite," she says casually.

After spending half my summer getting to know Evan's stunning sister, I've come to realize that Kate never says anything casual. She's smart as a whip and usually two steps ahead with a plan or two that she's plotting. I don't doubt her sincerity when it comes to our friendship. I know she likes me and has been a big supporter of my relationship with her brother, which she's had to defend. Deep down I feel their mother hates me for winning her golden boy's heart.

"Really?" I ask, touched that Evan would confide in her like that.

"Yes, he found some sea glass down on the beach yesterday and said it reminded him of your pretty green eyes." She leans over for a closer look. "You do have pretty eyes."

"Thanks. You know, I always wanted blue like Evan's when I was little."

"So did I." She bats her lashes at me and smirks. "Instead, I got my father's brown eyes."

I laugh and dig my mascara out of my bag. "I've been meaning to ask you, and please don't feel pressured to tell me or anything, but I've been curious about Evan's past."

She takes the mascara from me and says, "I'll do your lashes. Look up at the ceiling for me."

Following her instructions, I look up as she coats my upper lashes, not sure if I really want to know about Evan's mysterious past or not. Evan is amazing. I have no doubt that he loves me even though he hasn't returned the verbal endearment yet. Something deep inside is keeping him from opening up the way I want, the way I'm ready for him to and I want to know what that is, so I prod. "Something happened to him and I think it's why he had trouble at college." I leave it at that to observe her reaction.

She stops and looks up at the ceiling, pondering what I've said. "Evan hasn't told you what happened four years ago?"

"No," I shake my head, my stomach twisting in anxiety.

A smile appears, soft and understanding. "I promised him a long time ago that I wouldn't tell anyone. But you should know that although what he went through was painful for me and my parents, it changed who he is. It changed us all. That's all I feel I can share without breaking my promise to him."

I'm a bit disappointed, but not surprised by her words. My conversation with Ms. Chart the night I met her leads me to think the same. Whatever his secret is, he's keeping it that way for a reason, but I can't help my curiosity and hope he trusts me enough to tell me one day.

An hour later, we're ready with our hair styled, our party dresses on, and feeling bubbly like the two bottles of champagne we polished off. We walk through the breakfast room and out the open doors that lead to the pool. The deck area is beautifully decorated, his mother's attention to detail on full display. The party has begun and I see the first few guests ordering cocktails from the bar. Looking around, I don't see Evan, so I follow the girls to the bar.

"Katie, you look beautiful." I hear a male voice greet her from behind me.

"Hi, Daddy," Kate says with a bright smile, her eyes lighting up and arms going out for a hug. "Let me introduce you to my friends. Hugh Ashford, this is Sunny Ladell and *this* is Mallory Wray." She winks at me then looks back at her father. "Mallory is Evan's girlfriend."

"It's very nice to meet you." His eyes scan mine like he's trying to understand something. It becomes obvious his wife has told him about me. He probably expected a three-headed monster after listening to her. "I've heard a lot about you," he says, and it makes me wonder if he means from Evan or his mother, but I don't dare ask. "You're very lovely."

"Thank you," I respond. "I've heard a lot about you too, Mr. Ashford."

"That can't be good, but I'm not afraid of a little hard work to prove all those rumors wrong. And please call me Hugh." We laugh politely, and then he says, "I hope you ladies have a nice time tonight and please try not to send my guests to the hospital." He leans closer. "Three beautiful women, lots of old men with weak hearts, you could do a lot of damage at this party." He winks at us, leaving us giggling as he walks away to greet other guests.

He was not what I expected at all. *How is he the husband of the Wicked Witch of the Upper East Side?*

"I'll call and find out what's holding up the guys," Kate says. "Make yourselves at home. Food is over there. The bar is behind you."

"I should've used the bathroom before we came out. Want to come with me?" Sunny asks.

"Nah, go ahead," I reply, "I'll be here." Walking over the large deck to the edge of the grass, I look out at the sunset and think about Evan. The girls made me promise to spend the day with them to prepare, which meant a day away from him. With only a month left on the island, every minute feels precious. My heart speeds up in anticipation of seeing him soon, and I turn to scan the crowd once more. I'm left disappointed and a little anxious he's not here yet.

"Mallory, there you are." Although I recognize this voice of evil, Evan's mother doesn't sound mean . She actually sounds... *friendly*. Maybe this is the turning point, and she has come to accept me. Or maybe I should brace myself. I'm undecided when I turn around.

Claire Ashford is walking toward me with wide open arms and a smile on her face so big it could outshine a movie star's. She takes my hands in hers and holds them out to the side to look me over. "You look nice." She glances behind her then leans in closer, her expression darkens minutely as she says, "There's someone I want you to meet —a friend of Evan's."

Before she finishes her sentence, I see her and the name escapes me before I can stop it. "Kelly." *Stupid, pretty, blonde girl and goodbye kisses at the airport. My Evan.* Jealousy and possessiveness grabs a hold of me as the memory comes back.

"Oh!" Mrs. Ashford exclaims, surprised I know the girl's name. "I wasn't aware you already knew each other."

How could I forget it? The image of her, tears streaking down her tanned skin as she kissed Evan goodbye flashes through my mind. Even then I noticed that she is the opposite of me visually and that instantly turns my stomach inside out. *She's here for him, for my surfer, for my boyfriend, for my Evan. What if he prefers her?* "Shit!" I say, the word blurting out uncontrolled as an ache in my heart overflows into my veins.

Mrs. Ashford drops my hands and looks aghast, gripping her hand against her chest, stunned.

"I'm sorry. I just..." I can't finish. There's no reason for her to be here. *Is there?*

"So you know Kelly or no you don't?" Mrs. Ashford's patience has thinned since her greeting.

"I, um... I don't *know* her," I stutter.

The girl stands tall in front of me, a beauty by everyone's

standards and oblivious to who I am or how truly awkward this situation really is.

"But you said Kelly?" Mrs. Ashford questions.

"Yes, that's right. I'm Kelly. It's nice to meet you and you are?" The girl that I can't look in the eyes asks while offering her hand to shake.

"I'm Evan's girlfriend." The words flow from my mouth, insecurities instantly developing. I know it's immature to stake claim to him, but now I know why he did that big display of a kiss in front of Noah at the restaurant the other day. If he was here, I'd be doing my own public display of affection, marking him as mine right now.

Her tone is clear, with a slight high-pitched tinkering to it when she speaks. "*Oh*, I didn't know he had one. He never told me about you."

"Why are you here?" They probably think something is wrong with me considering the way I'm blurting things out, but I'm confused to why she's here. And she thinks she can show up like this. *Does Evan know she's here? Is she showing up unannounced?* Unless... A thought dawns on me and I stand more upright. My face contorting, hurt and doubt clouding my vision as my gaze lands on Mrs. Ashford who seems to be relishing in the moment with a pleased-as-punch smile and sparkle to her eyes.

"I wanted to surprise him," Kelly says, disregarding what I just said.

"Evan?" I ask as if I expect her to say someone else this time while still praying she means someone else.

"Yes," she answers, annoyed.

"Does he know you're here?"

"*Noooo*, I said 'surprise' him, but I guess we've all been surprised, haven't we?"

"The more the merrier, dear," Mrs. Ashford says, comforting Kelly by rubbing her arm.

I blink rapidly, hoping this nightmare goes away. It's all too much and I need out of this situation. "I'll let him know you came by. It was, um....yeah." That was my weak attempt at getting rid of her, and unfortunately, it doesn't work.

"Sorry for the confusion, Mallory, but Kelly is staying for the party. Isn't that fantastic news?" Mrs. Ashford purrs in victory. "I know Evan will be so happy to see her again."

"Mallory?" Kate appears at my side, stopping my escape. "What's going on?"

She sees my eyes flicker to the stupid, pretty blonde imposter and without missing a beat, Kate introduces herself. After a brief introduction and breakdown of the events, Kate lays it all out like only she can. "So, let me get this straight. You 'hooked up' with Evan back in May and now you're visiting him, uninvited I might add, this weekend? Just showing up out of the blue?"

Kelly glowers at us, but keeps calm, knowing Mother Ashford is on her side. She turns to Kate, and says, "Yes, it's a surprise visit, but I know he'll be happy to see me. We have a special connection."

"You're really going to stand here and say that in front of his girlfriend?" Kate puts her hands on her hips and tilts her head waiting for an answer.

"Kelly's been invited to stay for the party... *by your mother*," I add, further fueling Kate's fire.

I glance over at Mrs. Ashford who shifts and looks over her shoulder to avoid eye contact.

"When I arrived this afternoon," Kelly starts to say, "I discovered that—"

"Mmmhmm, I'm listening. Go on," Kate says, interrupting Kelly with her sarcasm. I love having her on my side.

"I discovered that Evan wasn't home, so I knocked on the main house and Claire invited me in. After hearing my plight, she also offered me a place to stay. We had tea together and I told her all about my brief, but meaningful, relationship with Evan and gladly accepted the offer from *your mother*," Kelly says, crossing her arms and twisting the metaphorical knife deeper into my heart.

"Of course, you would. And plight? *Really?*" Kate rolls her eyes, "Mother, may I speak with you?"

"No. I have guests to tend to. Excuse me, ladies," Mrs. Ashford says, avoiding Kate altogether and walking away from us.

Kate turns to me and says, "Kelly and I need to have a tete-a-tete privately, if you don't mind?"

Kelly's eyes widen and if I'm not mistaken, I spy fear behind her blues.

Quirking my eyebrows in curiosity, I look at her, but she silently tells me to go, and go I do. "Go right ahead." I narrow my eyes at Kelly one more time and see the stubbornness in her stance, ready for a showdown.

After rushing into the house, I run down the corridor, and into the safety of the bathroom. Out of breath, I fall back against the door as tears fall from my eyes. All my fears are being realized as his past comes back to haunt us. I lean against the counter, my palms flat on the cold marble, staring down into the empty sink. I take several deep breaths and try to calm myself, wishing Evan would just get here already.

A light tap on the door is heard and I jump, startled. I swipe under my lids with a tissue trying to hide the fact I was crying before I open the door.

When I see Kelly, I huff in irritation. "What do you want?" I want to wipe that condescending smirk right off her face, but I refuse to play this game with her.

"Mallory, I'm sorry this has been sprung on you. I wasn't aware he had a girlfriend and I feel terrible you've been caught in the middle like this—"

"*In the middle?* I'm not in the middle. I'm firmly at Evan's side."

"That may be true right now, but I thought you should know that he's been texting me all summer. We've even talked a couple of times."

I thought my heart hurt before, but now it shatters as I stare into the face of my undoing. I can't stop the tears, my humiliation and pain worn openly across my face.

She continues and I stay to listen. "If he'd given me any indication that he was taken, I wouldn't be here. I swear to you. I'm disappointed and hurt as much as you are—"

"No, you're not. You were a one week fling. We've been together for..." I stop mid-sentence, realizing that technically we've only been together for a couple of weeks, but we've been playing this love tug-of-war for over a month. I can't explain what Evan and I mean to each other, so I lie. I straighten my shoulders back and affront her. "We've been together over a month now and he's given me no reason to doubt him. So, if you don't mind, I'm taking his word over yours."

"I can show you the last text," she says, lifting her phone up. "Look right here. It says 'Miss you and can't wait for you to return.' " She flashes the phone in front of my eyes then quickly jerks it away.

Seeing it clearly with his name attached, I push past her, needing to find Evan and desperate to get away from this nightmare I'm living.

"I'm also hurt by this," Kelly yells down the hall as I round the corner. I think I also hear her laugh, but I can't be sure, and I'm not stopping to find out.

"Where are they?" I demand, looking at Kate.

"They were hanging out at Murphy's and Zach's. They're on their way. Take a deep breath, Mallory. That girl is not going to bother you tonight and she'll be gone in the morning."

"She has proof that he's been texting her—"

Sunny gasps. "No."

Kate is shaking her head. "She's a lying gold-digger. He hasn't been—"

"She showed me the text."

The group goes silent.

"Sunny, come with me. Mallory, stay put. We'll be right back." Kate drags Sunny into the house to obviously formulate some kind of plan, but this waiting is too much. Evan has some explaining to do and I'm willing to listen, but he's taking forever. My hands begin to shake with the possibility that she might be telling the truth. I turn to the bartender and order a shot. I need something to calm my nerves.

Torturous minutes pass with no sign of Evan. The bartender places another shot down in front of me and I debate for two seconds before I down it. I'm tapping my fingers anxiously on top of the bamboo bar when my phone rings.

I answer in a rush, hoping it's Evan. "Hello?"

"Hey there. I'm glad I caught you."

It's a male voice, but not the one I wanted. "Noah, now's not a good time."

"Bummer. I wanted to take you to the beach to see the big fireworks display. It's pretty awesome."

Tears threaten to fall again from his kindness as my

anxiety over Evans' blonde ex peaks. I can't make a scene at the Ashford's party and I feel I'm close to crossing that line if I wait around any longer. As much I want to talk to Evan, I can't stand here waiting to be humiliated in front of his family and a crowd. I'm losing my grip on my heavy emotions, feeling the betrayal of Evan engulfing my more rational thoughts. The only way we can survive this night is to abandon it until tomorrow. There's nothing I can say to Evan that won't come out as an accusation covered in my pain. There's nothing he can say to justify what I just had to endure at the hands of a girl that fits into his charmed life so well, a girl that his mother supports to be on my boyfriend's arm for all to see.

No, I can't do this tonight, not here. Not if we have any chance of not letting the situation destroy everything we want so badly. I make the one choice that seems reasonable when not entirely sober. I decide to go just for now, just for the night. I decide to go and give my alcohol-tinged insecurities time to taper off and for my hurting heart to heal. I'll go for me, but I'll also go for Evan, so he doesn't have to deal with the crazy that is sure to come if I see him now.

"I'll go," I whisper hesitantly, looking around, needing a savior, needing a friend, needing Evan to save me from this sinking sorrow that's overwhelming me, but he's not here.

"I'll pick you up," Noah offers.

I take a deep breath, and then say with a heavy heart, "I'm at the Ashford's."

"Oh, um... okay. It's probably best if you meet me out front in about ten minutes then."

"Okay." I hang up and call Evan, but it goes straight to voicemail. "Call me, okay. I need to talk to you, babe. It's important. Call me as soon as you get this message." I hear the tremble in my tone as I leave the voicemail. Turning around, my eyes lock on Kelly across the pool. She's charming the pants off Evan's parents. With one sideways glance in my direction, she makes it clear that she's here to stay, further cementing my decision to walk away before it's too late for me to have something to return to.

2

MALLORY

Ten minutes. Ten minutes of pure torture. Kate has done her best to pass the time, shamelessly trying to entertain me with stories of wild society parties she used to attend in The Hamptons. Sunny sets me up with another cocktail and I'm staring toward the side path everyone is using tonight in hopes of seeing Evan walk in sooner rather than later.

Kelly is keeping her distance from me. Wise move. She's also been working the crowd like she's already an Ashford. Her charm and etiquette is more polished than my average upbringing in Colorado afforded. She's all about the social graces and seems to be winning everyone over.

"They'll be here any minute now, Mal," Sunny reassures me, rubbing my back. "Don't worry. We know the truth. Don't believe that conniving witch."

Noah rounds the corner, making his way through the crowd after spotting me on the other side of the pool. He leans in toward my ear, still smiling, and says, "Hi, I waited out front. You ready, cuz this is not the most friendly of parties, if you know what I mean. Enemy territory and all."

"Yeah, I guess," I say, glancing behind him one last time

for Evan. I've had a lot to drink and I'm not feeling reasonable, much less in control of my emotions if provoked. Looking over at Kelly, I can tell she's waiting to incite. I don't want Evan's parents to hate me more than they already do.

Sunny reaches for my hand, a desperate plea in her eyes. "Mallory, please wait. He'll be her—"

"What the fuck are you doing here, Kalei? This is a private party." Evan and his perfect timing have arrived. He takes possession of my hand, and pulls me to his side.

My eyes land on *her* as she saunters up next to him, all fake smile and evil glints reflecting in her eyes as she glares in my direction.

"Here you are, Evan. I was wondering where you ran off to," she says, her hand taking to his bicep like it belongs there, rubbing up and down.

"What are you doing here?" he asks, looking at her like he's seen a ghost... a ghost from his past.

I step away from him, releasing his hand as I feel the invisible sucker punch to my gut at her familiarity with him, how her devious grin looks as if she remembers every touch they've shared, knowledge she's silently taunting me with as she sends painful blows to my already bruised ego. She knows his mother despises me and her confident smile messes with my inebriated mind. His words of surprise at seeing her are lost to the focus I have on her hand, to the way she's touching him. Even when he pulls away, their tie that once bound them is still evident. I need to flee the scene before I breakdown, before I show Kelly and his witch of a mother that they've won, that they've beaten me.

"Mallory?" he says, but in my alcohol-induced brain, his voice sounds distant.

Noah understands my reaction as he surveys the scene.

I can tell by the sympathy in his expression. "Mallory, I can take you home." His words are just as careful as his actions.

The attention we'd garnered from other guests fades, their interest falling back into their own cliquish conversations. Tears gather under my lids while listening to Kelly laugh at my expense. "Evan, your mother wants to speak with you." Kelly's charm school training mixed with her expert back-stabbing skills leave me stunned. It's only a matter of time before her magic begins to work on Evan.

I turn to go, recognizing when I've become a third wheel.

"Mallory, what's going on? Why are you leaving?" Evan's tone wavers between confusion and aggravation as he speaks to my back.

A quick peek over my shoulder is my undoing. He's walked away from her, but the drinks add to the emotional weight of the situation, blurring any clarity I thought I could hold onto. I turn completely around and look him in the eyes before I lose my pride and the last shred of my sanity in the middle of this party. "I need to go. I'm sorry, Evan. I just do."

"No." He's firm in his conviction like he has every right to say so. He comes closer. His eyes searching mine, his expression revealing that he knows something is wrong, something that might be bigger than the both of us. "We can talk. C'mon, baby, talk to me."

"Not here, not now." I look around at the attention from the nearby party-goers watching this scene as it starts swelling into a spectacle. His hand goes to my cheek, pressing to soothe the underlying trauma I'm feeling inside. His skin is warm against mine, his touch healing, and yet as the image of a text to an ex crosses my mind, it begins to burn. "Don't touch me." My demand is harsher than intended, and his hand drops away, but he grabs my wrist and pulls me with him without a word.

Noah grabs my other, yanking me to a stop, and stretching me in two directions.

There's no confusion left. Evan's anger is obvious. "Get your hands off of her!" He keeps his voice low, but solid. His restraint is clear because I can see how much he's ready to fight if he has to.

Noah releases me, and asks, "Are you okay, Mallory?"

I don't want to talk to Evan in the state I'm in because I'll end up saying things I don't mean. But this is not something that can wait. His past with Noah, Kelly, and how his mother makes me feel all needs to be resolved or settled one way or the other.

"I'm fine. I need to talk to him. I won't be long." I give the faintest of smiles to reassure Noah before turning back to Evan. "We should talk."

We walk to the front of the house and weave between the cars. His Maserati is trapped in on all sides, so we stop in front of it just as his frustration boils over. "Shit! I wanted to go somewhere private."

"Evan?" I keep my voice steady, keeping the emotional tsunami whirling inside at bay.

He locks eyes with me while his hands flex at his sides as if he doesn't know what to do with them. "Why is he here, Mallory?"

"Why is she here?" I point back toward the house.

"Who?"

"Kelly."

"What does Kelly have to do with anything?"

"You told me you wouldn't hurt me." My tone is flatter than I mean to sound, my eyes losing focus on the man I love so much, and only seeing the guy from the airport.

Looking deep into my eyes, he approaches. "How did I hurt you, baby?" His voice is much calmer, his eyes soft around the edges. He's always been a good actor, his skills artfully rewarded with an easy lay. Kelly is a prime example of his talents.

"That girl, Evan... I, I don't understand why you wanted to be with me so much, and yet you still needed a backup plan—a girl waiting in the wings for when we're over," I explain, tears streaking down my face.

"Baby, I'm sorry, but I wasn't—" His hands reach for my cheek as he looks at me miffed by the overflow of emotion.

"I don't want your apology!" My own hurt turns to anger and my hands start to shake again.

"I don't understand. Why are you acting this way?"

The tears dry on the spot at the insinuation that I'm in the wrong. Alcohol might not be the best remedy for the blues, but it always fuels an irrational fire, which is burning inside of me. "Why am I acting this way? Why am *I* acting this way? You have some nerve turning this around on me when you're the one chatting up your fling this whole time while spewing a guilt trip on me over Noah." I've been such a fool. I thought I could handle being carefree Mallory, but that's not who I am. Whether I'm in Colorado or Hawaii, I'm still the same person.

"What are you talking about?" His voice is raised as he narrows his eyes pointedly at me.

I have a feeling Evan Ashford is not called out on his actions much. "I'm talking about your girlfriend from the airport. Why'd you do this to me? Why not just fuck me and send me on my merry way like you send every other one night stand?" I hit him on the chest once and then again as I shout, "Why?"

"You're talking crazy. I don't know why she's here, but it's not because I asked her to come. You really think I'm that much of an asshole?"

"I think you knew what you were doing all along," I say, pointing at him. "You only pursued me because I rejected you at the airport. You pursued me because you're spoiled and can't accept no when you're told."

"I haven't done anything wrong. I'm telling you the truth, Mallory. You're drunk and blowing things out of proportion."

There are phrases that men say to women that are sure fire to set a woman off in a rage. 'You're drunk and blowing things out of proportion' is one of those. I close my eyes, attempting to gather my thoughts which are running rampant. When I open my eyes again, I can tell everything we have built teeters on the weight of this conversation. "You should have just fucked me the first day. I expected it then. I wanted it. But you, you had to make love to me and make me feel more than I wanted. This was supposed to be a fun summer. I finally got to be whoever I wanted to be, escaping my life back home. I wanted easy and frivolous. I wanted to have a one night stand and leave it at that, but no. You had other plans, like torturing me until you got what you wanted. Are you happy, Evan? You've broken me into a million little worthless pieces, the whole of me lost to the abuse of your charms and good looks."

I'm tipsy, maybe drunk, but now that we're laying it all out there, we might as well get the rest out into the open. Every little insecurity and twisted situation aired and in the end maybe we will survive or maybe we won't, but if we do, it will because we live in the truth.

"If I would've fucked you without expectations, we'd still be here today," he says, his voice much more cautious.

"There's something between us that neither can deny. Something stronger than our will and desires—"

The plan has formed. The solution to our problem lies in the wake of our beginning. We have to backtrack and make this all right, make it the way it was always meant to be. "You may be right, but we can fix this. Since you're obviously not ready to give up other girls then you can give me up. I've got the perfect plan. Fuck me, Evan."

"What? What are you talking about?"

"It's so simple. Don't make love to me. Don't be gentle. Fuck me without emotion, so we can move on with our lives, knowing that's all we were. Nothing more. Nothing less. Nothing gained. Nothing lost." I look down, believing this option is viable. "Just do this. If you ever cared about me, do it." I look up as the tears pool in my eyes again. "We gave it our best shot, but it's time to end this like it was always supposed to end." I hate the plea in my voice as it cracks, my heart warring between strength and devastation.

He holds my arms, squeezing them as we stare into each other's eyes, and says, "That's not going to solve anything, baby. Everything would be lost because we're way beyond fucking each other out of our systems. I've tried it and it didn't—"

"You tried? You mean..." My heart explodes inside my chest, knowing he's been preparing for my leave all along, plotting out his plan to rid me from his life. This reaffirms my own plan. Yes, I need for him to do this because then I'll see him differently. He won't be loving or nice. He'll be a user, an abuser, and a taker. I'll be able to walk away with those last images and forget the past and everything I thought we could be.

His grip tightens, and I see his expression change as

reality sets in. I'm slipping away, even if I'm physically right in front of him. "That's not what I meant, Mal—"

"I don't care what you meant! Let's just do this and then you can send me off with a kiss and fake goodbye and it will be like the last six weeks never happened."

"No, it won't, and I can't treat you like that. I care about you. Why are you doing this?" Tears fill his eyes as his hand touches my cheek.

I turn away, not able to watch him fall apart. I'm barely holding on myself. I can't be strong for both of us. "I saw the text. It was from you," I say, my voice barely above a whisper.

"What text? It's not real. We're real, baby. Kelly's nothing to me. She never meant anything to me and you know that. We—"

"It can be quick, fast, and meaningless," I say and look down the path toward the guest house. "We can just go in there and do it how we should have done it the first time."

I'm right. I know I am. I saw the text. His silence slices deep as he stares at me. He's probably having a mental field day trying to psychoanalyze this moment and I'll let him. Maybe that will make this easier if he feels in control once again.

This is it. I will finally find out why all of the girls leave crying after being with him. I know it's not from him 'making love' to them. Deep down, I already know why. Like all the ones who came before me, they give, he takes, and nothing more. So this shouldn't be a difficult decision for him. I'm offering what he wanted all along—no strings attached. I try not to think of the one that clings, connecting my heart to his, as I look at his wary face.

His hands hold my arms, his fingers flexing around them. Leaning down until he's eye-level with me, he says, "I didn't betray you. I wouldn't! So if you need to leave with Noah to feel better about a misunderstanding, then do it. We're done here." His body leaves mine and the balmy wind scrapes across my skin.

"So you're done?" This comes out more like I've been waiting for it to be over a while now, but I never was. I hoped for more. Our actions and pain have taken over who we were together.

Two tears slide down his cheeks as he looks back, his pain evident as he releases a deep breath. "If you're choosing to believe her over me, then yes, Mallory, *we're* done."

By texting her, his heart and mind betrayed me. His body would've followed soon after. *We're done.* It doesn't matter that he said it. *We are done.* This is better for me in the long run. *She* only made the inevitable happen sooner. She didn't have to show me the text. His past speaks for itself. I could see it, the connection they shared, in the way she touched him. She's in love with him and I can't ignore the fact that he's arguing a lost cause. That girl has proof of his betrayal. "I saw it was from your number, Evan. How can you stand here and lie to my face?"

Noah comes from around a parked Porsche, and says, "I've been asked to leave. I don't know what's happening here, but I think you should come with me, Mallory. I'll take you home."

"I'll get my purse." I turn without hesitation.

"You can't leave!" Evan follows me back to the corner of the house and I note his words are contradictory to what he told me minutes earlier. The music and laughter from the party is a quick distraction from my reality as I grab my purse from the table inside, and turn to make a quick exit back out.

Evan rushes to stop me. "Please. Please don't go like this. I'm not sure what happened tonight, but I can take you home and we'll talk."

"You said I could leave with him, so I'm doing it." I step around and rush toward Noah who's standing by the pool. Tears sting my eyes because the hard evidence of that text can't be discounted so easily. Evan hasn't questioned her or bothered to see the same thing I've seen with my own eyes, yet he's been questioning me, treating me like I'm crazy.

"Stop! Don't go!" Evan's voice carries over the music, drawing the crowd's attention.

I do stop. The man I hate myself for loving tells me to, so I do. I stop in my tracks and turn back to look at him, hoping he'll make this whole night go away, that he'll put us back the way we were yesterday. His face is beautifully pained. Worry creasing his forehead as he searches for the right thing to say. The words won't come tonight because he's been caught in his own web of lies, but then he surprises me. "I trust you, Mallory. But Kalei, you better not put a hand on her."

Noah grips my arm, and I turn to look at him, surprised by the possessiveness of his hold on me. "I would never hurt her. I'm not like you, Ashford. I know how you treat women. We all know what you did to my sister!"

There are moments in life where it slows to a crawl and everything becomes vivid, almost to the point of overexposure. A lump forms in my throat as the bright dots connect —Evan, Noah, enemies, Noah's sister, Evan's tragic past, words from Kate – 'changed who he is' –and I come full circle, blinded by the obvious truth.

"She's dead because of you!" Noah yells, pain and fury combined in those five shocking words.

Evan is shaking his head, a violence revealing the battle

behind his eyes, and I reflexively cower against Noah. Evan's expression drops when his gaze lands on me—every emotion playing out in a brilliance of spectacular colors. His secret exposed in front of everyone, in front of me. The most dazzling of lights turned off behind his deep blues, and darkness takes over. The window into his soul slammed shut.

Hugh Ashford steps in front of Evan, his hands up, his words direct, but trying to calm as he speaks to Noah. "I know you're upset, Noah, but you need to leave or I'll have you removed. This is not the time or the place for that discussion. That matter has been put to rest."

"My sister was put to rest because of your son. Your money can't bring her back!"

"Don't you talk about Lani! I'm dead fucking serious." Evan stalks toward him, and shouts, "After all we've been through, you have some nerve buying Mallory a surfboard. If I hadn't been there..." There's a distinct change in tone, but I can't figure it out before his anger surges again. "...I'm warning you to keep your fucking hands off her."

"You mean respect her like you do?" He laughs, but I can tell there's no humor to be found.

"Noah, stop," I beg, looking up at him, but my plea falls on deaf ears.

To my embarrassment, Noah continues, "Or more specifically, you don't want me to do her in the parking lot of a party. Is that what you mean, Ashford? Don't treat her like a whore?"

I stand there shocked, feeling humiliation cover my face as my cheeks pulse with heat, all eyes on me—judging, watching, assuming. Just as my gaze lands on Sunny's face, her expression showing the pain she feels for me, I'm drawn back to Evan as he lunges to punch Noah.

Murphy jumps in the middle and captures Evan's hand in the air, blocking the impact with his fist. "We're not going to do this, Evan, so calm the fuck down. This is a party, man," Murphy commands, standing between the two former friends.

Noah cups my face, forcing me to look at him. His words are urgent as he stares straight into my eyes. "I will never treat you like that. You mean more to me than that, Mallory." He pulls me by the arm and as if I don't have a say in the matter, I go stumbling behind him.

"Mallory!" Evan calls, and though I know better, my heart still aches for him.

Looking over my shoulder, Murphy and Zach have him restrained. My eyes catch movement nearby, and I see his mom and Kelly smiling in their victory. I move forward, needing to be free from the hate of their contemptuous eyes, needing a minute away from everything to do with a future snuffed out. They planted the seed and let us destroy each other. A conversation that should have happened during more sober times, forced itself into our lives, and now we'll pay the price for the hurt we've caused. Both of us walk away wounded in a battle over egos and lies, a battle that should have never been waged.

Just as I round the corner, a strangled cry halts my escape and every breath in my body.

"Don't leave me, Baby! I love you!"

3

MALLORY

I stop, his words halting every muscle in my body, my breath faltering as well, and look over my shoulder at Evan. But with Noah continuing to walk while holding onto one of my arms, and Zach suddenly taking my other, I'm dragged out of sight. *But I heard him.* Evan finally said what I'd wanted to hear from him. My heart lumps in my throat as mixed emotions play through my head, the realness of hearing him say those three words overtaking all the bad. When I close my eyes, his voice and words repeat in my head, '*I love you! I love you! I love you! I love you!*' But his words, in this traumatic of a moment, don't change the reality of the situation we're in. I'm still living this nightmare and Evan is gone. No matter what words were said in desperation, it's clear from the actions of tonight that we're done.

By the time we reach the valet guy, I'm staring at Noah, aiming all of my anger directly at him. "How could you say that? How could you embarrass me in front... in front of everyone like that?"

Stunned by my reaction, he says, "Mallory, he has to know you can't be treated like that. You shouldn't be. You don't have to settle. I may not be rich, but I would never treat you like you're beneath me or like a slut."

"You don't know what you're talking about. Please don't make me explain what you saw earlier." The tears drop from my jaw as his hand graces my cheek. I turn from him, causing his hand to drop away as well.

A gentle squeeze to my shoulder draws my attention behind me. I turn around knowing it's not Evan, but still wishing it was. "Evan?"

"No, but we need to leave right now. Evan needs time to calm down," Zach says, "and sober up."

Sunny runs up from behind him, but stays quiet at his side. Her anxious demeanor makes me nervous and I look back one more time, allowing hope to seep into my heart.

Zach is firm in his stance, his shoulders back, protective of both Sunny and me. "Noah, I think Mallory should be with Sunny tonight. We'll take her home."

Noah looks between me and Zach several times before nodding. His Jeep is parked behind him and the valet guy tosses the keys to him. He steps closer to me as Zach holds eye contact with him, slowly relenting and moving to the side.

Taking one of my hands gently into his, Noah says, "Mallory, I meant what I said. As if tonight wasn't enough of a warning for you to steer clear, let me tell you that the Ashford's have nothing but money and problems. Don't get—"

"That's enough, Kalei," Zach warns, stepping in front of me, between us. "I think goodbye will suffice for now."

Noah's nostrils flare and I expect more of a fight by the death stare he's waging on Zach, but he walks around without another word and leaves. Enough was said to know

where everyone stands on the issue of the Ashfords and
Evan anyway.

Sunny pulls me into a hug, and whispers in to my ear,
"Are you alright?"

I shrug away from my friend, lowering my head in
shame. "Can we go now?"

We get into Sunny's VW, Zach getting in the back and
she pulls away. I watch in the rearview mirror, willing him to
come after me though I wouldn't take him back right now—
or maybe I would, but he never comes, so no choice has to
be made.

EVAN

I fight for my freedom, but to no avail.

"Calm. The. Fuck. Down. Evan." My father enunciates
each word, whispering close to my ear.

I turn my head abruptly, realizing that was the first time
I've ever heard him swear *and it was at me.* When my eyes
meet his, I start to calm, but the thought of Mallory leaving
with Noah, leaving me, leaving at all, fuels the fire again. I
wrangle out of my dad's and Murphy's grip and make a run
for it almost knocking a lady into the pool accidentally. My
focus is set on finding Mallory. Only her. She's all that
matters.

I dash up the path, running faster than I ever remember
running, but I never had something worth running after
before Mallory. I have to reach her before she's leaves and
ends everything we have going, before ending us.

My phone buzzes in my pocket, but I don't stop until the
top of the driveway. "Fuck!" I yell, gasping for air while
watching Sunny's red tail lights fade into the distance.

Bending over, I rest my hands on my knees, breathing erratically, and swearing under my breath.

"Do you have a valet ticket, sir?"

I look up at the Valet guy, and ask, "Hey, there was a girl with long dark hair who just left. Did she leave with a guy in a Jeep or a girl in that old van?"

"The van."

I smile and breathe out, my body finding some relief.

"Cool. Thanks, dude."

My phone pings, reminding me that I have a voice message, so I drag my phone out of my pocket and enter my password.

"Mallory is coming to my house tonight. Give her the night. We'll explain about Lani. You need to figure this shit out that I'm hearing about a text." Zach lowers his voice and continues, "Come by in the morning. You guys need to talk when you're sober. Later, brah."

"Fuck!" I fucking want to slam my phone into the street, but I know I'll need it in case she calls me. *Please fucking call or at least text me, Mallory,* I pray to the stars above. The sky is way too clear for how muddled my life is right now. It's as if the universe doesn't realize how messed up my life is.

I dial Mallory's number, and of course, it goes straight to voicemail. *Double Fuck!* I leave a message. "Hey... ummmm... we need to talk, baby. I can explain. This has gotten crazy out of hand. Please call me back."

I hang up as I walk back down the driveway, down the path, through the partygoers, and straight to the bar. I shouldn't have shown up to the party buzzed from the pre-party at Zach's and Murphy's house. I should have known to have my wits about me. I shake my head thinking that it's sad that I need to go to these lengths to protect someone I care about from my own fucking family, but once again, they've proven my instincts true. Reaching around, I grab a bottle of Jack Daniels.

"Hey, you can't take that," the bartender threatens.

"Like fuck, I can't!"

"It's fine," my dad says to the bartender before turning to me. "Son, I think you should retire early tonight."

"What? And miss the party, Daddio?"

"It's not a suggestion."

"Whatever."

"We can talk tomorrow if you're up for it."

We stare at each other for a good minute. He's not backing down and I'm over this scene. I need to leave before I fucking hurt someone. Stalking across the crowded deck, I go into my house and lower the blinds while drinking straight from the bottle. I strip off my shirt and pants and take a piss, still chugging the warm whiskey. After climbing into bed, I prop myself up against the headboard and drink more, trying to drown the memories of tonight.

Images of Mallory begging me to fuck us out of her system stay with me, breaking my heart, and hurting my head. I've been where she was tonight. All my thoughts messed up and alcohol intensifying my emotions. Ginger and Tiffany come to mind as a perfect example of being messed up. But I had intentions that day that I would've never followed through with. I know that now.

What Mallory doesn't realize is that what we share will always override any casual fuck. We can't be washed away that easily. I close my eyes and mumble, "We're in way too deep for that."

4

EVAN

"I missed you."

"Hmmm." I moan without opening my eyes, the dreams of Mallory slipping away.

"Wakey, wakey, Evvvan."

My eyes flash open and I see Kelly hovering over me. Startled awake, I jump back as if she's about to attack me, which I guess she is technically. "What the fuck are you doing in here?"

She sticks her bottom lip out at me as if that look will work for her. She tries to stroke my hair, but I duck and free my legs from underneath her, and stand up.

"Evan, what's wrong with you? If you want, I'll let you tie me up. I know how you like to play rough," she whines, desperation edging her tone.

I continue to back up, but stop to stand my ground against this intruder. Crossing my arms, I say, "Actually, you don't know how I like it. You're the one who likes to play rough, not me! Now, get the fuck out of my house."

"Is this about that girl, your *'girlfriend'*?" she asks in a mocking tone.

I want to smack that condescending grin off her face for talking about Mallory like that, but I would never hit a girl. Fortunately for her, my manners are still intact and I still feel lethargic from the alcohol.

She stands up and looks at me for a moment, giving me a long, hard stare before rejection settles in. "You'll regret this, Evan. If I walk out this door, I'm not coming back," she states, putting her hands on her hips.

I smile. "That's a blessing, not a threat. Sayonara, sweetheart," I add, sarcastically.

She turns to leave, but suddenly I remember Mallory talking about an exchange of texts between Kelly and me.

I grab her wrist, surprising her. Her surprise morphs into an unattractive smugness, and she says, "I knew you couldn't resist me, Evvie."

My glare should say enough, but I back it with my words in case she doesn't get it. "I can totally resist you. Give me your phone."

"What for?" It seems to dawn on her as she speaks. "No!"

"Give it to me. Now!" I'm not playing games with her.

She twists in my arms just as I release her, and backs toward the door, smiling. "You know I was only kidding around with that girl, right?"

"*That girl* has a name and it's Mallory. You'd be wise to remember that. Show me the text."

"I don't kno—"

I pull it from her pocket before she has a chance to finish the sentence. She has a phone similar to mine, so it's easy to navigate. "It was just a joke, geez, lighten up, Evan. I actually did fly out to see you. Doesn't that matter? We were good together. I told my family and my friends all about you."

Ignoring her rambling, I scroll through her messages then I ask, "Did my mother put you up to this?"

"Put me up to what?"

She's playing dumb, and I know she's not stupid. My hard gaze meets her eyes and nothing more is needed for her to know I'm not fucking around and playing games.

"No," she says, "I met your mother when I showed up at your house. But I have to say, she doesn't like your *girlfriend* very much."

"Thanks for the obvious. You two met and bonded on a mutual plan to make me miserable or what?"

"I came here because I care about you, not to hurt you."

I arch an eyebrow to intimidate her. It works.

"Fine! Your mother is pretty fucked up by the way. When I showed up this afternoon and you weren't here, I knocked on the main house and the maid was talking to me when your mom invited me in. I told her about us and my surprise visit. She was delighted to see me and welcomed me in, Evan. She didn't tell me to do anything, but she might have encouraged me to go after what I want and I want you." She takes a deep breath then looks me in the eyes. "She thinks Mallory is one-night stand material. She's not like us. She doesn't have a place in our world. Can't you see that?"

"You don't deserve to even know Mallory, but she's not a one-night stand, just so *you* know. Everything is so fucked up now." I load one more page of messages and that's when I see it. "The last text from me is from May 25th."

"Yes, I know," she says, nodding.

I'm shaking my head in confusion. "Mallory and I weren't together then. I remember this text. It meant nothing. It was just something to say."

Kelly crosses her arms. "Oh, thanks a lot."

"But, why would she think this was recent?" I look back at Kelly again, hoping for the answers to magically appear.

"I kind of hid the date when I showed her the message," she says, cringing.

I squeeze the phone, wanting to crush it, but I need the proof. I grab my phone from the bar and take a picture of the text message making sure the date is visible. I toss her phone back to her and point to the door.

"We're done. Get out."

"That's it. Just give you what you want and that's it? You're such a user, Evan. I was a fool for thinking you..." I stare in annoyance while she continues her little rant. "... Agh! You're a bastard, Evan Ashford!" She storms out, slamming the door behind her as she exits.

I lock it, still a bit wobbly on my feet from the booze. Spying a tipped over bottle of Jack next to the bed, I pick it up and place it on the bar then make my way to the bathroom. I wash my hands, wanting to rid myself of any contact I had with Kelly then drop back into bed.

Laying in the dark, wide awake in the middle of the night, the silence that fills my room reflects the emptiness I feel inside. I look at my phone, staring at the photo of the text. "Fuck!" I slam the phone down on my bed and jump out of bed. I throw on a t-shirt and shorts and storm past the cleaning crew still taking the party decorations down. Running into the main house, I head straight up the stairs to my parents' room knowing they won't be asleep yet. I wouldn't have cared if they were.

Two knocks is enough warning, and I barge in.

My mother is taking her jewelry off on her side of the bed, but is shocked by my sudden appearance. "Evan! What are you doing in here?" Sensing my anger, she points at the door and yells, "How dare you barge in here like this. Leave right now!"

"No! I won't until you hear me out. Whether you like it or not, you're not going to control me anymore—"

"Evan, you need to leave this room right now or suffer the consequences," my dad warns as he comes out of the bathroom.

"I'm not a child anymore. This is *my* life!" I turn back to my mother with a scowl and demand, "You're going to apologize to Mallory for treating her like you did tonight."

"No, I'm not," she says flatly.

"Why? Why do you hate her so much? Why do you hate me so much that you would get rid of the one person who makes me happy? The one person who has made me *feel* anything other than numb in four years?"

She walks closer and looks at me, *really looks at me,* straight in the eyes. I know I've hurt her in the past with all my screw-ups, but damn, my heart is breaking because of my meddling mother now. I guess that makes us even.

"Honey," she says as her hands hold my face. "I love you. I could never hate you."

I shrug out of her reach, knocking her hands off of me. "You don't treat people you love like this—"

My dad pushes me back away from her causing me to stumble backward before I finish my sentence. "Don't you ever touch a woman like that! Do you understand me? You were raised better than that," he states firmly, his voice calm and controlled, but threatening. "Is this what we've come to? This is our family? We're all we've got and need to start respecting each other again." I stand there in shock, my gaze following him as he walks to the door. "This has been a long night. You're drunk, Evan. We'll finish this discussion tomorrow when everyone has had some time to think about their role in the events of tonight." He offers me the door though I can't say I feel I have a choice.

I leave willingly, but I'm still pissed that I'm not getting the answers I need from my mother. I hoarsely say, "Fuck you, Mom!" The door slams and locks behind me. I smile in a small time victory, knowing me calling her mom instead of mother will upset her more than the 'fuck you' I yelled.

Maybe it was a bad idea coming up here tonight. I need my dad on my side, but really, what's one more fucking mistake at this point.

IT TAKES me four more hours of laying in my bed, blinds closed, curtains drawn, and fireworks exploding in the distance, for me to finally sober up, and cool down enough to grab my keys and decide it's time to go find Mallory.

I should've been there at the beginning of the party and this shit would have never happened. Kelly and my mother wouldn't have been able to get to her like they did. I could've taken my dad and Murphy if I really wanted to. Okay, maybe not Murphy, but my dad if I tried, but I've put him through enough. On bad advice, I let her go, but I'm thankful she ended up going with Sunny and Zach.

Tonight was a clusterfuck of crazy. When Kalei brought Lani up, it threw my mind into a whirlwind. I had frantic thoughts of Mallory leaving me once she found out the truth.

I drop my keys as my head swims in regret, knowing I didn't fight hard enough when that asshole was dragging her away from me. I may owe Kalei a life, but he can't have Mallory in exchange. She's mine.

A tailspin of thoughts send me into panic mode as I remember Lani's lifeless body, the call to 9-1-1, and the last time I saw her face before they took her away. Like so many times before, I run to the bathroom and throw up praying the memories of that day are ejected from my body along with the bile.

I stand, leaning on the counter for support, and look at myself in the mirror. I close my eyes hoping to forget again, hoping to forget Lani.

When I open my eyes, I'm pale. That's to be expected since I was sick, but I'm also different. There's no physical evidence of it, but I know by the way my heart aches that I'm in love. Unlike Lani, Mallory is here, Mallory is alive. She's flesh and blood, soft skin and warm kisses. I close my eyes and tilt my head back toward the ceiling, reasoning that if there is a Heaven, than that's where Lani is now. I look to her behind closed lids and silently apologize. *'I'm sorry I wasn't there for you when you needed me most.'*

A tear escapes as I continue this most foreign of acts— saying a prayer. *'I'm sorry I couldn't love you the way you deserved, how you wanted, how you needed. There was nobody else, like you thought, but my heart was too young. Your death shouldn't have been the thing that made me recognize your love for what it was—kind and trusting. I'm sorry I couldn't give you the same. I'm sorry I couldn't save you.'*

With this most simple of acts, a prayer and apology, I feel a change. I start to heal, just a tad.

I rinse out my mouth and brush my teeth. I wash my face and dry it and look in the mirror once again hoping to find someone else, a better version of myself. *'I'm sorry I couldn't be there for you, Lani. But I can be there for Mallory and I'm not going to lose her this time.'* Feeling more focused than I've felt in a long time, I've been hoping for this new beginning for years and I won't waste another minute.

I'm solid and motivated. I pick my keys up and run up the path to my car. The party is over and the guests have long gone. So I back out of the driveway and speed down the road. It's past 2 a.m. and the streets are empty, hopefully the cops are sleeping on the job.

I drive fast in the still of the night to my best friends' house, causing a dust storm on the dirt driveway when I brake suddenly, throwing my car into park. I jump out and rush to the door. I have ten feet to go when I spot Zach and Murphy sitting on the dark front porch. Zach cocks his rifle and stands, aiming it right at me. "Hold it right there, son," he says with a put-on southern drawl.

I halt in my tracks, hands up automatically like I'm the bad guy and I've been busted. "What the fuck? Is that a rifle, Zach?"

He keeps it steadily pointed at me. "It's actually a 70th anniversary Daisy Red Ryder BB gun with original lariat and lead BB's," he says, stroking the toy gun proudly.

"Whatever, dude," I shift, dropping my arms to my sides. "Where's Mallory? Is she asleep?"

Murphy steps forward as I start walking toward them again. He crosses his arms across his chest like a huge bouncer, and says, "I'm sorry, dude, but you won't be able to see her tonight. You both need to sober up and have this discussion with clear heads."

"I'm not fucking around. You know I need to talk to her, to explain Lani."

Murphy holds his position. "Katie's orders. I can take you any day, but I'm scared shitless when my girl is mad at me. So it's a no-go for tonight."

I stop and look between them several times. I'm pissed. I'm frustrated. "I'm serious. This isn't funny anymore, guys. I really need to see her. I need to talk to her, to tell her everything. She's probably in there thinking I'm a murderer."

I walk forward again, and Zach says, "I'm warning you, Evan. Don't come any closer or I'll have to shoot."

I walk closer not heeding his warning, and mock him, "You're gonna shoot me with your toy...*Fuck!* That hurt! You shot me in the damn hip, you, asshole." I grab my hip, putting pressure on it to try and stop the stinging.

"I warned you," Zach says with pride, stroking the barrel of the BB gun one time before lowering it.

Murphy laughs and says, "He did warn you."

"You guys suck cock! Will you at least ask her if she'll come out here and talk to me?"

"No can do. Like I said, we were given strict orders to protect this house and the cargo inside aka, *the girls*, from you. You can come back tomorrow. Not early because I'm really hoping for some action tonight and we'll want to sleep in—"

"Shut-up, Murphy! That's my sister you're talking about."

"Oh, yeah. Sorry, forgot about that." He smirks again and then rubs it in. "You got one hot-assed sister, man."

"I'm not talking to you anymore. You're dead to me," I say this with a straight face, but he knows deep down I'm kidding with him.

I focus my last ditch efforts on Zach, the reasonable one of the group. "Zach, can you help a brother out? I'm dying here. She's my..." I stop and look down embarrassed by what I almost admitted.

But he encourages me. "She's your what, Evan? Tell us."

I look him in the eyes and know I'm making headway. He has a kind nature and is a romantic at heart. I open my mouth and tell them both the truth. "She's everything I never thought I'd find in a girl. I love her." My voice unintentionally softens as I say these words aloud for the third time ever. The first time was while she was sleeping, so she never heard and the second time was at the party in front of everyone. One day I hope to say to her directly and only her.

They both smile at me like two chicks *oohing* and *ahhing* over this confession which is totally humiliating and not manly at all. "I suggest you tell her that," Zach says. "But it has to wait until tomorrow. It's best this way. Kate has already explained the situation to her."

"I open up to you assholes and you still don't let me in. Fuck you, guys," I say, flipping them each a bird and stomp back to my car. I get in, slam the door closed, and pound my fists on my steering wheel three times. That's when I see my phone on the passenger seat and immediately call her. It goes straight to voicemail, so I text her: *I need to talk to you. Please.* I call it a night at that. There's nothing more I can do at this point and I don't like leaving Zach's place unrewarded, but I do it anyway. Time is the only thing that can bring us back together and I'm counting every second.

Thinking I've lost her eats away at me. On the drive back, I'm tortured by these negative thoughts. By the time I get back home, I've managed to pull out some of my hair and am fighting back tears, which really pisses me off.

I sit on my back door step and inhale two cigarettes, trying to relax my nerves before I climb into bed. I'm desperate to will this nightmare to end. In bed, I lay with visions of Mallory to comfort me: Mallory's lips, Mallory's smile, the light sprinkling of freckles across Mallory's nose, kissing her belly button, Mallory's hands, and Mallory's hands on me.

5

EVAN

"Dude, wake up!"

I hear my subconscious yell at me.

"C'mon, the swells are ripe this morning."

Apparently, my subconscious wants to go surfing.

"Open the door, Dude!"

I bolt upright.

Zach.

My eyes are blurry and heavy, not ready for the day, but my heart is racing not only from being startled awake, but because it's morning. Morning means Mallory. I run to the door, unlocking it, and fling it open in hopes of seeing true beauty standing next to my best friend.

"Ech! It's just you," I say, distaste filling my mouth.

Zach grins. "Yeah, thanks. Grab your stick. Let's go."

I grab a t-shirt off the floor and shake my head while scrounging around the place for some shorts. "Can't. I need to talk with Mallory. This shouldn't really be a surprise to you."

"You can't," he says as if I should know this already.

I stop and look at him. "Why can't I?"

Zach rubs his hands over his unshaven face and hesitantly says, "Because she's gone. I mean, she already left my pad this morning."

"Okay, so I'll go to Sunny's."

"They're not there. They're out today, so grab your board and c'mon."

As my stomach twists, I look at him beneath a furrowed brow and can tell he's hiding something from me. "Spit it out, dude. Where is she?"

He fidgets with the blinds then pulls them open. I squint from the brightness of the sunshine flooding my place.

"Zach, just say it." I'm getting really pissed off.

"They went to the Southern Shore Finals."

"Why would they..." I close my eyes, rubbing over them with the palms of my hand. "*Noah?*"

I hear Zach sigh in resolve. "Umm, you know, I don't think that's the reason. Sunny mentioned that Mallory had told Noah she would go a while back, but I really think they went because it's such a big event and Johnny invited them."

"She never told me." My mind is spinning wildly through images of her being dragged behind him... away from me last night.

I find a pair of trunks on the floor of my closet and strip off my boxers before pulling them on.

"I really doubt she's going for Kalei or maybe she didn't get a chance to tell you with all that happened last—"

"She told me she'd be spending more time with him. I guess that's what she meant." I bite the inside of my cheek in frustration, debating what I should do now.

"It's not exactly illicit. She's with Sunny and he's gonna be busy with the contest. Gotta say, you know he's going to revel in the fact that she's there."

"Yep," I say, knotting the drawstring and grabbing my board. "I need to think. I need to hit some waves."

AN HOUR LATER, the waves have flat-lined. We sit atop the glassy surface of the water, boards under us, legs dangling in the water, isolated by fifty yards or more between us and the next surfer.

Zach lies down on his board and closes his eyes. "This sucks."

"You can say that again."

"This sucks."

I roll my eyes. "What happened at your house last night?"

"Well, I was making sweet love to my woman and then she did this thing with her tongue—"

I lift my foot up under the water and tip him off his board. As soon as he breaks the surface, he yells, "Fucker."

"Don't fucking torture me. Tell me, Z!"

As he climbed onto his board again, he says, "Kate told her about Lani. She seemed to understand. Noah's bitter and upset. He used you as a scapegoat."

"There's no changing the fact that I let her die."

"No, you didn't," he says, paddling closer, facing me as I stare out at the horizon. "She drowned, man. You couldn't have saved her. You tried."

"I shouldn't have let her surf. She wasn't ready—"

"You teach people for an hour and then send them out into the water every day. Why would she be any different? You can't stop the perfect storm. You couldn't predict a wave would place her right over that sinkhole. The best swimmer would find it hard to fight that."

"I should have been paying closer attention. I should have been there."

"Listen, Evan. You can beat yourself up for another four years or you can start living the life you were supposed to live in the first place. You can deny it all you want, but I know that a lot of what eats you up is that you didn't love her. Yeah, sure, you liked her, but she loved you and you feel guilty for not loving her back."

"I don't want to talk about his." I turn around and dig in, ready to paddle to shore, but he grabs the rail of my board.

"Too bad! I'm tired of this shit messing with your head. Get it out."

"What do you want me to say?" I'm frustrated and push away from him. "I'm outta here."

"You can paddle away, but we're going to talk about this." I stop paddling and rest my cheek on my board lulled by the feel of the gentle waves that are starting to build again below me. Zach moves closer and almost in a whisper, says, "Her death is not your fault, Evan. You couldn't have saved her."

I sit up abruptly, pointing at him, and yell, "I'm a fucking surf instructor. I'm CPR certified. I should've been able to and I should have never given her the board." Frustrated with myself, I hit the board under me. "Fuck! The truth is that I was going to break up with her. I'd been planning it that whole week. I bought that board as a consolation prize, hoping it would ease the blow of the break-up, but I hadn't found the right time to say the words." I close my eyes and remember how happy she was when she saw the surfboard. "She made me take her surfing right then. The waves were big, too rough. I knew better and yet I let her paddle out. Heck, I also paddled out wanting to rip it up." I look at him. Zach's face is calm, non-judgmental, so I continue as he listens. "By the time I reached the shore, I didn't see her. That's when I saw the board spiraling around that sinkhole; that fucking sinkhole that wasn't there two days earlier."

"You can't fight fate, E. It was her time." He paddles to stay even with me, and adds, "The lawsuit was settled over three years ago. Now it's time you settle it in your mind."

"The Kalei's should've sued me. I let their daughter and Noah's sister die. My dad paying them off in exchange for Lani's life does not mean it goes away, like everything is even; tit for tat shit. That blood money doesn't erase the image of her underwater." The image of her haunting me again after so long, stabbing me in the heart. The words are quiet as I tell my friend everything I've buried for years. "It was like she was in a peaceful sleep. I hadn't noticed how her short hair had grown out until I saw it floating around her still face. I hadn't noticed how beautiful she had become. I hadn't noticed anything because I was so fucking selfish. So caught up in my own world that I hadn't taken the time to notice."

"You were eighteen. Everyone is selfish at eighteen. Hell, you're supposed to be selfish at that age."

Squeezing my eyes closed tight, I try to wash the image of Lani away from my memories while inwardly berating myself. "I used to force myself to think about her, to constantly remind myself of my failings. That first year in England, I only fucked dark haired girls, closing my eyes, and imagining it was her. A symbol of how I'd fucked up."

"That doesn't even make sense."

"I know, but it made some kind of sense to me then, though. I was so screwed up. I think I still might be." I look straight ahead, ashamed, but finally admit, "I was Lani's first...*and only*."

"Mallory has dark hair—"

"I've never seen Lani in Mallory. Mallory gives me peace. She's different. I feel calm, whole, when I'm with her. I can feel my heart again. I thought it was gone. God, I sound so lame." I'm embarrassed for opening up like this.

"No, you don't and I have a feeling that that's the first time you've ever told the full story."

I look over my shoulder realizing the waves have picked up. I position myself forward on my board, and say, "Yeah, maybe." I start paddling, but before I steal the first wave, I look back at him. "Thanks for listening, man." The tip of my board rises up on the wave as it grows in height and I paddle hard, focusing all my energy on this one wave. I pop up onto my feet and ride it in. I feel good, freer, lighter. I do a few cut backs across the water that's returning me to shore.

When I get into my car, I text Mallory before heading home, but she doesn't respond. I don't blame her after how my mom treated her, or with all the shit I've laid on her.

AFTER TAKING A LONG NAP, I jump in the shower. When I walk out, I find my dad sitting on my couch. I stop and look at him, not knowing what I should say, if anything.

He leans forward resting his forearms on his knees, and breaks the silence. "I want to take you to dinner." He looks out the window, his discomfort clear in his actions. "I want to spend a little more time with you before I leave tomorrow."

"Okay."

"Meet me at the car in ten," he says as he walks toward the door. "Oh and, Evan?" He stops and looks back over his shoulders. "Invite Murphy and Zach along. I'd like to get to know your friends better."

"I will. Thanks."

I get dressed knowing this is a unique opportunity. When I was in New York I didn't see him except when I was in the office. I hated being confined in that office, another reason why I left.

My father loves his Porsche. My appreciation for driving finer vehicles is inherited from him. After sliding into his Carrera, we spend a few minutes in silence. I break it this time. Only seems fair. "You have to leave tomorrow? Not much of a vacation this year."

"Your mother said she told you about the board and the possibility of a handover to a management firm. I want to be present to make sure that doesn't happen. If I take my eye off the ball even for a second, I could lose Ashford Holdings, and I'm not willing to let that happen. I've worked too hard to be handed a retirement check and told to go away."

"Dad, I don't really understand how this works, but I'm assuming it's because it's a public company. So, you have to answer to the board?"

"Yes, the board represents our shareholders and clientele, but our family still holds majority stock. If the board gets their way, that could change. That's why it's important for you to be a part of this meeting in August. Can you do that, son? Will you help us so we don't lose our company?"

I gulp hard, the importance of this upcoming meeting starting to burden my shoulders. I glance at my dad as he's driving and see the worry, the concern in his eyes. I've lived frivolously for a long time now. My parents have given me the time with little argument. It's time I give something back in return. A meeting is easy. I'll fly in and fly out. Then I'll be back in paradise in no time. "Yes. Kate and I will fight for the family."

He exhales his relief, reaching over and grabbing my

shoulder, giving it a tight squeeze. "Thank you, Evan. I knew I could count on you."

"Of course, Dad."

Zach and Murphy are already seated at the table on the patio of the restaurant. They never turn down a free meal. After a quick greeting between us, Murphy stands, holding his hand out to my dad who takes it. "Sir, thank you for inviting me to dinner, Sir." His nerves are clearly showing. I'll let him sweat it out on his own. That will teach him for dating my sister and Hugh Ashford's daughter.

My dad removes his hand from Murphy's before sitting down across from me and next to him. "Thanks for coming and please try to relax. I'm not here judging you, but I do have some questions for you concerning my daughter."

We order our food and a pitcher of beer. As my father quizzes Murphy regarding his intentions toward Kate, I sit back anxiously waiting for Sunny to text Zach, as she promised. Mallory hasn't left my mind, but I'm looking forward to this time with my dad.

The surf contest has ended, but Zach has told me to lay off the calls and texts today. She's 'working' on her and needs more time. The problem is that I've been on edge thinking about her—needing to be near her. At this point, I might even take her saying goodbye to me just to hear her voice again.

I hear Murphy pleading his case to my father. "Yes, it is early in our relationship, but I feel strongly for her. I respect her decisions concerning this fall. I have one more semester of school and then will be making a lot of big decisions myself."

Murphy's conversation with my dad draws me back to the restaurant and I watch this six foot four, two hundred plus man quiver like a teenager.

My dad pats Murphy on the back, and says, "I appreciate your good intentions and I look forward to spending more time with you in New York when you visit."

"Thank you, Sir."

"Please call me Hugh," my dad says, laughing.

Zach's phone rings. The smile on his face tells us it's Sunny without him saying a word. He stands and walks a few feet away. His eyes dart to mine then he looks down.

I can tell something is wrong when he straightens his back. My stomach tightens and my posture matches his. Mallory. I stand, my worry getting the best of me. As soon as the phone is away from his ear, he says, "I need a ride to the hospital. Can someone give me one?"

"What's wrong," I ask, my heart beating hard in my chest.

"Sunny hurt her hand again while helping Johnny."

I exhale, relieved it's not about Mallory, but my dick move is noticed by all and now relief turns to guilt. "I'll take you." I offer because my friend needs a ride and Sunny is pure good and deserved better than to be overlooked by my messed up emotions.

"Thank you," Zach says.

My dad stands as I do, and tosses money on the table. Then he says, "Evan I drove you. I can take you both to the hospital."

I'd forgotten that minor detail.

Zach looks at Murphy then back to my dad. "Murphy drove, Mr. Ashford. He can drive me."

"No, no. We should all go. I know you're all friends with her."

"Thanks," Zach adds, turning around and walking toward the exit.

We're close to the hospital, so the drive is short. Murphy

drops Zach off in front of the ER. My dad parks and even though I'm concerned about Sunny and what happened, I'm suddenly nervous I might see Mallory inside. Will she talk to me? Will she even look at me?

Murphy walks up behind us as we enter through the sliding glass doors. Zach is at the counter talking to a nurse and I scan the waiting area for those familiar green eyes. I'm disappointed when I only find two men watching the TV in the corner. Turning back to Zach, I lean against the counter next to him. "Any word?"

"She'll be out in a sec. On the phone she said she was helping Johnny with a table when she twisted her wrist, tweaking her hand that she hurt before."

"Is she getting a cast?" My dad asks. His own worry is showing through his expression. I appreciate his concern for my friends.

"Zach!"

We turn toward the direction of his name being called and find Sunny smiling as she hurries down the corridor and into his arms. Johnny is behind her and a girl I don't recognize. Mallory is not with them.

I'm trying to be sensitive to Sunny's pain, but the pain in my heart is building, wondering where she could be.

When she releases Zach, she leans over the counter toward the nurse, and asks, "Am I free to go?"

"Not just yet," she replies while staring at her monitor. "We need to make a copy of your insurance card and for you to pay the co-pay first."

Sunny digs down into her pocket and pulls out her ID and bankcard but there's nothing else except a stick of gum. She looks up, her expression falling. "It's in my van which is parked at the beach. Johnny drove me here."

"We'll need the card or you'll need to pay half the bill

before I can release you," the nurse adds, a sympathetic smile appearing.

My dad steps forward and asks Sunny, "Do you remember who your insurance carrier is? Maybe we can call them."

"No, I can't. Last time I was here, I was out of it from the medication they gave me."

The nurse looks up, her lips tightening as she ponders. "I can't release her without the co-pay or fifty-percent of the total as a deposit."

Dad turns toward Sunny and says, "Come over here and we'll call your parents."

Sunny, Zach, my father, and Murphy all go together. I stay with my back pressed against the counter and cross my arms.

"I know this is a touchy subject, but Mallory told me what happened at the party."

I turn and look at Johnny, the girl with him joining the others.

"She hasn't heard my side," I say, looking down at the shiny linoleum floors. "She won't talk to me."

"She cares about you. I know that much."

"Don't know if that's enough anymore."

A quiet contemplation settles between us.

"Mallory left with Noah after the contest," Johnny adds.

My head practically spins on my neck when I turn toward Johnny. "What?"

He takes a deep breath and a short exhale, nervous to speak. "Don't freak out. Okay... It's completely innocent, but she went to celebrate with him. He won Southern Shores and his family is having a luau for him. She said she'd never been to one."

"He won?" I look at him as if his previous statement will

change. It doesn't. "Fuck, he did it! He finally won," I say more to myself than to Johnny.

"It's huge! He'll get sponsored and compete in the series down in New Zealand," Johnny adds.

Murphy joins the conversation. "Yep, Southern Shores stepped it up this year. They'll sponsor him for the surfing season there. I bet he'll have to leave soon." Murphy laughs, looking at me. "One less thing you'll have to worry about, my friend."

This is a lot to process. I can't believe Noah is leaving the island like he always wanted and that makes me grin. The small part of me that remembers our friendship, knows this was his dream and its coming true. "Man, even my cold heart has to smile at that shit."

With Noah leaving soon, I try to trust that Mallory is only celebrating her friend's victory with him and it's not a celebration of any other sorts. I attempt to convince myself of this, though deep down, I feel major jealousy that she's chosen to spend time with him, especially after last night. It makes me wonder if she's thought about me at all. Worse, I'm now worried I may never get the chance to make this right with her.

My dad calls me over to sit with him away from the others. When I do, he says, "Sunny's parents aren't answering, but they found her insurance details from the last time she was here. I'm going to cover the bill. I know she can't afford it and I don't want her stuck here for hours. While they print the paperwork, I'd like to talk business with you. I'm leaving tomorrow and don't know if I'll have time before then and I have a conference call tonight."

"No, it's fine. What's this about?" Dread settles in well aware that we're going to be talking about a job back in New

York. All the reasons I usually have handy to explain why I should stay in Hawaii are escaping me.

"I'd like to talk about your plans first. Are you going to return to school?"

I lean back in my chair, sliding down in my seat. Turning to look him in the eyes, I say, "Um… yes. I missed the deadlines for Yale, and U of Hawaii. I looked into The University of Colorado, but I missed their last admissions deadline by three weeks."

He's sitting upright, but his tone is relaxed. "Is that where Mallory attends?"

"Yes."

"So, it's more serious than your mother thinks?"

"Yes. I'm considering going back with her."

"And what does she think about that? I don't think she can afford to support you."

When I look at my friends they are staring at me, shocked by my revelation.

Shrugging off the uncomfortable feeling of all eyes on me, I respond the best way I know how. "I haven't told her that I'd looked into it because I didn't want her to be disappointed. I don't want her stressing, thinking she'll have to support me. I can get a job."

"Sounds like you're talking from your heart, but you're using your head. I think Mallory might be good for you although your mother is not convinced. You should talk to your mother soon because she has strong ideas about your future." He sits back and looks out at the beach across the street. Just when I think he's deep in thought, he turns to me and states, "You're in love with Mallory." His gaze meets mine. "That's what you said or rather shouted in the middle of the party last night."

Feeling awkward, I search for a much needed distraction. But my friends suck and leave me in the hot-seat by acting like they aren't eavesdropping. I feel my face heat and face him straight on. "I love her, dad."

He smiles, the corners of his mouth gently edging up, and says, "Well, since you can't attend school with her, how about earning some money with the promise you'll enroll somewhere in the spring? I can offer you $125,000 a year starting out as an active Board Member with Office Responsibilities. You can earn $42k by Christmas. That's a good deal, son."

"What does 'Office Responsibilities' mean?"

"I have to somehow justify a board member receiving a large salary. You'll work in the office like the rest of us. You don't have your degree, so I can't give you clients, but you can train in that time period." He reaches over and pats my hand. "I want you to seriously consider this job. It's a solid offer and works well for building your resume. Then in the spring, I expect you to pick a school and graduate. If it's from Colorado then so be it, but I want you to finish your education."

It is a really good offer, very generous, and I'm family, carrying on the Ashford name. There are built-in burdens that come along with that title alone.

"Mr. Ashford?" the nurse calls him to her station. "You know by signing, you're responsible for her bill in full if she doesn't pay?"

"Yes, that's fine," he says with a nod of his head.

"Ashford, as in Evan Ashford?" A filing clerk standing behind the nurse questions.

I step up to the counter as my dad responds, "Yes, that's my son."

The clerk looks embarrassed as everyone stares at her. She shakes her head and slams the cabinet drawer closed.

"Oh, I've just heard the name before... must be from the files or something. Sorry to interrupt. Just sounded familiar."

My dad turns back to the nurse after signing the paperwork.

She tells Sunny she can go and the group starts walking out the door. I start to walk, but pause, unsettled by the clerk's familiarity with me. My name is trashed in Hawaii, the Ashford name filling the papers and becoming gossip fodder. Usually that doesn't weigh on me much, my own life feeling protected among my group of friends and hangouts where I'm not judged by my sins. But her eyes told me the lies behind her words. She definitely knows my name and now I'm curious to know why.

Needing answers, I turn back and approach the desk again. "May I speak with you?"

The older nurse in the chair raises her eyebrows at the younger clerk and smiles. The nurse must think I'm flirting with the clerk.

She straightens her scrubs, and says, "Sure," with a heavy gulp. "It's time for my break anyway."

When she walks out from behind the counter, she leads me outside. "I shouldn't have said anything."

"That means you know something about me. Please tell me."

She steps to the corner of the building. An ashtray pushed up against the building indicates this is where the medical staff smoke. She pulls a pack of cigarettes and a lighter from her pocket and lights up.

I watch with trepidation, wondering why she knows me or more specifically, of me. She blows out a big puff of smoke and begins. "I could lose my job for telling you confidential information, but I ran across a file the other day. That's why I was surprised to hear your name."

"A file with my name in it?"

She nods. "It was Lani Kalei's file."

Exasperation drops my shoulders, and I say, "Yeah, that. I'm sure my name is all over her file."

She looks around, making sure no other eyes are on us before she speaks again. "I have full access to patient records. I also read the papers after the accident. Lani's record is sealed, marked confidential. But three days ago, the newly renovated files department opened and we had to re-file all of the old ones into the new department. That file was among twenty others that were re-classified. We had to create a new folder for it because the judge's request to seal the Kalei file expired three months ago."

"You mean it's public?"

"No. No medical file is public, but it's accessible with the right permissions in place and I've seen it since I had to re-organize it. As I said, I could get fired for telling you this, but I know the battle you've fought with the press. They made you out to be her killer, but you aren't."

"I couldn't save her," I say, my head shaking. "I tried though. I tried so hard."

"You couldn't have saved her."

"I should have."

"I've seen the damage this has done to you publicly and I can only imagine how it has affected you privately, so I'm gonna get to the point. Lani Kalei didn't die from drowning. I saw her death certificate. She had a small tear in one of her heart valves and that is listed as the cause of death. The doctor-on-call's final diagnosis was clearly written. She didn't drown."

"What? I was told..." I close my eyes as my mind drifts back into the darkness of those fatal hours.

"If she had drowned, I believe your CPR tactics would've

saved her. But, the autopsy report shows the tear had grown, causing the blood to flow backward into her aortic valve and that's what actually killed her. I think it was just bad timing that she was surfing."

"What?" My dad's voice startles us both.

The clerk stubs her cigarette out in the ashtray, visibly shaken as if she's been busted.

Murphy bumps me from the side as he takes a protective stance next to me.

She stutters as she starts to explain for all of us to hear. "I mean even if Lani would've been sitting on a couch watching a movie, she would've died that day." She shifts nervously. "Both she and her family were aware of the tear prior to the accident. She'd seen a doctor in Honolulu the fall before the accident."

Staring at the pattern of the bricks of the building behind her, my disbelief over the bomb that's been dropped hits me hard. "No way! She would've told me. No way. Noah would've said something." I look her in the eyes. "They sued me," I say, needing my dad to make sense of this for me. "They took us to court because I let her drown. They blamed me. I blamed me. How is this possible?"

Realization weighs on my dad and he crosses his arms over his chest, his eyes revealing his own disbelief. "We settled out of court." When he looks back at the woman, questions now fill his eyes.

"I'm wondering if this would have come out if the case would have gone to court," she says.

After a heavy sigh, my dad looks back to me.

I remain silent, stunned by this revelation. *I didn't kill Lani.* "I didn't kill Lani." Reassuring myself, I say, "I didn't let her drown."

"No, man, you didn't. CPR wouldn't, couldn't have saved her," Murphy adds.

"Damn it!" My father's face flushes red— angry, but focused. "This can't be right. This has torn my family apart and destroyed my son."

The clerk backs up at the sudden action. "I can lose my job," she pleads.

My fists clench at my side as flames fuel the fire burning in my heart, and I say, "I'm going to fucking kill Noah Kalei."

6

MALLORY

JULY 4TH

"I don't understand why it's best *not* to talk to him," I stomp then stumble on my unsteady legs.

"Because you're drunk. That's why. You shouldn't be all emotional and drunk when you talk to him. You'll only make things worse. Let's just go to bed. Get some rest. Things will look a lot different in the morning," Kate explains, waiting at the door for Sunny.

"Will you guys stay with me?"

Both of their faces soften and Sunny says, "Sure."

In the dark, Kate says, "It was an accident, you know. I don't think my brother's to blame for Lani's death." She goes on telling more of the story, more than I've heard before.

An accident. It was an accident where Evan tried the best he could, but walked away from it damaged on the inside. I need to see him, need to talk to him. I jump out from between Kate and Sunny, my legs tangling in the covers, and trip to the floor, hitting my head on the bed frame.

With my hand pressed firmly against my head, I sit up in pain.

Sunny rushes down next to me. "Are you okay?" she asks, gently moving my hand away for a closer look. "You need to be careful. You're still a bit bruised around the old stitches."

"I don't know...that was..." The words jumble around my head.

Kate grabs my arm, pulling me back onto the bed. "Sit for a minute. You're in no condition to—"

Scrambling out of her arms and into the bathroom, I vomit, feeling my stomach convulse. A minute later, Sunny sits next to me and rubs my back as Kate pulls my hair into a rubber band, knotting it on top of my head, both of them silent.

I feel horrible and I only want this nightmare to end. After another thirty minutes of heaving, my body is feeling better and the girls leave and go to bed. I'm relieved to have a moment to myself. I can't seem to get my thoughts straight and I'm still spinning a little when I close my eyes, needing to rest. I'm exhausted, but I want to talk to Evan. *He said 'I love you'*. But he didn't say it. He yelled it for the whole world to hear.

Using my arm as a pillow to cushion my head, I lean on the side of the tub. My eyelids are heavy and I can't muster enough energy to move my weakened body.

I wake up with a start, my body aching from the uncomfortable sleeping position. Other than the pain I'm feeling, Evan consumes my thoughts. I push up off the tub and use the wall to help me balance. Unsteady on my feet, I walk down the quiet hallway, my hands on the wall as I tiptoe, careful not to wake anyone. I rummage through the living room looking for my purse but don't find it then check the kitchen without any luck either. After filling a glass with water, I rinse my mouth thoroughly before drinking more down slowly.

Reality sets in as I stare out the window over the sink. I lost my boyfriend *and* my damn phone tonight. I want to cry, my world not crumbling but crashing around me. The revving of an engine draws my attention to the front of the house. I hurry the best I can, opening the front door only to find Murphy, Zach, and a dust cloud in the driveway.

"Was that Evan?" I ask, desperate to know.

"Yes," Zach answers calmly.

I hurry down the steps and shout his name, but the taillights fade into the night, the car too far to chase. Turning around with my hands on my hips, I demand, "He was here to see me?"

"Yes." Zach's cool demeanor is frustrating, and pisses me off.

"Why didn't you let him?" I say with tears filling my eyes again. My eyes burn and I can barely see they're so swollen from all the crying I did earlier.

Zach stands and walks closer to me as Murphy sits down in a chair on the porch. "He's not thinking clearly, Mal. I know Evan well enough to know that when emotions are fueling him, it's best to stay out of his way. You've helped him—"

"Why does everyone keep saying that?" I scream in frustration, tired of hearing the same thing and not understanding the meaning behind it. "How am I helping him when I seem to only cause him pain?"

Zach ponders this thought before answering, "He battles himself as much as the rest of the world. We don't know the real deal with this text, but let him figure things out tonight and you should do the same. I'll be honest. I want you to work it out and be happy, but it's up to you two to sort that shit out before you rush back to each other with your hormones raging. We've all seen how you guys *'talk'* and it's not working for you anymore. This time when you talk you really need to talk, Mallory. And you should know where your feelings lie beforehand. Because from what I've seen, when you two are together all reasoning flies out window."

I should be offended by his directness, irritated at the very least, but Zach is speaking the truth, so I can't hold it against him. As the dust from the driveway settles, so does my anxiousness. "I don't want him to think I don't love him because I do. Knowing about Lani now and the hell he's been through...I want to be there for him, but the texts, Zach. Fucking Kelly and that text! His mother." I wipe a tear away. "It feels like everyone is conspiring against us."

Murphy leans forward, and says, "It sure does seem like it. Well, not us or Sunny or Kate, but everyone else."

"But why?" I hope he can give me the insight I'm so desperate to discover. "You're dating Kate and they don't have a problem with you, right?" I sigh in regret. "I'm sorry. I didn't mean for it to sound like that."

"I know what you mean. I know you don't think bad of me, so don't worry about it." He stands and walks to me, and his hand rubs my arm. "Evan's the son. He's the one they've groomed to take over, discounting their daughter's abilities. Kate's fucking smart as a whip. I wish she'd get a job with a competitor and hand their asses to them on a plate." He walks to the edge of the porch, sits on the railing, and says, "You're in an all-out-war here. So listen to Zach. His advice is sound. Don't go running to him because you feel sorry or guilty about Lani. Seriously think about what you want from him or if you're even willing to sacrifice for this rela-tionship because you're going to have to sacrifice. You're living in two different worlds and something like seven hours by plane. That's a lot of distance. Make sure when you make up, *if you make up with him*, it's because of who he is... who he really is at the core and not the bullshit you've been fed."

Murphy jumps off the railing and laughs. "Fuck, I'm starting to sound like Z here. I really need to start thinking about getting my own place. I'm obviously seeing his ugly mug way too much. I'm going to bed. Katie still awake?"

I look at him with a light smile. "No, I think she fell asleep a while ago."

"Well fuck. Guess I'll be sleeping after all." He walks into the house, but stops at the door, and says, "Goodnight."

"Yeah, night," I reply.

"Go in and get some rest. You're looking really pale, Mallory," Zach says, leading me in and shutting the front door behind him. "You can still have my bed."

"No, get Sunny from the sofa. I'll sleep on the couch."

He hugs me, and whispers, "I'm not going to humor you. You're both smart enough to know that you're meant to be together. Just make sure it's for the right reasons, okay?"

"Okay." I hug him, appreciating how good he's been to me. I'm glad Sunny has found such a great guy and Evan has him as a best friend.

Zach carries sleeping Sunny from the couch, leaving me to settle into the living room for the few remaining hours of night. I look at the chair, wishing I could snuggle with Evan as we had once before, the memories of that night still fresh on my mind. But I can't. It's too painful right now. Too fresh. Tonight's fiasco should have never happened. Lies have tainted all that's been good between us, but lying in the dark, two things become clear to me. One - I need answers regarding that text. And two - I need to know that he'll defend me to his family if it comes to that. I can't fight for us by myself.

I fall into a restless sleep, nightmares filling my head. "Holy crap!" I sit up, shaking and sweating.

"Are you alright?" Sunny asks, dropping the newspaper to her lap.

"Um..." I pat the couch, still trying to come to terms with where I am. "Yes, I'm fine. I think."

Sunny looks at me funny then turns the paper around and says, "Look, Southern Shores is today. Johnny called and asked if I'd help him at this t-shirt booth he's working. I think you should come. It's a major surf contest and they're usually a blast."

She sits forward, lowering her feet to the ground, and asks, "I know that you and Zach talked last night. Have you given any thought to what he said about time?"

"I tried, but I was exhausted and fell asleep. It was almost three in the morning, but I do agree that if we decide to give us another chance, we should do it knowing that stuff like this can't happen again. We need to be built on trust and honesty."

"Are you ready to make that kind of commitment?"

"Yes," I readily answer. "But I want to make sure I'm with him for the right reasons. The chemistry is there and I never question that. I think his commitment to me is there. I love him, but I don't want to end up hurting him either. I can't be with him because I think I can save him. I don't want to be his savior. Everyone else seems to want that from me. I want to be his partner. I want him to heal because he finds it within himself to want to heal. I want him to move forward, because he sees a better tomorrow for himself."

"I think that's a good way to look at it and you're definitely not a replacement for Lani. It's pretty damn obvious how much he cares about you."

"But you know what I went through when Will cheated on me. That was tough to handle and I'm already in deeper with Evan, so I need to know about that text. I know this sounds silly and contradictory, but at the same time, I really want to trust him, so I might have to take his word on this one. I'm not sure what to do. And if you say 'give it time,' I'm going to smack you, Sunny."

She stands up and walks to the opening of the hallway. "Mallory, don't rush things. You have a lot going on in your head that needs sorting. I really do think you need to give yourself some...*time*," she says with a chuckle as she suddenly runs down the hallway into Zach's room, avoiding the pillow I throw at her.

"I hate you, Sunny!" I yell, partly joking...okay, fully joking, but damn it, I need someone to tell me something different.

I shower and get dressed in some of Sunny's clothes. After searching frantically for my phone and still not finding it, I concede and tell Sunny I'll go with her to the surf contest.

As she's driving, I look down on the floorboard and see my purse, relieved to find it. I pull out my phone and then drop my head back while closing my eyes in frustration. It's dead.

I'm supposed to be giving the whole 'us' thing serious consideration, but I can't stop the ache in my chest over the pain he must be feeling about how things went down last night. I sit back in the seat and start thinking about all that I know about Evan. There's so much more to him than most give him credit for, but I see him, the real him under the arrogance and privilege, and how much he has to offer the world. I will never forget how he's shown me happiness and made me feel desired and alive. Glancing to Sunny, I ask, "Can I use your phone?"

Her expression reassures me that I've made the right decision. She doesn't give me a hard time or make any faces or jokes about not being able to stay away from him. She hands me the phone. "I don't have Evan's number, but he's with Zach."

I scroll until I find Zach's name and push the button. Four rings and then I'm sent to voicemail. Unsure of what to say, I waver and sigh. "Hey Zach, it's Mallory. Um..." Looking to Sunny, her smile is sympathetic. She sees my struggle. "Will you let Evan know I called? Thanks." I was disappointed I didn't say more, but with my emotions still swirling, it was hard to get that much out.

On the drive to the beach, Sunny doesn't pressure me for a conversation she knows I'm not ready to have. She gives me *time*.

When we arrive at the beach, we both squeal when Johnny greets us with a tight, squeezy hug. He seems happy, which makes me smile. I wonder for a split second if it's because he's seeing Sunny, but then he introduces us to Lorelei, and that thought is instantly replaced. Johnny rests his hand on her lower back as she stands to shake our hands. She's pretty—Hawaiian in heritage with long hair and beautiful, dark gleaming eyes. When Johnny talks to her, his face lights up, and my heart melts seeing him so smitten. He seems to be getting over Sunny just fine.

"Lorelei has this cool vintage looking t-shirt line. We have a booth set up and get swarmed between each heat."

"I really appreciate you coming here to help me out today," Lorelei says, smiling at us.

It's good to be busy and will hopefully take my mind off

of my own problems, but I know deep down that it won't take my mind off Evan. Nothing could right now.I put on a smile for them, and ask, "No problem. Glad we can help. Where do you need me?"

Sorting the folded t-shirts by size and color makes me feel useful. I thought I wanted things off of my mind, but I should have known that was impossible. I do the assigned task and let my mind 'go there.' Reliving the events of last night isn't fun, but I find chinks in the flow of the evening that lead me to the only conclusion I can live with: it doesn't matter what the text said. Ultimately, I do trust Evan. He doesn't need to lie to me because he doesn't have a reason to. He loves me. I know because I feel it in my own heart. Plus, when he professed his love publicly the other night, I was sure half of Hawaii heard him.

Watching the surfers out in the water, I hear Noah's name announced in the heat as the lead in the contest.

Noah!

It was Noah who wronged me, us. Noah spied on us and then used that information against Evan which also ended up embarrassing me in front of everyone including Evans' parents. He sacrificed my reputation for his own emotional gain. *And all for what?* Because he wanted to tear Evan down again? My anger rises to the surface. What seemed cloudy and convoluted now seems so clear. Suddenly it's as if the world has shifted back to a time where Evan and I belonged together. And damn it, I want Evan. He's my sexy surfer and I love him. It's time I fight for him.

'Noah Kalei wins the final heat and the Southern Shores champion title,' the announcer blares through the speakers scattered on the beach.

I look up, focused on the main stage thirty yards away. "Perfect timing." I consider rubbing my hands together in an evil fashion and releasing a crazed cackle, but I save the dramatics for another time. I don't want to seem deranged when I see Noah or he won't trust me enough to listen. And boy is he about to get an earful! I start walking, a newfound confidence surging through my veins.

7

MALLORY

I track Noah down behind the winner's stage where he just had beer dumped on him.

He's doing an interview, but as soon as he's done, I call, "Hey Noah." I keep my eyes on his, not looking at the large trophy in his hands, purposely not acknowledging his win.

"Mallory!" He hurries over and hugs me, lifting me up off the ground, spinning around, and planting a kiss on my cheek. I won't give in and wait for him to put me down. His brow furrows, but he recovers quickly and smiles. "I won! I really won."

He holds out the shiny trophy for my appraisal. I keep my tone flat. "Yeah, so you did. I wanted to see if we could talk for a minute. I mean, I hate to interrupt..." That's not true at all. "...your celebration back here, but—"

"I'm glad you're here. Yeah, let's celebrate. Have you been to a luau? You told me before you want to go to one before you leave. My family is having one tonight. I want you to come with me."

"Oh, um, I don't think that's a good idea. I'd like to talk

now," I say, knowing there are a few choice words I want to say to him, but unlike him, I'd prefer to say them in private.

Looking over his shoulder at his dad, who is beaming and shaking hands with other spectators, he turns back and says, "Well, I kind of have to go now. Come with me. We can talk there."

I'm too angry inside and need to right this wrong that has gone on too long. I can't let this slide any longer, so I agree. "I guess I'll come for a bit, but we need to talk—"

"Great! Meet me over in the parking lot in ten, okay?"

"Fine," I say, my chipper tone to most would render me untrustworthy, but he takes it at face value. I need to get this over and done with, location is irrelevant to me. I turn on my heel and walk back to the t-shirt booth. *This is right*. This is what I should've done over a month ago. *Evan was right*. I can see the lies behind Noah's eyes so clearly now and I can't wait to call him out. His victory party just might turn out to be my own personal celebration.

I let Sunny know I'm going with Noah. She's shocked by this revelation and warns against it, but I can't let this opportunity slip away. "What am I supposed to tell Zach if he asks about you? You know he's with Evan today."

"I don't want you to lie, but I need to settle things. I can't let this drag out any longer."

"Like settling a score?" she asks, eyebrows raised.

"Don't be so dramatic!" I laugh. "I've got to resolve this, not for Noah, but for me...*and Evan*. It's time I set things straight with both of them and since I'm not with Evan, I'm starting with Noah."

I meet Noah in the parking lot at his Jeep. He has the engine already going and the trophy loaded in the back with his board strapped on top. He's excited and the sheer happiness on his face is kind of contagious. The friendship we've shared is starting to override the memories of the tug-of-war he made me play against Evan. When he takes off down the road, his tires leave a trail of rubber on the cement behind and I hold on to the side for safety.

"Mallory," he starts, raising his voice above the wind blowing through the open-air Jeep. "I wanted to tell you that I'm sorry about last night at the party. I shouldn't have said those things in front everyone. My temper took over. I'm sorry."

"You humiliated me, Noah," I say, anger coating my tone. "Why would you do that? Why would you hurt me like that?"

"I didn't mean to hurt you. I was trying to show everyone that Ashford treats you like every other girl he's ever had sex with. You're not special to him like you are to me. You were blinded by the money. I get that, but he's all surface and show, Mallory."

A gasp escapes me at his insult and I feel disappointment color my expression. "You think so little of me. I guess this is good to find out now." Feeling betrayed, I want to leave, hiding how his words, his true feelings, hurt me, but I don't. I have to be strong and finish what I started by coming here with him. I take a deep breath. "Listen Noah. I'm gonna say this once, so pay attention. Evan means a lot to me. I'm not gonna lie or downplay how important he is. What I share with him is real and he treats me well, better than you think. He treats me like he loves me and that's all I want from someone I'm with."

He pulls into a lot and parks, killing the engine and hopping out. I get out and meet him at the front of the car, trying to keep him focused. Clearly he's not focused on me at the moment. I can't blame him for that, though. I do feel a lot of other blame can be placed squarely on his shoulders. "We need to talk about this now."

"We'll talk, but my family is waiting. Let's go over and say hi, and then we can take a walk on the beach and talk." He turns and walks ahead, across the short green grass of the park toward the beach picnic area.

I trudge behind him and watch over the next hour as his family grows in numbers and he has to spend time with each arriving member. I swim in my own irritation, unfriendly, and unwavering in my anger waiting on him.

The sky turns dark and I'm tired, extra pissed, and ready to talk, so I call him over.

He jogs toward me, apologetic. "I'm sorry, but winning today is my dream come true. I kind of got caught up in the party. You want a beer or something?"

"No. Can we finish talking, please?"

He rolls his eyes, shaking his head as if he's been waiting for this confrontation all along. The way he's playing this off fuels my irritation. "Why are you so mad?" he asks. "I was honest with you, which was more than Ashford was and you're throwing it in my face. So go ahead and shoot, Mallory. I can take it. Just know before you get pissier, I actually like you."

"You're being so self-centered." I mimic his eye-roll. "This... this expectation you seem to be holding onto between us, it's got to stop."

"So Ashford finally got to you. I knew he would." His cocky side starts to come out. "I kind of expected it sooner. He must be losing his touch."

My hands fly to the air, representing my temper that I lose control of. "Evan didn't work on me or turn me against you, Noah. You did a fine job all on your own. Last night proved that to me."

"He's got you fooled," he says, shaking his head in disappointment. "You leave in a month. Do you really think he's going to be faithful once you leave? Hell, he wasn't faithful with you here. You heard that girl at the party. He's been talking to her all along—"

"No, he hasn't. I know it's a lie. I know it."

"How? How can you tell? I've seen him lie with a confident smile on his face, believing his own bullshit."

I look off toward the ocean and the reflection of the moon on the choppy waters before crossing my arms and looking back up at him, staring him in the eyes. "He didn't cheat. I believe him. He loves me and he wouldn't hurt me."

"He only declared his undying love for you because you were leaving with me, baby," he says as he reaches for me, stroking my cheek.

"Don't call me that and don't touch me! You only pursued me because Evan was interested. You covered your lies in the charade of a friendship. Were we ever real friends, Noah? Did you ever really like me? Because if these are your true colors than you win and I lose because I trusted you."

"You're no loser and we met before I knew about Ashford being in the picture, but even I can man up, unlike him, and admit, it did make the chase more appealing." He chuckles, looking away briefly. When his eyes target mine again, he says, "Then I wanted to fuck you to prove a point to Ashford. But I didn't take that further because I actually care about you." His hand touches my cheek again and his voice is softer as if that will take the sting from the words he confessed. "He's a fuck-up, Mallory. I'm a winner. I got the trophy to prove it today." He laughs. "I know you feel the chemistry between us. Give us a chance."

I turn from his touch, the contact prickling my skin as a warning. "I said don't touch me."

Offense is written all over his face and his jaw hardens, all hope disappearing from his eyes. "I think you're right. Let's skip the foreplay and celebrate my win with a first place fuck." His large hands reach around my body, grabbing me by my ass and pulling me roughly against him. Just as he leans in for a kiss, I start to struggle, but his hands hold me firmly in place, so I can't back away or take a swing at him like I really want to do.

I finally manage enough strength to shove back, which is like pushing off of a brick wall—unmoving, and intimidating.

"Noah!" I scream, shocked by his abrasiveness and audacity, wondering how far he would have taken things if we weren't surrounded by others.

"C'mon, baby. How long are we gonna pretend we don't want this?" he asks, signaling between us. "I've seen you check me out more than a few times."

I feel dirty, dumbfounded by what an asshole he's become. But with his new found confidence, that I assume he got from winning the surf contest, I realize he's serious. He actually believes I want him. My hand goes out to stop him. "So let me get this straight. You think I've been 'pretending' to not want to sleep with you? For real?"

"Oh, there'd be no sleeping involved, sexy," he says smugly, grabbing me against him again.

I don't know if it's his face, his gall, what he said about me at the Ashford's party, his complete lack of respect for Evan being in my life, or maybe all of the above, but the emotions that have been simmering inside of me the last twenty-four hours boil over when he calls me baby again. Only Evan has earned that right. Feeling strong—mentally and physically—I slap his face, a knee-jerk reaction before logic catches up.

When the palm of my hand makes contact across his cheek, the sting is immediate, like a bed of tiny needles piercing my skin. I stumble back, grabbing my hand and squeezing it into a fist to fight the searing pain. "Holy Hell!" My eyes begin to water as the pain holds steady.

Noah's laughing, but it's the loud snarl from a few feet away that grabs my attention. There stands Evan and I lose all feeling of pain as my eyes connect with his, my heart soaring as everything becomes clear in that moment. Evan is everything that matters. He's mine and I'm his and all of our good intentions are good enough.

His eyes hold only love for me as he comes closer. Taking my hand in his, he brings it to his mouth and kisses it. The sense of relief I feel from his tenderness heals all wounds. I just want to leave with him, escape to our own world, wishing I could take away all the bad that's ever been and love him forever.

But Evan has different ideas about how the next few minutes are going to go. And just like how he's passionate about me, the flip side to that passion is his hatred for Noah. When I see his expression, eyes glaring at his enemy, I know it's too late. My heart is pounding in my chest, my head spinning as I try to figure out how I'm going to stop a war that's already begun.

8

EVAN

"Evan, Stop!" I hear my dad yelling as I make a dash from the hospital to the car. I see red after what that hospital clerk told me and I've got to go and now!

Zach and Murphy catch up to me. They block my path, and Zach, the voice of sanity says, "Kalei's entire family will be there. We'll be out numbered."

Murphy hits him in the chest. "You chickening out, brah?"

"Fuck no, but he has a big fucking family and I don't feel like spending the next week in the hospital."

I fume, no reasoning left in my mind. I'm ready to take Noah on once and for all. "This has been a long time coming. I'm going with or without you." I cross my arms over my chest and throw down an ultimatum. "You in or out, Z?"

"If you're going, you know I'll be there, man."

I shake his hand and nod once.

"Evan!" my dad calls just as I'm about to leave. He walks with purpose with his eyes focused on me. "I know you're angry, but is chasing Noah down really going to give you the answers you need to feel better? The result you want?"

"Absolutely!" I lock eyes with his, trying to match the intensity I've seen him use many times in the boardroom.

He grabs me, pulling me by the neck toward him, forcing my forehead against his. With our eyes still engaged, he lowers his voice and says, "You've been absent from my life for too long. Don't go waging a war that could end in your demise. I don't want to lose you a second time."

I reach my arms around his neck and nod in understanding. "You won't. We'll win this round. I need to do this, but I need to know I have your support." In that moment, I realize I'm about two inches taller than him. He's right. I've been so absent from my life that I don't remember growing up? "Are you with us?"

"I can't support violence, so I hope you cool down. But you've been hurt. We all have, so there's nowhere else I would be right now. If you're there, I'm there, but I'm driving." He backs up and starts for his car.

Murphy says, "You're really going, Hugh?"

He stops and smiles. If I wasn't paying attention, I might have missed the devious glint in his eyes when he says, "Yes, I am. Not the smartest decision I've made recently, but my boy has been wronged, so I need to be there for him."

Trying to keep my mouth from dropping open, I tense my jaw instead. I hold back the feelings of joy wanting to overcome me, trying to save it for later. As much as I want to savor in the fact that my dad is willing to go to protect me, to help me, and to support me simply to be there for me, I can't get lost in the niceties of the moment. I need to hold onto the anger and pain I feel inside by being broken by the Kalei family.

Murphy and Zach chuckle. Murphy says, "Don't worry. I've got your back, Sir."

"That's good to know because I'll probably need it."

I know my best friends well enough to know they're in the car behind us psyching themselves up, probably placing a wager on who gets the most hits in. I can appreciate that. But my father and I sit in a tension-filled silence. As we pull into the parking lot, with my hand on the door lever, I whisper, "Thank you."

He looks over at me and nods his head. I jump out and start running toward the gathering of Noah's family. I hear Zach behind me yelling to my dad, "You sure you're ready to fight."

"Damn sure, but try to talk first, boys. Always try to talk it through first."

"Okay, old man. Let's go serve some justice," Zach says, patting my dad on the back.

"Well, all-righty. Let's go get those lying bastards," Murphy says, elevating his voice as we jog to the luau on the beach.

A commotion up ahead draws my eye. I spot Mallory...*in Noah's arms*, but I can't hear what's being said as she pushes him away and slaps him across the face. "Holy Hell!" she screams as she stumbles backward. He's laughing at her, which pisses me off even more, but then the scene before me registers.

I stop shocked by what is playing out before my eyes. "Holy shit," I say, stunned when I see Mallory slapping Noah Kalei. That's my girlfriend taking care of herself. *And to think I foolishly thought I'd be saving her.* I knew I loved her, but that right there shows me the firecracker that she was that first day I met her. My girlfriend is a fucking badass.

But there's no time to revel in her greatness because the

damage he's caused me and my family weighs heavy on my mind and my hands fist. I start running again, ready to settle all past pains and lies. And as much as I love that I didn't have to point out what an ass he really is, it also doesn't change my feelings of wanting to punch his face in for touching my girl.

When I reach her, I take her hurt hand in mine and kiss it gently. Looking at it, it's red, but she's gonna be fine. I place another kiss on her knuckles and whisper into her ear, "We're gonna talk, but right now, I need you to back away, baby."

"Why?" she asks, her gaze shifting to Noah then back to me.

Keeping my voice low, for her ears alone, I kindly ask, "Will you please back up for your own safety?" I turn ready to attack Noah, verbally first.

Mallory grabs my arm and moves closer. "No! Why? I don't want you fighting."

I turn back to her, hearing the plea beneath the demand. "Can you please listen to me and not be so stubborn this time. This isn't about you...Well, it is about you, but it's mainly about the lies these motherfuckers had me believe."

Noah crosses his arms after taking a step forward. "Who you calling motherfucker, fucker?"

"You, because you are," I spew back at him.

"Actually, speaking of mother*fuckers*," he starts smugly, "your mother does have a fine as—"

My dad cuts in, his face as stern as his tone. "That's my wife, Noah! Kindly refrain from talking about her."

Kekoa Kalei, Noah's father flanks his son's side, as well as a few of his cousins that make up his gang of misfits. Kekoa tries to reason with Noah. "Son, he's right. Don't be disrespectful."

"That's a joke." I step forward pointing my finger between Noah and Kekoa. "How could you do it? Lani loved me and you let me think I killed her, like it was my fault she died. I didn't have a chance and you knew that all along. That's disrespectful to her memory."

"What are you rambling about, Ashford?" Noah asks, his feet anchoring into the sand with his body on the defense.

"I know about Lani's heart. I know how she really died. The tear in her heart caused her death, not my inability to save her." My hands fist at my sides. "You knew and you didn't tell me. We used to be good friends, Noah, best friends. How can you be so fucking cruel?"

"Listen, Hugh, I don't know where you and Evan got this information, but it's not—" Kekoa starts.

"Don't, Kekoa! We know the truth now. We settled with you out of court because I believed your pain, I saw the anguish in my son as you let him believe he caused your daughter's death. I wanted to end his suffering in public. He was persecuted in the papers and you allowed that, you lied." I watch my dad standing tall and powerful, sure of his every word.

I nod, agreeing with him when I'm struck by a surprise blow to my left cheek and fall to the ground, sand flying into my face.

"Evan!" Mallory screams.

When I look up, all hell breaks loose. The cousins attack Zach and Murphy, and I snap up, putting my hand on Mallory's middle to push her behind me. "Move back, baby!"

I run forward, landing a right hook across Noah's shocked face and follow through with a left punch to his stomach, which sends him stumbling backward. I see Murphy in my peripheral tossing one guy into the sand. I glance to my right and find Zach already rolling in the sand with another, appearing to have things under control. I look for Mallory, who's standing there horrified with her hands over her mouth. When I turn back, Noah is in full swing motion. I'm too fast for him and I duck. He stumbles a bit, landing his fist straight on my dad's jaw. My dad flinches, but quickly resumes his composure and swings, taking Noah down with one smooth direct punch.

Kekoa rushes to his son's aid while yelling profanities. All the fighting ceases and the cousins, bloodied and breathing heavy, return to their side of the respective line drawn in the sand.

Kekoa helps Noah to his feet and gripes at my father. "You hurt him. You should be asha—"

"You've ruined my son's life for the last four years. The truth is out and you no longer have him to carry your daughter's death as his own burden anymore. Descended from royals my ass!" He looks at me and smirks then turns back once more to Kekoa. "I expect my money to be returned. If you need to make payments then contact my lawyer and he'll set that up. It's blood money now. Please do the right thing here and remove the guilt that weighs on my son's heart by paying it back or we will sue you for everything you own and more."

The murmur of his family and friends collectively gasping from this news is overshadowed by Mallory rushing to my side, whispering my name and words of concern. My father's words of support mixed with hers make my heart and confidence soar. I feel more myself than I have in years, the weight of guilt finally lifted. I wrap my arm around Mallory's trembling shoulders, and hold her to me. She's crying and I love her so much that I hug her even tighter, lucky to have the opportunity again.

My dad looks at us, and a small smile plays out. "It's time to go."

We turn our backs on Noah's family celebration without fear or worry of them striking because they know we now have the upper hand.

Noah gives it one last desperate attempt. "*Mallory!* C'mon. He's only gonna use you and toss you aside. Come back."

She flips him the bird over her shoulder, but never turns around to look at him. "What an asshole," she replies without remorse.

"Guess your hand is okay," I tease.

She wiggles it around. "I'm gonna live."

I load her into my dad's car then jog over to Zach's. My father is about to sit down when I call, "Hey, Dad?"

He stops before getting in. "Yes?"

"Uh, I wanted to..." I stumble through my appreciation with my hands tucked safely into my front pockets. "...I wanted to say thank you for... what you did back there, all that you said."

"You're welcome, Evan. You okay?"

"I should be asking you that?" I say, looking at his jaw. My mother is gonna be pissed when she sees that.

"Eh, I've been in worse—"

"You've been in worse? You're not really the fighting kind, Dad," I say incredulously.

"I could hold my own back in ancient times," he says, and chuckles.

"You still can from what I just saw." I glance back at his car and see Mallory sitting inside, waiting for me. "Maybe we can grab a beer together sometime and you can share some of those stories."

"I'd like that. Let's do that when you're in New York next month."

I nod and we shake hands, but I pull him into a hug. We part with deep sighs, a little bit awkward from this big show of affection.

"Drive your girl home," he says, handing me the keys.

"Okay, thanks."

"Don't put a scratch on that car or I get yours." He smirks and I can see a bit of myself in him for the first time.

After I get in the car, I look over at Mallory briefly before driving away. Out of the corner of my eye I see her spreading her fingers then squeezing her hand closed, so I ask, "You sure you're okay?"

"I'm fine. It just stings."

Reaching over, I'm about to touch her hand, but pause, not sure if I should go there. I sigh, tired from the day, mentally exhausted from dealing with the truth about Lani, and physically beat from the fight. But somehow I find the will to smile. The girl next to me means more than I ever thought possible and she's here with me now.

I pull out onto the road and continue driving. It's only a few minutes and both us seem okay with waiting to have a conversation that may define us forever. Upon arrival, I park at the beach and we both get out at the same time. I hang back, suddenly feeling awkward about where we stand, letting her take the lead. I don't know how I'll deal if she walks away forever. So I want her to be comfortable in her surroundings because I want this conversation to bring us back together.

With my heart in her hands, I take a blanket from the trunk as she pulls a pack of cigarettes from her pocket. Flicking one up, she pulls it from the paper container with her lips and I immediately pull a lighter from my pocket and stride over to her offering her the fire. She leans in like she did the first day, all attitude and beauty, until the stick is glowing and then she walks down to the water's edge. I silently follow.

"I haven't been back here since I drown..." She doesn't finish the sentence, but exhales a deep breath. She doesn't have to say more. I know what she's thinking. I watch her with bated anticipation as she bends down to put out the cigarette in the wet sand at her feet.

After spreading the blanket out, we both sit, but the distance is felt between us. Apparently, she needs the space.

"It seemed fitting to come back here," I say, keeping my voice from wavering. It's tough because I want her back, but it's up to her if she's going to trust me or not. "The right place to deal with some of our... fears and issues."

Seeing her again, it's easy to admire her beauty, but tonight I need her forgiveness. I just pray to God she'll hear me out. "I'm sorry, Mallory," I whisper, trying to find my voice. "I'm sorry that you have to deal with my past and for the way you were treated at the party."

She doesn't look at me, but her movements and tiny fidgets finally still. After another long moment of silence in the space that divides us, she says, "I'm sorry for how I acted. I'm embarrassed. I overreacted and shouldn't have put you in a situation of having to 'end' us... I was trying to make you out to be the bad guy because I'm not strong enough to leave you. Forcing you to be the bad guy was easier than having to deal with the bullshit your mother and ex were throwing my way."

I look at the water, hoping the right words come, but I don't have the time to wait. "Don't apologize. You have nothing to be sorry about, but I do. I want you to know I sent the text in May. I'm sorry I sent it and I regret how this has affected you. You never deserved to have to deal with my mistakes."

She remains staring at the water in the distance. "Evan, you don't have to explain."

"I want you to know the truth. I don't want you to ever doubt my intentions."

She sounds as if she's amused, but she's not smiling when she says, "I wish I could have held my emotional breakdown for another time, but well, cheating is a sore subject with me."

Averting my eyes back to the moon's reflection on the water, I explain to ease the pain she's feeling. "The text was sent after we'd met, but days after when we weren't speaking. You stormed out of my life full of anger. I thought you hated me. I returned a text from her and only wrote what I did to appease her, not meaning any of it. I shouldn't have sent it, but I did."

"You continued the lie you like to tell the girls? The love'em and leave'em game-plan that was working so well for you?"

"Working well until I met you, yes." I smile. I don't think she's mad and I realize even that short time apart has made a difference.

"I have proof of when I originally texted it, if you need to—"

"I don't need to see it," she says.

Looking at her, I see for the first time how fragile she really is as her eyes well with tears. Her tough exterior has broken down and her cool kid vibe has vanished. She wraps her arms around her knees and rests her chin on top. "Listen, Mallory, I'm not going to lie here. I'm not any good at this. I'm not good at relationships or fighting with girls, I'm not good at saying I'm sorry or for being what someone else needs. I've been selfish for a long time now, so know that I'm trying. I'm trying to be who you want me to be and who you deserve."

"I don't want you to be anything you're not. That's part of the problem here. I'm not your parents or your professors. I'm not the outside world with expectations of you, except for one. I expect you to be true to me and being true to me means not cheating or lying to me." Her hand touches my arm, bridging the gap. My heart races at her touch as she finally looks into my eyes. "But our friends made me realize I wasn't being true to you. I believed Kelly's word over yours and that's not the person I want to be, not with you. Yet today when I woke up, I didn't need explanations. I didn't need you to clarify the situation. I don't believe *her*. There were holes I couldn't see yesterday in the heat of the moment. I'm sorry I questioned us when you held strong."

She moves a few inches closer, leaning her head on my shoulder. She doesn't make a production of it and this feels natural, like nothing bad has ever entered our world. "I'm sorry and I'm hoping you'll forgive me," she says.

"You have nothing to be forgiven for because you did nothing wrong. I've done what you did at that party. It was like if I did something extreme it would make the bad go away, cover it up, but doing that doesn't work and I learned that lesson the hard way." I take her hand in mine and whisper, "I don't want anything like that to come between us again. I love you, Mallory. I'm *in* love with you."

When she looks up, her lips part as her eyes glass over with tears and her words fall quiet taking in the joy of hearing mine. "Please," she says, her request barely heard, "say it again."

"I love you," I say, freely without hesitation.

Weaving our fingers together, I look only at her, the sight

of her the only thing that matters and makes sense in this chaotic life. "I should've told you before now, before the party. I felt it. I always felt it. When I made you those promises that we'd be together, that was my heart speaking to yours, not just words. I'm in love with you, Mallory, and I should've exposed my true feelings a long time ago instead of internalizing them."

Her tears fall over the barrier of her bottom lids and drop onto her lap as she tucks her head downward. I wrap my arm around her, holding her tightly to my side. Her body trembles against mine as she cries, releasing all the pent-up emotions of the last couple of days. Leaning forward, I kiss the top of her head several times.

When her body relaxes—the anxiety, fears, and tears subsiding—she looks up at me, her smile struggling between pain and happiness. "I love you so much my heart hurts."

"Mine too, baby." It's the truth.

We lay down, my arm acting as her pillow as she snuggles into my side. The beauty that surrounds not lost in the emotions of the moment. The soft wind blows and the nearby trees rustle in the breeze. The gentle sounds of the water caress the sand, and distant seagulls call to each other. After a while our breathing levels, and I whisper, "I can never leave you either. I love you too much for that."

I feel her cheeks move up in a smile on my arm then her breathing deepens. Her body relaxes with mine and we fall asleep under a full moon in paradise.

9

EVAN

I wake with a start, unaware of where I am. But a deep breath of relief escapes me when I realize I'm holding Mallory. All those same sounds that lulled us to sleep last night signal our whereabouts now. I turn and look at Mallory's contented face as she rests with ease next to me. Looking into the distant water, I see the start of an amazing sunrise.

"Mallory." I gently nudge. "Mallory, wake up."

"Mmmm," she hums, slowly squirming to life. Her eyes flicker open as reality sets in. "We slept out here." It's more a statement of amazement than a question.

I sit up, helping her up next to me. My voice is still groggy with sleep, but I say, "Yes, we did. I guess we were both more tired than we thought."

She rubs her eyes and in this most innocent of movements, my heart lurches when I remember that in one month I won't get to appreciate such a simple act.

She looks up at me, her lids still heavy. "I didn't sleep much the night before, you know, after the party."

"Neither did I. At least we got a few hours last night. I

want to watch this sunrise together and then I'll take you home."

She nods, leaning back against me for support.

"Can I ask you something?" I'm kind of worried about her answer.

"Yes."

Staring ahead, I ask, "Why didn't you call me back yesterday?"

"Oh, um, my phone is dead since I haven't been home, so I couldn't charge it. I tried to call you, but... well, I don't have your number memorized since I have it programmed into my phone. Then I used Sunny's phone to call Zach, but he didn't answer. I left a message for you to call me back."

"I didn't get it. I would've called you if I had. I'm sorr—"

"No." She scrunches her nose and looks embarrassed. "I'm the one who's sorry. I'm sorry about the party and I'm totally humiliated by how I acted. I drank to help me calm down from how Kelly made me feel and ended up being buzzed and not thinking logically. The time apart may have been painful, but it served a good purpose. It gave me time to sort through the events on my own and realize how much I screwed up for believing her over you." She looks into my eyes, and says, "I regret so much, starting with going to the surf contest. I need you to know that I only went to help Johnny and Sunny out. When I was there, my thoughts cleared and it was so obvious. Noah wasn't a friend to me if he could say all the things he did. I was so stupid."

"No, you weren't. He's just an asshole."

She smiles then continues, "I think he was genuine at first, but I became something else to him, something he wanted to win away from you. He even told me that yesterday before you showed up." Her face is anguished. "I only went to the luau to tell him I had him figured out and that's when things got out of control. I guess you saw how it went down from there."

"We don't need to rehash what we did wrong, but when Zach told me you went to the luau... I can't lie. It hurt that you were celebrating with him."

"I feel I owe you so many apologies, and I do. I'm so sorry. I should have talked to you first. At the time, I felt it was the only opportunity I had to tell him off. Going there was selfish, but it also showed me who Noah really is." She briefly looks away, lowering her gaze to the ground. "I saw a person I didn't know at all and if you wouldn't have shown up when you did—"

Something dark comes over her. When she looks up at me, I ask, "What's wrong? What happened?"

"Don't worry. He was handled and I learned I'm stronger than I thought I was," she says. "I'm tired of talking about him." Taking my hand, she brings it to her chest, holding it tightly. "The only thing that's important now is that you know I love you, Evan, and I'm sorry I didn't trust you. That won't happen again. I promise."

I nod and then kiss her head, needing to be satisfied that this has tested us and now it's clear where we stand—firmly at each other's side.

We gather our stuff, dusting the sand off us and the blanket before going back to the car. I wait with the passenger's side door open for her, but she stops before getting in. "I'm glad you brought me here. This feels good again. What about you? How are you feeling?"

"Seems like a lot of bad stuff has happened on this island, but it's where I felt I needed to be last year. My heart doesn't feel as heavy today," I say, kissing her on the forehead when all I want to do is kiss her on the lips. She slides into the passenger seat and I drive her back to Sunny's.

After stopping the engine, I wait, unsure if I'm invited in or not. She gets out, but stops to duck back in and ask, "Coming?" She doesn't sound unsure at all.

I jump out, knowing she wants me with her. Inside, she empties her pockets onto the table and plugs in her phone. Turning back to face me, she smiles, and says, "I have to be at work in an hour. We have to clean the place from top to bottom before we open today. Will you stay with me until then?"

I sit on the couch, resting my forearms on my knees. "I'll drive you."

She tilts her head and the smile on her face is so sweet and sincere that I sit upright and smile in response. "So, *us*, we're all good, right?" she asks.

I gulp before walking to her, relieved she's feeling the same and still wants to be a part of *us*. I bring her into me, engulfing her frame against mine.

Her arms have already made their way around me, but she doesn't move, not even to breathe. When she finally looks up at me, she's deep in thought. Her eyes in that moment are darker than I've seen, her pupils wide, taking me in, pulling me into their depths. She drops her gaze, hiding her face against my chest and says, 'I love you and that's enough for me."

"I love you, too, Mallory."

"I know you do. I knew all along." She sighs then asks, "Did I screw us up?"

"No," I reply, tilting her chin up so she has to look at me. "It's not that. I don't want to hurt you and I feel like that's all I know how to do."

She laughs softly. "You know how to give love, Evan. I just don't think you know how to receive it."

"I think the same could be said of you."

"What a pair of fools we make."

"Fools in love."

"Yes, fools in love." She walks into the bathroom, starts the shower flowing, and comes back. "Maybe we should start over."

"I want to be with you."

She gives me that smile that pierces my soul with its beauty and then says, "I know. I also want to be with you, but maybe we should live for now and not worry so much about what's next."

I step closer, taking her by the hips, and say, "Have fun in the present?"

"Yes. We can stop worrying about tomorrow and live for today."

I don't really believe that either of us is capable of this, but I agree in theory so nod. "Can I still tell you how much I love you? I mean now that I've yelled it so the whole island knows, I don't know if I'll be able to stop myself from saying it. You'll probably get sick of hearing it. Besides, I like the way the words taste on my tongue."

"And how do the words 'I Love You' taste, Evan?"

"They taste like you."

A huge smile appears, and she says, "Then never stop saying them because I will never get enough of hearing that."

"I hope not because I'm going to be saying it a lot." I press my lips lightly against hers and whisper into her mouth, "I love you." Our mouths meld together and I deepen the kiss, opening, allowing our tongues to greet each other.

She presses her hands against my chest, slightly pushing until our lips agonizingly separate.

"I still need to shower the beach off of me and probably

brush my teeth. You wanna join me?" she asks, her expression full of sexy innuendo.

"If I do, I can promise two things. You'll definitely not be getting clean in there and you will be late for work." I grow hard waiting for her response and say a silent prayer for this to go my way.

She rubs her hips against my erection, and says, "I know we weren't apart that long, but I miss the feel of you. I want you, Evan. All of you. I want to feel you inside me."

"I want you more than you know." I place my hand on my chest right above my heart. "This is the tip of the fire that burns inside of me. Only for you, baby." She melts into me again as we continue kissing.

But then she stops as my hands wrap around her middle. "Wait, we can't. I promised Alana I would be there ready to work and I don't want to disappoint her."

"Okay," slips from my lips, yet I feel anything but okay about letting her go.

"Do you hate me?" she asks, shyly looking up at me from beneath her lashes.

"No, I can't hate you, but I might be disliking you a lot around noon when I can't walk because I'm in so much pain down here." I reference my cock.

She laughs as if I'm kidding with her.

"C'mon, it won't be that bad." She looks at me dreamily and the playfulness disappears as she says, "We always have tonight."

"Yes, we do, but what if we're really quick?" I pull her hips against mine, making her feel what she does to me. Nuzzling into her hair, I take a deep breath, thankful I get to do this to her then smile at the thought of what I plan to do to her later tonight.

Pushing her toward the bathroom, I smack her ass. "Go shower before I give you no choice, sexy."

She giggles then runs off to the bathroom.

I walk back to the couch and sit down, but I'm uncomfortable so I adjust myself.

A minute later, she peeks out from behind the bathroom door. "I love you." She pauses then asks, "You sure you're okay?"

I could answer that in so many ways, but I keep it simple. "I'm fine." But really, I'm elated, unattended boner or not. I've got my girl back and that trumps everything.

WHEN I DROP her off at Big Kehones, and we kiss briefly, saving everything for later. With that in mind, I smile, knowing the best part of a fight is the making up part and that's coming tonight. I start to harden at the thought of our reunion.

I go home and crash until early afternoon when Kate comes in and demands that I spend time with her and our parents. I've made peace with my dad, but haven't seen my mother since I barged into their room telling her to fuck off. I need to face her and deal with her head on. So I grumpily climb out of bed and get dressed again. Kate makes a pot of coffee and I join her with a cup on the back step.

She eventually stands and without looking back down at me states, "I'm going to work for Ashford Holdings."

Surprised by her announcement, I stand up in shock. "What? When'd you decide that?"

"I was offered the job graduation weekend."

"Does Murphy know? I thought you...loved him and all that stuff?"

She turns, now surprised by my question. "I do love him, Evan. The two aren't mutually exclusive."

"But he's here. Does he already know?"

She looks back out at the view. "Yes, I told him the day I came back to the island." Her tone turns defensive. "I can't help the location of the job. It's in New York. We always knew that's where the family business would stay rooted."

Rubbing my forehead, I try to process this new information. "I didn't think you wouldn't work for dad. I guess I thought that maybe you were changing your mind on some things since you met Murph. You told me before that this relationship is different."

"Liam has another semester—"

"Liam?"

"Yes," she says, putting her hands on her hips. "His name is Liam."

"I know his name is Liam, Kate. He's my best friend. But since when did you start calling him Liam?"

She rolls her eyes. "As I was saying before I was rudely interrupted, Liam only has one more semester of school left. I need a job now and I've been planning to enter the family business since I was ten. You know that's why I got my business degree. I'll admit that he's made me triple guess my decision, but it's not rational for me to give everything up for someone I'm dating." She leans against the small house. "I'm thrilled you've found Mallory, but you two have more time to figure stuff like this out since you're both still in school."

"She's leaving though." I say, suddenly remembering I'm supposed to be focusing on the present not the future, but I can't because I want her and I'm pretty sure she wants me.

Kate adds, "She's only going to school and would never cheat on you."

"I'm not worried about her cheating. It's kind of pathetic, but I worry about other guys being there when I'm not."

"*Ahhh*, you're jealous. You're afraid if you're not there twenty-four seven that some other guy is gonna hone in on her. Well, lil bro, they might, but it would be immature of you to move up there only to keep that from happening."

"I guess dad talked to you about my job offer?"

"They talked to me about it in May, but he told me this morning that he finally spoke with you."

"You're thinking I should take it?"

"It's four months, Evan. It's great experience and decent money."

I walk a few feet, tucking my hands into my pockets and stare out into the ocean.

"If it's meant to be, it will be," she says before turning and walking around to the main house. "C'mon, let's go be a family for a little while." She waves me over, hoping I'll follow. I do, but begrudgingly because I need to settle some things with my mother.

A cheese and fruit tray is set up with a pitcher of lemonade on the table and I walk by, helping myself. My mom pokes her head up from her lounger in the sun next to the pool. "Good afternoon, Evan. I'm glad I got to see you today." She smiles and her face looks years younger with the simple gesture.

Laying down on the chaise next to her, I lean back, studying her for a moment. My stare is more intense than I intend, so I look away before stating, "Mallory's important to me. You can't treat her like that anymore, especially if you want me in your life."

She sits up, her legs sliding over the side so she can face me. "I didn't realize it was that serious."

"You didn't realize? I think you did *and* I think you saw an opportunity when Kelly came knocking on your door."

Her hand goes up to shield her eyes from the sun, and she says, "Kelly is quite an ambitious girl all on her own."

I stand up, pointing an accusing finger at her. "I'm not going to take your shit, Mother!"

My dad, who has been wading in the pool nearby threatens, "Calm down, Evan. You won't speak to your mother like that. She's only concerned about your future."

I look at him in disbelief. "You're kidding me, right? She almost ruined my relationship with the only person I've actually cared about and you were right there encouraging her." I know I'm supposed to show respect for my elders and all that, but I'm stunned that he can stick so close to his moral code in situations like this. I look back at my mother. "Mallory and I are stronger than that disaster the other night." I sit back down, fully realizing we are. I'm breathing heavily to relax myself because if I don't, I'm gonna fucking punch something—in through the nose, out through the mouth, in through the nose, out through the mouth.

Kate interjects, "Evan is right, Mother. Mallory's a great person and she's really good for him. He's changing. You need to recognize that it's because of her. She makes him happy."

"Kate, sweetie, it's like that boy you're seeing. He's a great guy, but he's not your future. Your future is in New York, not this island and certainly not with a—"

"Don't do this!" Kate yells. "Don't ruin the happiness we've found! *Please*. Please don't."

My dad hops out of the pool, grabbing a towel and wrapping himself up, and goes to Kate, bringing her into a hug. "It's okay, honey."

"No, it's not. I feel like I'm having to choose between my

family and my boyfriend and it makes me feel terrible that I might choose him instead."

We all remain quiet as she cries on dad's shoulder. My heart breaks for her and then I get angry... again. "You're doing this to us. You're not allowing us to be happy. Kate will do—"

"That's enough, Evan," my mother says. "We're obviously not going to see eye-to-eye on this, so we just need to drop it. I want to have a pleasant afternoon with my children before I leave."

Kate's head pops up. "When are you leaving?"

"I've decided to fly back with your father tonight. I don't like him being all alone in New York," mother says, pulling her cover-up on over her suit. She cares. That shows how much she cares. She's likes to be there for him, always in support of him. Her kinder, more caring side that I've seen in the past, though rare, is showing.

I can't help but rejoice inwardly that I can have Mallory back in my bed tonight. This revelation produces a smile that's hard to hide.

"Yeah, I know you're all torn up over me leaving," Mother says, tapping me playfully. "I know this doesn't matter now, but I sent Kelly away last night."

As I look at her face, she's smiling at me, trying to edge me into a better mood. It works slightly when I hear this news. I say, "Mallory is here to stay. You need to accept that, Mother."

We exchange a brief moment of understanding, a flicker of love flashes across her eyes that I haven't seen in awhile. We both nod, acknowledging our positions before she gets up, walks over to a chaise lounge on the grass, and settles down into it. My father joins her and as Kate and I stare at the back of their chairs, their hands fall together as a united front.

Kate wipes the evidence of tears from her eyes before looking up and meeting mine. She whispers, "Tell me it's going to be okay, Evan. I need to hear someone say it."

I move my hand and take hers in mine. We're a united front also. "It's going to be okay, Kate. We don't have to be with them all the time to know what our hearts feel. That knowledge alone can tide us over when we can't be together."

After another hour of hanging around in the pool with my dad and sister, my mother sunbathing slightly away from us, my dad suggests, "Son, you have time for a quick walk before I need to leave?"

I follow him down the stone steps to the beach. We stand calf-deep in the water, throwing sticks and shells out into the deeper ocean.

"I wanted to know if you've given the job any thought?"

"A little."

"Obviously, you and Mallory made up. How's that going to play into your decision?"

"I'm not going to lie. She plays heavily into it, but I think you're right. I think it will be good for my resume and I can use the money the following semester to move to Colorado."

"That's a yes then?" he asks, excitement coloring his words.

"Not yet. I need a little more time, but I'm seriously considering it."

He pulls me into a hug, patting me on the back, and says, "I know you'll make the right choice. And, Evan?" I look at him when he calls my name. "I think you'll do a great job."

"I want to make you proud of me again," I whisper, knowing it's time for me to grow up.

Two hours later, Zach calls and tells me to meet him and Murphy down at Pray for Sex, a hard-to-reach little strip of beach about forty-five minutes from my house. Mallory is going to ride out with Kate and Sunny after work.

After catching what seems like the perfect set of waves, the boys and I lie on the sand and rest. I smile with my eyes closed, feeling like today has been damn near perfect. I woke up with my girl back in my arms while on the beach, my parents know my stance on my relationship, and I've got a good job offer on the table. Life is good. *Fuck, life is great!*

10

MALLORY

What is it with that man? It's just not right. How can he be built like that, have the face of a model, and still be so romantic? I smile knowing I can't leave out his skills in the bedroom. Nope. No Sirree Bob, those definitely can't be forgotten. "*Ridiculous!*"

"What's ridiculous?" Sunny asks.

"Huh?" I reply, my eyebrows rising as the only form of acknowledgment to her presence.

"Mallory? Earth to Mallory?" Kate waves her hand in front of my face instantly pissing me off.

"Stop, I can't see!" I swat her hand away, keeping my eyes focused on the ocean... or more importantly, on the man *in* the ocean.

"You can't see what? My brother?" Kate asks sarcastically.

"You've got a little drool on your chin there, Mal." Sunny swipes her finger underneath my chin and announces, "Got it!"

"*Whatever.*" I continue watching Evan deep out in the ocean with Zach and Murphy as they float on their boards waiting for a wave. He waves his arm in the air and I giggle knowing that's for me.

"Holy Shit! She's got it bad, Sunny," Kate says, laughing again.

"Mucho bad!" Sunny declares.

Zach and Murphy wave and the girls start giggling. I nudge them both with my elbows since they're on either side of me and I smugly declare, "See! It's not only me!"

Murphy takes the next wave, standing tall across the top of the water and doing body builder poses for us. We all laugh at his antics. Before he's even to shore, Zach claims the next wave, cutting across the eight-footer low and steady. He performs two one-eighty degree jumps before taking the nose straight into shore.

"That's my man!" Sunny runs to meet him.

Kate has already met Murphy in the water when Evan finally grabs the last wave of the set. I wrap my arms around my knees, holding myself back in anticipation. The sun is starting to work its way toward setting and my eyes never leave my surfer on the horizon making his way back to me. The waters are rough with the odd crashing wave this evening, worrying me as Evan falters on his board. He makes a quick recovery and slashes through the water, as if showing it who owns who.

He jumps off into knee deep water, grabs his board, and walks up on shore. I stay seated, still admiring him and all his beauty from this short distance. He bends over removing the leash to his board, and then stands up, making eye contact with me. His expression is playful, and he winks then shakes the water out of his wet hair. It's in slow motion like on "Baywatch" and completely captivating. When he looks back up, he waves at me and I blush. That Sun God is mine. All mine, and my cheeks burn with the thought.

I slowly stand, dusting the sand from my shorts, and saunter over to him. He's got me all worked up and feeling sassy. I feel more than sassy, but I'll let him find that out later. Standing in front of him, I drink in the view and lick my lips in appreciation.

"Hey, sexy, what're you thinking about?" Evan asks, then lifts me up by my waist, devouring my lips with wet kisses before I have a chance to answer.

I wrap my legs around him, run my fingers through his hair, and then wrap my arms around his neck. His tongue moves with authority yet pure gentleness as his hands grip me possessively, turning me on even more. My hands slide down over his strong shoulders, and squeeze his biceps that are flexed and tight from the ocean workout. My fingertips dance across his chest in the small space between us and I feel up his abs while pressing myself against his hard center, purposely pushing into him for his pleasure and mine.

"Fuck," he moans into my mouth, leaning back to look at me.

My feet touch the ground again as I watch a rivulet of water trail down his sun-kissed chest, and then I follow it... with my tongue.

"Mallory? Oh, yeah, wait...yeah, that feels good, but I'm getting," he whispers into my ear, "hard, baby. Unless you're going to provide some cover for me, I suggest we stop *for now*."

I stand back up, but it's very clear he's already affected. "Oh babe, you'll need cover, that's for sure."

He grabs me, pulling my back against his chest and pressing his hard-on against my ass.

"Seriously, dude, you couldn't wait to get in the car before sportin' that boner?" Murphy chides him.

"Guess not. I blame Mallory." His breath covers the back of my neck and goose bumps cover my skin.

"Oh, sweet Jesus, can we go? I really don't want to hear about Evan's boner," Kate says, pulling Murphy behind her to his car.

"Guess we're going. Laters!" Murphy laughs and tickles Kate, sending her into giggling fits.

"I have a surprise for you," Evan says then places a sweet kiss on my neck.

"Oh, really?"

"My parents left today. I want you back at my place tonight."

I turn in his arms, feeling his excited cock against my stomach now. "*Oh really?*"

"Yes, really. Will you?"

"I don't want to be anywhere else. Let's go, now," I suggest, emphasizing my point by rubbing against him.

Sunny gets up and tries to hug me, but I remain, pinned to Evans' hardness. She looks between us and then says, "*Ewwww!* You two are seriously gross. Mallory, I'll see you tomorrow." She slaps my ass causing me to yelp. "Have fun, ya crazy kids." She laughs as she walks back to Zach, taking his hand. Zach runs back to the beach and retrieves his and Evan's surfboards, and gives a nod of acknowledgement, and they also leave.

"Looks like the coast is clear, my dear," I say, looking around at the empty beach.

"C'mon, maybe if we hurry we can beat the sun."

"Racing the sun can be dangerous business. You sure you can handle that?"

"Oh, I can definitely handle it." He suddenly lifts me up, throwing me over his shoulder. He sets me down on the passenger's side of the Maserati then opens the door and drops his wet trunks to the pavement without a care in the world. He slips on a pair of cargo shorts he grabs from the floorboard and runs around the car to get in.

The top is down and the evening is breathtaking as we drive along the coast on our way back to his place. I unclasp my seatbelt and stand with my hands in the air, the wind whipping around me as I scream freely into the wild Hawaiian breeze. Giddy happiness is coursing through my veins. Life is better than ever.

I plop back down in my seat while appreciating Evan.

"What?" he asks, smiling back.

"Just admiring." He laughs to himself, a little embarrassed by the attention. I'm hot and horny for the boy and if I want to eye fuck him, I will. Speaking of fuck, "Have you ever had sex in this car?"

He tilts his head and looks at me like I'm being ridiculous. "No, this is my *caaarrrr*." He drags out the last word like that thought is unfathomable.

"Oh."

"*Oh?*"

"Yeah. Ooh." I drag my finger leisurely down his leg, insinuating so much more, and trail it back up. When I reach the top of his thigh, I flatten my hand and push forward, rolling it over his cock, which responds like a pro.

His hand immediately lands on top of mine, stilling it. "What are you doing, baby?"

"Exploring." I smirk and offer, "Would you rather me explore with my mouth?"

His eyebrows bolt up in surprise, but he quickly collects himself. "Exploring, huh?" Looking back at the road, he says, "We'll be home in twenty minutes. You want to wait 'til then?"

"No, I don't." I lightly press, squeezing his erection for emphasis.

"Fuck, that feels good. How do you expect me to concentrate on driving when you're doing that?" His eyes briefly close, then he pops them back open. "Mallory, I don't think this is such a good idea." He leans his head against the head rest, and I can see himself mentally willing his erection away.

I unsnap my seat belt and lean my head down toward his legs. Watching his handsome face as his mouth drops open, I tease and push the button to make his seat go further back. When I lift back up, I position myself, partly over the console, leaning over him. Running one hand through his wind-blown hair, I slide the other down his chest, for balance and to make my intentions very clear.

"Mallory, I don't think this is very safe—"

Covering his mouth with mine, I make sure my head doesn't block his view of the road. He returns the kiss, his mouth instantly opening for me. I peek and find him focusing his gaze past my cheek. Ahhhh, my surfer is a multi-tasker. Well, let's test that theory.

Leaning back a little, I smile and then kiss his neck as a distraction while I undo his seatbelt and unbutton his shorts. I can multi-task too. I hear him moan right before he says, "Mallory, what are you doing to me? Baby, we'll be home soon. You're going to make me crash the car."

I ignore his warning and gently touch the tip of his length, which is exposed through the opening of his shorts. "Babe, lift up," I whisper my request directly into his ear. Balancing myself with one hand on the door and one on the console, I smile when he lifts, pulling his shorts down to the middle of his thighs.

He briefly looks up at me wavering above him, my hair

swirling in the wind, and he smirks. "I'm breaking one of my rules for you." He looks back at the road above my left arm.

"Sex in the car?"

His eyes flash back to mine. "Is that what we're doing?" he asks, surprised.

"Abso-fucking-lutely, baby!"

"Damn! This is even crazy for me." He shakes his head, clearly amused. Evan grabs my attention when he says, "You lead and I'll drive. Now show me what ya got, sexy."

I pull my skirt up to my hips, maneuvering one knee between him and the door. It's a tight space but the my other leg is jammed against the console, which is awkward and a struggle. This is not comfortable at all, but I'm hoping to be righteously distracted in a minute. I untie the bikini strings on the side of my bathing suit underneath my skirt, and remove it, throwing it onto the floorboard.

"Is that a challenge, Evan?"

"Abso-fucking-lutely!"

I pull a condom from my pocket, my hopeful plans from this morning coming to fruition.

As I tear it open, he nods at me in disbelief, but it turns to happy snickering as I roll it down his length, slow and steady.

"Touch me with your fingers," I demand because I can tell he's turned on by me being the one in control right now. "And rub it on yourself."

He takes two fingers and swipes between my legs then pulls them up to show me. With a devilish grin, he puts them in his mouth, sucking the tips between his lips then says, "Oops, I don't follow directions very well. I've been a bad boy. May I please touch you again?"

Holy fuck, he's hot!

And I'm even wetter, ready for him. I try to move down,

but realize that's impossible in this position, so I rearrange myself on him, putting my back against his. Facing the road, I lift up and slowly lower myself back down onto him. The lack of warning causes him to moan and the car sways to the left.

"Shit, you should've warned me," he says, straightening the wheel and regaining control of the car again.

I drop my head against his shoulder and using the leverage of my hands on his thighs, I lift back up and slide back down. Enjoying the fullness, I wiggle when he's all the way inside of me. Quickening my pace causes me to moan against his neck, completely lost in him, and the love we're making.

"Oh, fuck," he mutters, "I need to pull over."

My head bolts upright, and I shout, "No! Please don't. I'm so close already."

I keep my rhythm going as he struggles to steer the car.

"Baby, I need to pull... shit! Yes, just like that. Again."

"I need harder," I say, "rougher."

His right hand takes to my hip helping me slam down just the way I need to feel him. We swerve again when his driving becomes more erratic.

"God, you feel amazing, Mallory. I love you."

Although, I've never been big with the exchanges of *I love you's* during sex because they never were heartfelt, this time it feels different. I need to hear it again because it lights my insides on fire hearing it from Evan. "Say it again," I command, keeping pace with his movements.

He quickly kisses the base of the back of my neck, his tongue coming out momentarily to lick, and then he sounds out each word with an accentuating thrust. "I. Love. You. Mallory."

I peak when he says my name, the base of his cock

meeting my clit with each push. I'm loud, but the wind drowns me out.

"Fuck! Grab the wheel!" He says, trying to stay calm, but failing. I take the wheel just as the last of my little tremors subsides. With all passion and power, he grabs my hips and slams me up and down on top of him twice before letting himself go. I love the feel of him moving inside of me, knowing I bring him so much pleasure. He cries my name as he orgasms and I feel his hands back on the wheel then the car comes to a stop.

As soon as he shoves the car into park, he tells me, "Turn around."

I do, moving my legs so I can face him, straddle him. He takes my face into his hands and kisses me, relentless in his pursuit.

"That was fucking fantastic. God, what a rush!" he exclaims, smiling at me with lazy eyes.

Swinging my leg back off the console, I fumble into my seat, pulling my skirt back down. "We should definitely fight more often, if that's what the makeup sex is like." I laugh.

He leans across the console, kisses my ear, then whispers, "That wasn't the makeup sex, baby, that was the sex on the way to the makeup sex."

My thighs clench at the prospect that it might be better than that, which seems entirely impossible to me at this very moment. I look over at him and he's somehow, without me noticing, already disposed of the condom and his shorts are buttoned. I start to laugh, always impressed by his smooth moves. I pull to fasten my seatbelt just as I hear a siren behind us.

"Shit! Buckle up, Mallory," Evan says, looking in his rearview mirror as he clicks his own belt back.

I try to be covert and snap my seatbelt down, but when I

look behind us, the cop is already eyeing me then he scribbles in his tiny pad.

"I can't get in trouble, Evan. I could be suspended from school if I do." I'm seriously worried and freaked out right now.

"Don't worry. Let me handle this."

"*Miiisssterrr Ashford*," the officer says, dragging out his name sarcastically. The young officer takes his shades off, crosses his arms, and asks, "Do you want to tell me what you were doing back there?"

Evan looks at the steering wheel as he starts to speak. "I know I wasn't speeding if that's what you're asking." We both look at the officer waiting to hear his reply.

"You're right. You were only going fifteen in a forty, which is also a traffic violation. We have speed limits for you to understand what's expected of you while driving. You became an obstruction to other cars on the road. I can give you a ticket for that."

"Officer Mills, if you're going to give me a ticket for driving too slow then do it, but I don't think you are. So let's get to the real reason you pulled me over."

"Evan, don't be rude. He's a police officer."

He leans back, confident in his actions, and squeezes my knee. "Relax, baby. He's not going to give me a ticket."

"You're right, Mr. Ashford. Miss, I'm gonna need you to step out of the car." The officer's tone is firm as he stares down at me.

"What?" Evan's head almost spins he turns to look at the cop so fast. "No! She didn't do anything wrong."

Now I'm scared, but slowly unfasten my seatbelt and start to get out of the vehicle.

"She wasn't wearing her seatbelt, Evan. That's against

the law. You know, click it or ticket just like the signs say?" He says this with an incredulous laugh.

Evan grabs my arm stopping me from getting all the way out then turns back to Officer Mills. "Give me the ticket instead. I know you've wanted to for a long time now. This is your chance."

The officer sets his palms down on the car door. In a lowered voice, he explains, "She was the one not wearing her seatbelt—"

"How do you know that? It was fastened when you showed up." Evan is losing some of his confidence as he speaks.

"Well, I know because she was on your lap doing what appeared to be breaking a different law that gives me the right to take her down to the station, but I thought I'd be kind and only give her the seatbelt ticket as a warning."

Oh shit, he saw us having sex. I fall back into my seat almost in tears. If this gets back to my school... Oh God, how embarrassing!

"Fine, you win!" Evan begrudgingly announces, putting his hands in the front of him in surrender.

"Really?" The officer perks up.

Wait, I'm confused. What the hell are they talking about? No more discussion? He's only giving me the one ticket?

"Yes. Stop gloating and come by the surf shack tomorrow after three. I'll make sure she's there," Evan goes on making absolutely no sense to me whatsoever as he talks to the cop.

"I'll be there. You can count on it." Officer Mills stands back up, smiling and says, "Sorry for scaring you like that, Miss, but it was totally worth it." He hurries back to his car almost skipping with glee.

"What the heck was that all about?" I say, hitting him in the arm all irritated and confused.

"Heather."

"Who's Heather?"

"Heather's the one that just got *you* out of an indecency ticket." He peels out on that note forming a dust cloud behind the car as he weaves back onto the main road again. After letting out a large chuckle, he says, "I work with her. She wanted to give her dad a lesson for Father's Day, but she was broke so I hooked her up with one. She owes me a favor. That favor is now a date with Officer Mills."

Feeling a huge wave of relief wash over me, I settle back into the soft leather seat and watch the sunset ahead of us. Evan holds my hand and I catch him stealing glances my way. Despite the police drama, I feel great.

Evan also looks satisfied and happy. That might be because we just had sex, but I like to think his heart and mind are mutually content.

11

MALLORY

Our car adventure, my long day at work, and his day of surfing has worn us out. Evan and I have Chinese food delivered and watch movies on pay-per-view the rest of the evening. It's nice. It's a normal couple thing to do, spending time like this, but I can't seem to remedy the unease in my stomach.

I pull a cigarette and lighter out of my purse and let him know I'll be out back. I feel his gaze on me as I walk across the room and out of view.

After sparking up, I sit on the small step overlooking the ocean.

Thoughts of his lifestyle come charging back to the forefront of my mind. Am I holding him back from what is surely a bigger life than he could ever have with me? Will his parents cut him off for choosing me? What do I really expect from him? Of us?

"You want some company?" he asks, bringing me back to the present when he sits down next to me, stretching his legs out in front of him. He analyzes my burning cig, his expression turning concerned. "Since you're not really smoking that, do you wanna share?"

I hand him the cigarette, careful not to drop ashes on either one of us while passing it over. As I lean back against the doorframe, I watch his lips wrap around it and inhale. He appears peaceful as he relaxes. It's the same relief smoking provides me. He taps it twice then exhales from the side of his mouth while keeping his eyes on me. With a small smile, he asks, "Why are you smoking anyway? I know you only smoke when you're stressed, so tell me what's on your mind, baby."

I gulp, knowing I've been busted. I want to tell him all my inner thoughts, but I don't want to concern him with my worries.

He hands the cigarette back to me and picks up my other hand, turning it over and kissing my palm. It's such a sweet gesture that I know right then that I should talk to him.

"I've been thinking..." he says at the same time as I say, "I think we should..."

We laugh in awkwardness and I stub out the cigarette, tossing it in the sand bucket next to me.

"You go first," he says.

"No, you go," I insist, hugging my knees to my chest.

He takes a deep breath, and says, "I don't know what I was talking about this morning. I want to be with you. I want to be with you fully, not half-assed or only in the moment. I want us to give this our all." He looks back at the ocean nervously, obviously, not wanting to be rejected.

I sit up, taking his hand from his lap and kiss his palm, allowing myself the pleasure of lingering there momentarily before sitting up and exhaling my relief. "Thank God because I seriously don't think my heart could handle not knowing if we're real or not, just messing around or really giving this a go."

I smile as I stand up then sit down, straddling him, making sure we're pressed against each other for pleasure. He wraps his arms around me, pulling me closer and kissing me, and his length grows under me, making me squirm from the sensation.

"I love you, Evan. So much." My voice is huskier than intended, wanting to be with him so badly.

"I love you, too, baby."

I smother his words with my mouth as we kiss again, more urgently and needy than before. As my tongue swirls purposefully with his, our bodies began to slowly rock, and he pulls me down onto him harder. I reach for the hem of his shirt, yanking it off over his head and our mouths crash back together.

As soon as I start to grind, he abruptly stands up, and rushes us to his bed. It's unmade and he trips on the sagging blanket that is half on the floor already, a mess from an earlier nap or restless sleep. The bed breaks my fall and he holds his weight as if suspended by his arms alone to catch himself, not wanting to crush me as he falls down on top. I can see every muscle move under the taut skin of his form. Lowering himself down, he rolls to my side.

I cup his face to take in the moment, to take in all of him, like this, to see him looking at me with desires only I can ease. He's not holding anything back anymore. His eyes give him away, but I need to hear him confirm what I'm feeling, to know he feels the same. This tightrope is too precarious to linger on for long, so I move forward, risking it all, knowing he could destroy my heart if I'm wrong. "Babe?" I ask when his eyes start to close and he leans in to kiss me.

"Mmm," he responds, his voice low, lips gently sucking on the skin at the nape of my neck.

My original thought escapes me under the intense heat of his lips on me and body caresses. I finally manage to mumble, "Foundation."

He licks and nips my neck, all things gloriously sensual. "Foundation?" Hearing him repeat the word reminds me of what I was thinking. I pull away, an inch or so, and wait. He lazily opens his eyes, and asks, "What?"

"Us?" I softly breathe. "Do you think we have a strong enough foundation for us to last when we're apart?"

His hands are under my shirt messing with the clasp of my bra, but he stops. When he lifts his head up, he looks straight at me and sighs then slowly climbs up the bed causing our legs to tangle with the sheet and blanket. Stroking my hair away from my face, his hand graces my cheek. "Yes, I do. Whole-heartedly."

"This morning you thought we should—"

"I was giving you an out, Mallory. I thought after all that happened, you might want to slow it down, but the 'I love you's' and this... I just can't stay away. I won't." His eyes glance away as he takes a deep breath, the weight of the conversation showing in the heaviness of his sigh. When he looks back, determination is written all over his face. "I checked out Colorado—"

Emotions bubble to the surface and tears fill my eyes. I prop myself up on my elbows surprised to hear this. "You did?"

"I missed the deadline. I'd been thinking about going back to school, but couldn't seem to reason myself into it until early last week." He gulps, and a tear crawls down my cheek causing me to blink which makes another one fall.

"Don't cry, baby." He wipes under my eyes gently with his thumbs.

"Why didn't you tell me before?"

"I didn't want to disappoint you, but it seems to be the only thing I'm good at these days."

"That's not true. You're everything to me, and definitely not disappointing."

That brings a smile to his face. "Well, I wanted to know what I was doing before I talked to you, to have a game-plan in place. I was also hoping the school would make an exception because of my transcript. I tried. You've got to believe that I tried. I made a bunch of phone calls to admissions and to the professors in the Psych department, but they're firm on their deadline."

Sliding onto my side, I press my cheek to his chest right above his heart, which is racing. Squeezing him to me, I say, "I can't believe you'd move for me."

His fingertips dance across my back. "You were right before. You're settled there and graduate soon. I'm floundering out here, escaping, but I don't have to anymore. I've found," he starts, his voice not even loud enough to be called a whisper, "a purpose."

I roll onto my back, pulling him on top of me and kiss him with everything I've got. His hips automatically start to move against mine, but our legs are still tangled in the blanket. Surprising me, he jumps to his feet and I feel a rush of cold air blow across my body. Pulling me by the ankles to the end of the bed, he commands, "You—Get naked!"

Without hesitation, I get up and start removing my clothes as he gathers the bunched sheet and blanket and throws them to the floor. I toss my shirt and drop my skirt. Apparently I'm too slow because he snaps the thin fabric of my panties at my hips before I even have time to remark, then my bra is gone from my shoulders, flinging through the air and landing on the couch.

He pulls his own shorts down, displaying his eager erection then takes my hand and pulls me into the bathroom. I stand against the closed door as he switches the shower on waiting for it to heat. His eyes are on me, eyeing me up and down, making me feel vulnerable, exposed as he drinks me in. "Come here, baby."

I go to him knowing when our bodies are pressed together nothing else matters. All that troubles me fades away, leaving me with the perfection of the moment.

Trailing light kisses across the side of my face, his sweet words of desire flame between us. "You're so beautiful." The words fall from his lips and I weaken under them.

"I need you, Evan," I say, embracing the spell he's put me under.

"How do you need me? I want to give you everything you need."

"I crave the feeling of you inside of me, making me feel whole again."

My confession doesn't scare him away, but brings him closer. He kisses me while maneuvering me into the shower under the warm flowing water. Soap in hand, he lathers it up, and runs his hands tenderly down my body. Gliding over my breasts, his thumbs run across my nipples, making them stand for his attention. His hand slides down my stomach and between my legs, causing my breath to catch. Leaning closer, he whispers, "Breathe because I can't when you're not."

"It's all so surreal and perfect. I struggle to breathe when we're like this."

"Take all of mine along with my heart then."

That's the moment I realize I don't need anything else

from him. I've already been given more than I ever thought possible—all of his love and devotion.

But even with all the swooning I'm doing over his sweet words, I'm still hot for the man and he's in front of me wet and naked and seriously hard to resist, so I don't. I reach my hand down to touch him in very naughty ways, but he takes my wrist and tsks me. "Eh, eh, eh! I have something else in mind."

"You've got my undivided attention, Mr. Ashford," I say while enjoying the warm water hitting my back.

He reaches around and slams the water nozzle off then opens the door. Cold air clashes against my heated skin and I instantly wrap my arms around my body. With his sexy smirk in full force, he says, "Go to the counter and show me how much you want me, baby."

Although I'm wet, from head to toe, and cold, I'm hot on the inside and my breath is becoming harsher, making it more obvious that I'm turned on. I'm highly aware that Evan Ashford is the one who put me in this state. But I kind of love it when he gets all bossy on me. I walk toward the bathroom mirror and turn around then slide up on top of the counter, backing myself up against the mirror. His erection is sturdy, but it's his expression I lust after the most. He's beyond turned on. He's ravenous for me.

Putting my feet up on the counter, I keep my knees together until his gaze trails down. Parting my legs, I give him a nice view as I touch myself. I've never done this in front of anyone else and definitely never imagined I would be doing this so comfortably in front of someone watching me so intently.

His eyes are focused on my small movements as I tease him while teasing myself. My mouth opens as the feeling intensifies, my eyelids becoming heavy with lust from watching him enjoy the show. I lean my head back against the mirror, closing my eyes and blocking out every thought I have except for one—Evan. Knowing this is a bad substitute for him, I still need more, so I slip a finger inside. But I need friction and one finger isn't going to do it, so I add another.

A moan frees itself from deep within as I start to lose myself in the sensation. I'm ripped from my fantasy only to have it replaced by him in the flesh. He pulls me off the counter and spins me around to face the mirror, encouraging me to bend forward. When I do, I look into the mirror and see him ready, condom in place. Positioning himself, our eyes connect in the reflection, and then he enters me— confident, strong, and steadfast.

From this angle, it's all so overwhelming and my eyes flutter closed. Though he's not rough, he's not gentle either. I rest my weight on my forearms as he pushes in then pulls out, each thrust given with passion and ease. One of his hands rests on my back as the other holds my hips in place.

"Look up. Look at me," he says between jagged breaths.

I open my eyes as his hands slide up and around to my breasts and he takes hold, picking up his rhythm again. He squeezes and I push back into him with this new leverage, eliciting a moan from both of us and slam back again as he thrusts forward.

"Touch yourself again," he says.

"Uh huh," I hum, staggering for control.

After stabilizing my body with my other arm, I touch myself, but this time going right for my most sensitive spot. When I open my eyes, I see his are dark, taking me in and I lick my lips.

"I like that." His voice is a bit hoarse, affected by our activity.

Slowly, seductively, and yet innocently, I lick my bottom

lip again, then dig into it with my top teeth until it hurts, the pain mixing with the pleasure he's giving me.

Evan stops thrusting, his tongue licking his own lips as he watches my mouth. He slams into me and groans, "Oh fuck, I'm not gonna last."

His eyes shut tight as his orgasm overcomes him. Closing my eyes, I concentrate on the feeling of this, of him, of Evan invading my every sense as he continues moving inside me. I'm too blissed out to scream when I'm swallowed by desire. I can't speak or say anything remotely comprehensible, but I manage a few audible moans and then collapse onto the counter top.

His body rests lightly on top of mine, my breasts pressed against the cool marble top. I lay my cheek against it hoping to slow my speeding heart and stabilize my breathing. His stubble covered cheek rests against my back for a moment trying to steady his own breathing.

"So, you want to be a psych major?" I ask, picking up our conversation where we left off earlier with a giggle.

He chuckles which reverberates against my body. "I thought I would start using my skills for good instead of evil."

We both laugh together as he helps me up, disposing of the condom at the same time. He turns the faucet on warm and grabs for a washcloth that sits neatly on the shelf under the counter. He wets it, and asks, "May I?"

I nod, surprised by the sweet gesture, and part my legs. He rubs the terry cloth softly along my inner thighs then strokes upward—cleaning me, caring for me.

He wipes himself off, tosses the washcloth on the side of the tub and carries me back into the bedroom. Setting me down on the bed with my head on the pillow, he runs to retrieve the earlier offending sheet and blanket, covering me up and tucking me in. He slips underneath without disturbing the covers protecting me from the chilly air conditioning.

I roll onto my side and he does the same so we face each other in the moonlight.

"I think our foundation is solid."

I give him a small smile and say, "Yeah?"

"Yeah," he says, kissing my nose. "Like the Rock of Gibraltar."

"Rock solid."

"I love you, Mallory."

"I love you, too."

12

EVAN

Time is elusive. I can't count on it any longer. Ever since Mallory came into my life it is either racing by or crawling; sometimes it even stands still. I've lived the life of unpredictability for so long that I don't recognize a lot of what my life has become, which is disappointing.

I need to make some changes and I think the first is to weigh the pros and cons of the job in New York. Even if I'm too lazy to write them down, I should at least take a tally in my head. I also need to talk to Mallory about it. Over the last two weeks, since the party, we are inseparable. Apart from work, we spend every minute together, almost to the point of ridiculousness. But we like where we are right now. Actually, *we love it*. This is how it should've been from the beginning.

We spend the next two weeks talking, laughing, sharing, and exploring each other. We don't fight. There aren't even tiny moments of irritation. We're happy. It is as simple as that. It seems that all of the hurdles that once stood in our way have been jumped and left in the past.

We don't talk about my mother. I wanted to on several

occasions, but I'm not willing to give away any second of happiness with Mallory to deal with that issue. So, I don't. I greedily hoard her all to myself and can tell she's doing the same with me.

I've discovered what true beauty is, especially when I see Mallory first thing in the morning—sleepy eyes, lips barely parted, and snuggled into my side—I realize I've never known it at all. She is pure beauty and awe in my eyes, but I feel her splendor in the way she is with me as well. She expresses her love so openly through touches, whispers, her giggles, and blushes. I try my best to make her feel how she makes me feel.

But nothing takes away that nagging feeling that has moved into the back of my head and set up camp—her impending departure. Although I have concerns over whether I should take this job in New York or not, I push them to the back, right next to thoughts of her departure, and focus on our time together.

Today, I have big plans. I'm spending the day with Ms. Chart. We grocery shop and she's showing me how to make lasagna from scratch in the main kitchen. She said this would impress Mallory, so I'm making the effort to learn for both of us . It's not a monumental step, but it is a little one toward my independence from the life of luxury I've led thus far. One thing I am positive of is that once I'm back in school and then after graduation, my parents aren't going to gift me a private chef. So this little lesson into the culinary world will come in handy.

Mallory arrives at my house at exactly 6:48 p.m. I've been counting the minutes for the last hour. They've been dragging except for the time I spent with Ms. Chart.

When Sunny drops her off on the lower portion of the driveway, I greet her by wrapping my arms around her waist and holding her to me. "I missed you," I say and kiss her forehead because I like to, but she also really likes it, so I do it often.

"I missed you, too. It's kind of getting out of hand—"

"What is?"

"I just don't like being away from you. All I think about all day at work is how much I wish I was with you instead or thinking about what you're doing at that moment. It's silly really," she says, looking up at me, her hands resting on my upper arms.

"That makes me feel a little less insane because I do the same exact thing all day. Come on. I have a surprise for you."

"Really? What is it?"

"Why is that the first question people ask when someone says they have a surprise for them? You know the answer to that."

"It wouldn't be a surprise then?"

"Ding ding ding!"

We walk around to the table by the pool and she stops, causing me to also stop. "Did you," she starts, but goes quiet then starts again, "did you do all this for me?"

I turn back to the table and smile, proud as a peacock.

"A romantic dinner for two? This is stunning, Evan," she says, squeezing my hand.

"So are you, baby." I take her over, pulling her chair out and tucking her neatly up to the table. I pour each of us a glass of Chianti and then dish out the salad.

"Let me serve you tonight," she says, "You went to so much trouble for me. It's the least I can do."

"No, that won't do at all. I'm here to wine and dine you tonight."

"But you already own my heart."

I narrow my eyes at her playfully, and pout a bit. "Will you please let me do this for you?"

She agrees to let me handle the night. As usual, our conversation is easy. I find myself analyzing, maybe even over-analyzing her every little move: the way she eats, the way her smile envelops her face when she laughs from the gut, the way she blinks slower when we talk more intimately, and the way her hands move with such purpose, but sometimes give her uncertainty away.

"You haven't been treated well by past boyfriends, have you?" I ask, already knowing the answer.

"You already know I was cheated on."

"That's not what I'm asking."

She looks down and rolls a cherry tomato around on her plate before stabbing it. "Evan, I don't want to waste our time together talking about stuff that doesn't matter." She feeds herself the tomato while watching me as she chews.

"Okay," I say, not wanting to upset her. It's clear I'll need to treat her special so she carries that with her back to school. I want her loaded and bogged down with happy memories from this summer and I'm hoping they can override all the bad ones she's collected.

"I was thinking I could visit you in Colorado... if you want"

She sets her fork down and smiles. "Really?"

Reaching across the table, I take her hand in mine and look her in the eyes. "For purely selfish reasons, of course."

"Of course," she says, giggling. "But I can live with that."

We enjoy the leisurely meal and she can't get over that I had made this all by myself. It was under Ms. Chart's direction, but my hands had done all the work. After letting our meal settle, we walk the beach, hand in hand.

"Evan, I have two weeks left..." she starts, but pauses

before continuing again, "...I know we don't like to talk about it, but I feel like we need to."

I stand in front of her holding both her hands and say, "Then we should talk about it."

"I don't know how things will be when I leave. How we'll be or what will happen to us." She steps closer, hugging me, taking a long breath before adding, "I'm scared for us."

After taking a deep breath, I nod because I feel the same.

The sincerity softens her expression in the moonlight. "You told me once that we were more than just a summer of fun. Do you still believe that?"

As I look down into her soulful eyes, worry creases her brow. "I don't think you understand how much I love you, Mallory. I've never loved anyone like this before. I don't even allow myself to think about you leaving because my heart hurts and my mind goes into some kind of freakish negative overdrive thinking about every possible thing that can hurt us or separate us."

Feeling the weight of my fears tumbling down over me, I let her go and walk into the water until it drifts up to my ankles before flowing back out again. I squat down staring beyond the break point for a minute before returning to her. "Am I enough? I need to know. If I'm not with you in Colorado, are you willing to try this long distance thing?"

She slides her hands up my chest and around my neck pulling me to her. "Oh, Evan, we're so worried about getting our hearts broken that we didn't realize that's how the other feels. I'm more than willing to lay my heart on the line for you. I already have. I don't think it will be easy, but I think we can make it."

Her warmth is all I need and she knows this, so she kisses me. I open my mouth even though I know our conversation is not over.

She stops, tilts her head to the side, and asks, "When we say things like 'make it', what are we trying to achieve?"

We stroll back to the house, needing the time to think about what that means, what we mean. One thing that I've always loved when talking to Mallory is that she's also a great listener and usually only asks questions she really wants to know the answer to. And I want to give her a meaningful one.

"I think it's a little soon to talk marriage, but I think even in my screwed up head, I'd like to be married one day and have a wife and family." Taking one step up the back stairs to the house, she is now eye to eye with me. I lower my voice, feeling sentimental, and say, "I'd like you a part of that future."

Wistfully she sighs. "You do?"

"Mmhm, I do."

"Mr. Ashford, you say the sweetest things to me."

I laugh at the formality. "So how attached are you to that name of yours, Miss Wray?"

"Oh, ummm… I've been called Mallory my whole life so I'm kind of attached," she jokes, knowing what I mean, but I don't bother correcting her. We may be crossing lines that neither of us is quite ready to cross yet.

We go inside silently and snuggle on the couch. I wrap my arm around her, and we lie in the dark looking out the expansive windows, both lost in our thoughts. Mine are wrapped up in the crazy concept that I will probably be someone's husband, maybe even a dad, one day. Crazy because two months ago, I thought I wouldn't even see my twenty-fifth birthday and here I am thinking of a future—a future with the lovely Miss Wray in my arms.

13

EVAN

Sleep comes easily for us. It's the mornings that are hard. We're safe in our cocoon, our bubble, safe in each other's arms, but we know we can't stay like this forever. So each morning we wake up earlier than necessary to appreciate a few extra minutes of time together. Sometimes that's spent holding each other or making love, but it renews our bond and strengthens our connection.

I drop Mallory off the next day and head into work. It's the busy season for the hotel and my schedule is packed. I'm basically full time, which reminds me that I could be making a lot more money for the same amount of hours if I go to New York, and the novelty of this job wore off a long time ago. At one time I loved the constant attention I got. Now I dread it. It's shallow, superficial stuff. I'll admit that I used to perpetuate this playboy summer fling image, but now I'm actually trying to work. So the handsy housewives and the teenagers crushing on me have become a bit of an annoyance. The co-eds pick up on the no-go vibe I send and don't even try.

With Mallory on my mind, I think of all the guys that

frequent Big Kehones, but don't allow myself to dwell because it will drive me mad. Kind of similar to the thoughts I have when I think of her back in Colorado with all those college guys. There are approximately fourteen thousand of them—I might have done some research in my spare time.

I pop up on the board to show the class how to do it one more time and then give each a giant foam board and send them out to the ocean.

Close to six o'clock, the gang shows up. They stop by to say hi before heading to the bar down the beach. Keeping my hands and lips to myself with Mallory when they stopped by was fucking torture and the distance puts me in a bad mood, but I don't want to piss off the bosses and I really should be paying attention to my clients. *Fuck!* Since when did I start giving a shit about work?

I don't get the shack closed up until seven-thirty. That's almost two hours of missed drinking opportunities with my friends and time lost with Mallory. When I finally jog over to meet them, I find them under an umbrella shaded table. The guys are sharing a pitcher of beer and the girls all have tall fruity looking drinks in front of them.

When Mallory sees me coming, she runs to meet me. Jumping up, she grabs hold of my shoulders, and wraps her legs around my waist while attacking my mouth. I catch her and feel the heat of our connection that always exists between us. Her body relaxes in my arms and we both deepen the kiss. When she releases her mouth from mine, she says, "God, I missed you."

I give her the smirk I know drives her crazy and she attacks my mouth again until we're both hit in the head with flying chunks of cocktail fruit. Then Murphy yells, "Dudes, this is a public beach. Save the humping for later."

Everyone cracks up, including us.

She slowly unlatches her legs from around me and I pick a piece of pineapple out of her hair, obviously from one of their frou-frou drinks. Our eyes shift from the fruit in my hand to meet each other's mischievous gaze. Then we burst out laughing. "I might have to save this for later," I say, winking at her.

"I'm gonna hold you to that, baby." I love it when she calls me baby.

We continue drinking at the bar, getting more buzzed for another hour before Sunny asks, "So, what's the deal, you two? School starts in less than a month. What's the game plan, Stan?"

All four of them stop whatever they're doing at the time and are suddenly very attentive as they stare between Mallory and me.

Mallory turns to me, so I respond, "Well, as you guys know, we're together. I know we've kind of disappeared—"

Sunny chides playfully. "Kind of? That's an understatement. It's almost time for the girl to leave the island and this is the first time I've seen her in almost two weeks outside of work."

"I've totally bogarted her time, but," I pause, suddenly feeling the pressure of their eyes bearing down on me, "honestly, we haven't figured a lot of it out yet, but we're together." Then I try to seamlessly add to the conversation. "I might move to Colorado."

Mallory gasps, "What? What about the deadline?"

Zach leans his elbows on the table, staring at me in disbelief. "When did you decide that?"

I look at him, more wanting to deal with my girlfriend's reaction, not his right now. But I do because I know this seems out of the blue. "I said I might. That's all."

Turning back to Mallory, confusion is written across her

face, so I squeeze her hand in comfort. "I've just been thinking about it," I whisper. "There would be a lot that goes into a move like that, especially since I would have to find a job and stuff."

Sunny clears her throat and elbows Zach. "We should give them some privacy."

Zach stands, and says, "We're gonna go watch the last of the sunset, dude. Catch ya laters." He takes Sunny's hand as she jumps off her barstool and kisses him on the cheek.

Our eyes go to Kate and Murphy who are also standing, seeming ready to bolt. When I look at him, Murphy says, "I'd tell you what we're gonna go do, but I know you don't want to hear about it. So we're just gonna go."

"Yeah, probably not," I quip, scrunching my nose up in disgust.

They turn and start walking toward the parking lot, but we see Kate rubbing his shoulder blades under the tank top he's wearing and hear her say, "You're getting fuzzy again, hot stuff."

I instantly feel the bile rising. "What the fuck is wrong with her?"

Mallory laughs, but it's a nervous laugh which brings me back to what we were talking about.

"Hey," I say, resting my hands on her legs and turning in my chair to face her. "I said I've only been thinking about it. I'm not pressuring you into anything. I love you and being here at work all day has made me think about making some changes."

"Where would you live?" She asks concerned.

I laugh, "I guess not with you."

"You think we should live together? That's crazy! I mean, we love each other yes, but living together? What about my roommate Sarah? She wouldn't want a guy moving in with us and I can't bail on her senior year."

I throw my hands up to stop her from getting upset. "I'm not asking you to. I just made a joke, that's all. Obviously, it's not the time to talk about this."

"But you wouldn't have said it if you hadn't thought about it. Talk to me, Evan. Let's discuss this." She takes my hand into both of hers and rubs her thumbs over my knuckles.

With my free hand, I run it across her cheek memorizing the gentle curve of her cheekbone and letting my thumb linger on her bottom lip. She relaxes against my hand, closing her eyes momentarily, and giving into the feeling. I watch her intently not even realizing I'm staring.

"What?" she asks, soft spoken, but surprised.

My gulp is heavy, giving away my emotions of the moment. "I...I just love you so much, Mallory."

"I love you, too. What's wrong?"

"I don't know what came over me. It was like..." I laugh, embarrassed. "It's silly. Never mind," I say, shaking my head.

"No, please. Tell me."

Weakness isn't one of my strong suits. Being this open is hard for me. She deserves nothing less, but that doesn't make it any easier. I can't weigh a guilt trip on her because of the near future. She needs to go live her life, not worry about me and my sappy side. I stand up. "Come on, let's go."

The bartender's voice is louder than the tropical music playing overhead. "Your brah's left ya hangin' and stiffed ya with the bill."

"Shit," I mumble under my breath and wave. "That's cool. I'll take care of it."

I walk to the bar and he hands me the tab. "Really? I had two beers and get hit with a ninety-five dollar check?"

Mallory peeks over my shoulder, and offers, "You're right, you shouldn't have to pay that. I made decent tips today, I can pay it."

"Keep your money. I know you worked hard for it. I can pay for it no problem. I was just griping about it is all."

"No, I really want to help," she says, reaching for the bill, but I grab her hand to stop her. "Let me get the tip then."

Grabbing her hand before she tries to drop a twenty on the bar, I fold her hand around the bill and kiss it before clarifying, "Honey, I don't want you to pay for any of it. I got it."

I pay the bill and the tip and we walk back toward the surf shack. She's quiet, concentrating on something. For as solid as I feel in our commitment to each other, I still worry if she's happy. "Do you want to share your thoughts?"

"You've always been able to read me so well, Evan. Any guesses?"

After taking a long pull of the sea air in through my nose and exhaling loudly through my mouth, I venture a guess, "Colorado?"

She shakes her head, "No, but we should talk about that some more again. The logistics and all of that." She looks down shyly at her bare feet in the sand, and wiggles her toes. "You called me 'honey' back there at the bar."

"Yeah. I'm not following."

"That's so, so sweet of you."

"Aw, come here, honey." I wrap my arms around her and peck a light kiss on top of her head. "None of those other chumps ever called you by a nickname?"

"No, I've always just been Mallory."

"Well, I call you 'baby' a lot."

"I know, but when you call me baby it's like sex rolling off your tongue. It's all implications and promises. But when you called me 'honey' it was like you were speaking straight to my heart."

"It's little things like that that make you so special. Don't ever let anyone tell you different." I tilt her chin up and barely touch my lips to hers. "Honey." I kiss her. "Baby." Kiss. "Honey... mmmm." I hum with my lips pressed against hers. I steal one more kiss interrupting the perfection that is her mouth. She moans into mine and I know I've done good.

Her lips intensify against mine and I taste coconut, alcohol, and... pineapple. Oh dear lord, please have mercy on me as I'm about to fuck my girlfriend right here in the sand in front of a bunch of tourists who are meandering all around this beach. She presses her hips against me and I lose all sense of self. I pick her up, tossing her over my shoulder, and make a run for the shack while fumbling in my pocket for the keys. They fly from my hand in a clumsy move and land in the sand.

I set Mallory down acting all calm, 'acting' being the operative part of this sentence, because at this point there is nothing calm about my throbbing cock. Squatting down, I forget all about the keys because I'm sidetracked by her bare legs and slide both my hands up the inside of her thighs slowly, methodically, and seductively. Up a little more and I slip one hand up the inside of her cut-off shorts, appreciating the feel of her silky skin. I move my hand just a bit further and... no panties. My girl came out to play tonight and play we shall.

Dragging my gaze from the hem of her cut-offs up to her eyes, I see the internal struggle she's fighting to keep them open. I watch her face, lips parted for deeper breaths and standing still as I slide even further until I'm touching her most forbidden. She's already so ready for me, which is such a fucking turn on.

Reaching back down, I grab the keys from the sand and stand up. After unlocking the door, I smile then pull her in quickly, shutting the door behind her. I reach under the counter and grab the emergency flashlight, turn it on, but away from facing us.

Then with swift movements, my body is against hers trapping her between me and the door. I'm hoping my intentions are obvious, but in case they aren't, I push my hardness against her and swivel my hips for emphasis.

"*Oh, Evan*," she moans, "I want you so bad, but can we do this here? Won't we get caught?"

Can we? "Umm, I thought we were heading in that direction already." At this point, there's no stopping me now. It's sort of a fantasy of mine that I've never fulfilled, even though if you believe the rumors, I'd sound like a liar about now. But she'll be the first in here and that makes it even hotter. All kinds of crazy fun ideas come to mind on the possibilities this shack holds for us, but then I come back to a upsetting dose of reality. This has never happened to me before. I've been so caught up in deciding to stay in paradise, move to Colorado, or go to New York that I must have lost focus of the more important things in life. "Shit! I don't have a condom, baby," I exclaim while squeezing her breasts.

She moans again and kisses me, pulling away long enough to say, "It's okay..." Then closes her gorgeous green eyes again and presses her mouth against mine, picking up where she left off.

I ply my lips away from her, but keep my hands in place —right on her fantastic breasts. My hips are still pinning her against the back of the door as well when I start rambling, "I want you so much, but we should be safe." She stops and looks at me, moving my left hand to touch her face and feel her smooth skin. "We've never talked about it, but I know you're on the pill. I've seen you take them, but I haven't been tested in a couple of months and I think—"

She holds a condom between her index and middle finger, and says, "I meant, it's okay because I brought protection. You didn't seriously think I was going to forget your playboy ways just because I'm a little tipsy and you have a fabulous cock, did you?"

I chuckle, embarrassed by my false assumption. "I'm glad you're responsible even when you're tipsy. Now give me that," I say, grabbing the condom from her. "You're a dirty little girl, Mallory. I'm impressed."

"I don't want you impressed. I want you to want me."

"Oh, I want you!"

"Show me. I'm about to explode looking at you all sexy and shit."

"Oh, baby." I attack her neck with my mouth. "I kind of like the begging. Maybe I should torture you a bit," I say, pausing to undo her shorts, "longer." Once I'm inside the denim, I move my fingers back and forth taunting, teasing her. When I drag my hand leisurely out, I bring my fingers to my mouth and take a long, slow lick, never breaking eye contact with her. Her mouth drops open as I say, "*Mmmmm*, Mallory, I think I have a very bad girl on my hands. First, you have an all-too-convenient condom on your person—"

"My person?" She mocks before I take the two fingers I just licked and place them on her lips.

"Then, I find out that you premeditated your naughtiness by choosing not to wear any panties. On top of that, or should I say underneath all that, you're already wet and ready for me. Is that what you planned to do tonight? You want me to fuck you? Or, maybe you want to fuck me?" I play with her oh-so-very kissable bottom lip as I lean very close to her ear, and whisper, "Tell me what you want and I'll do it for you."

Her breathing tells me how she's feeling. It's deep and lustful and such a fucking turn-on, but I want to give her what she wants. I always want to give her what she wants.

Between shallow pants, she breathes out, "I want to get lost in you and for you to lose yourself in me."

"I'm always lost in you." I kiss her hard and push her shorts the rest of the way down.

I pull her tank top up over her head and don't bother talking anymore. I want what she wants just as much.

With one hand roaming anxiously over her body, the other unties the strings of her bikini top as she mewls into my mouth. After tossing it aside, I drop my shorts with the one hand and get the condom from her. Taking a desperate step back, I roll the condom down my length. I scan the shack quickly because as much as I want to take her against the door, it's old and I don't want her getting a bunch of splinters or marks on her back from the raw wood. An obstacle like that would've never bothered me before if I was doing this with anyone else.

All the foam boards are upright in the racks along the wall. One of my favorites that I borrow is here because I've been meaning to wax it for weeks. It's lying across the top of two workhorses. I look back at Mallory and raise an eyebrow in question, suggestion, and insinuation then smirk at her.

She readily moves over to it and perches her bottom on top, which positions her at the perfect height for me. Moving between her legs, I slow things down by cupping her cheeks and kissing her with care. When that first sweet sound is pulled from within her from my actions, I know she's ready and I push into her. She wraps her arms around my neck and one hand feeds into my hair, pulling just enough to keep me balanced between pleasure and pain.

It only takes a minute before I need more of her and I can tell she's ready for a solid fuck. I grab her hips and thrust faster and harder, not bothering to muffle my moans of enjoyment. I thrust a few more times and feel her being pushed across the surfboard and further from me. Starting to fall into the abyss of sexual bliss, I thrust harder. Her hands slide from my body as she slides off the back right into a pile of life jackets, screaming in surprise as she lands on the cushioning.

"Shit, I'm sorry. The board hasn't been waxed in a long time. It's slippery when wet," I say, rushing to help her up.

She giggles, thankfully finding humor in the situation. "Well, I'll say. Guess we have that in common."

I was so close sixty seconds before and want to get back there, so I look around the shack hoping to remedy the problem at hand. But the shack sucks for good sex until I spot the surfboard wax on the counter. It even has the word sex on the label. I grab the pineapple scented one and rub it against the top of the board in a fluid, but meticulous motion.

MALLORY

Standing there, I watch him wax the board in a fury of motion and it makes me smile to see him so desperate to get back to the sex part, falling off a ridiculous, but funny interruption.

He turns, and demands, "Get back on the board."

There's no questioning, the humor has evaporated and the shack heats up instantly. I position myself on top of the board again, my hand pushing the remaining wax bar to the side. I look down at it and an idea comes fast. It's crazy and erotic and something I've never done and never thought I would do. But being here with Evan, looking at the sweat glistening on his chest, his expression hungry for me, with him I want to experience everything. He makes me want to push my sexual boundaries. With a sly smile and a nod toward the wax, I ask, "Wanna play a little?"

He doesn't hide his surprise. "Fuck, are you serious right now? You want me to use the wax on you?"

"Mmmhmm." Just like the other times with him, I'm not nervous.

"Okay," he whispers then turns around to pick up the wax again. "Lay back," he instructs.

I lay down as he grabs a lighter from the counter behind him. Holding the flame under the wax, I watch it flicker as the wax begins to melt. When he moves it over my chest, his eyes connect with mine, and he says, "It's gonna be hot, baby. Tell me if it's too much."

"I will." The first drop of wax hits my skin above my right breast, stinging and shooting pain through my body. I arch up, my head falling back as I gasp before holding my breath until the pain subsides.

"Baby?" he asks, his brow furrowed in concern as he leans over me. "Too much?"

The dim light seeping into the room and the dulling pain heightens unexpectedly into pleasure. Shadows highlighting every groove of his muscular arms and shoulders as he hovers with me as his entire focus. The ache from the hot wax turns into an ache deep in my being, consuming me. "*No*, again, please," I beg this time, needing him now.

When his expression changes from worry to desire, I know he'll give me everything I crave. I hold the rails of the board as he flicks the lighter to life again. My legs squirm, waiting, but his careful concentration feels more like a calculated torture. I watch with baited anticipation as a drop finally releases, falling through the air. With a sharp unintentional intake of air, I close my eyes and respond to the blissful torment. "Ahhh."

My eyes open when he roughly drags his fingers between my legs, bringing my attention back to him. "You're so wet, Mallory."

Without warning, he pushes me onto my side then drags my hips to the edge of the board. "Hold on, baby," he warns as I feel his hardness at my entrance.

I grab the edge of the board again as his grip on my hips tightens and he slams into me, the surfboard moving in reaction with my body.

It was all leading to this, the foreplay readying me for him. Words of want and need escape me. "Yes! Oh, baby, yes!"

Not a minute more, he gives into his own need and comes. "Fuck, Mallory!"

Evan grabs my ass and squeezes with one hand and then slides it over my hip and stomach until two fingers slip into my wetness and rub.

He owns all of me and controls my every breath and orgasm, manipulating them to his will. I give in entirely, not wanting to fight the incredible feeling any longer. "*Ohhhh, Evan.*"

His hand stays until my body settles.

EVAN

Physically tired yet mentally exhilarated, I lean forward

and rub her back then help her up, directing her to relax on the nearby chair after I lay a clean towel down for her. I gather our clothes, handing them to her and pulling on my shorts. She slowly dresses, but looks satisfied and rightly fucked, which only serves to make me want to fuck her again, but I hold myself back.

A banging on the door makes me jump startled by the intrusion. Mallory covers herself in shock. I hear my boss yelling, "Ashford! Open the door!"

She hides behind me, pulling her tank top over her head and her shorts on as she whispers, "Who is it?"

"My boss," I state flatly, annoyed.

He knocks louder. "I'm not kidding, Ashford. I can get a key. Open the damn door right now."

Shit! "I guess I need to open it." I look her over once to make sure she's dressed then ask, "Where's your bikini top?"

"I have no idea," she replies all nervous.

I kiss her on the lips quickly then cock an eyebrow up in amusement. "No worries. Just stay behind me." She tucks herself behind me as I open the door and walk outside together.

"This is hotel property, Ashford. You know how many rules you're breaking by being in here?" He eyes Mallory up and down a little too long for my liking. I look behind me and see the white cotton top clinging to her perky breasts. When I turn around, I hold myself back from a quick cross punch to that smarmy expression he's wearing while staring at my girlfriend.

With my hand firmly in place on her lower back, I push her a step closer to me and hold her against my back, shielding her from his prying eyes. I straighten my shoulders back, and say, "We were just leaving."

He crosses his arms over his chest, and says, "Yes, you

are because you're fired. Clean out your locker and leave the property."

"Fired? I'm fucking good at what I do. You can't do—"

"You're replaceable and not worth the hassle and time I have to spend trying to get you to fall in line with our company's standards. The decision has been made. You have fifteen minutes to get your stuff and leave. Your skills are no longer required here."

He walks a wide berth around us into the shack and stands like a guard at the door. "Hand over your key, Ashford."

I'm kind of stunned and stand there a moment longer in shock, but then I feel Mallory's breath against my back which makes me realize this job doesn't really matter. She's leaving, I have a job in New York if I want it, and I have a future because of her. "Okay, whatever, man." I roll the key off of my keychain and hand it over, offering a handshake after. He accepts the olive branch, and I say, "Thanks for the job. I actually did enjoy working here, but I understand. I broke the rules."

"Yeah," he says, nodding his head incredulously at me. "Rules are in place for a reason."

Turning back to Mallory, I take her hand, and ask, "Do you mind waiting for me at the car?"

She nods. "I'll meet you there."

We both start walking when he says from behind me. "Hey kid, glad to hear the truth come out about that girl." He looks down then says, "Take some advice. Go back to school, Evan. You're too good for this place anyway." He smiles which makes me smile and chuckle back.

"I intend to."

After cleaning out my locker, I walk to my car with my spare clothes and shower stuff under my arm. My body comes to a complete halt when I spot my car under the large parking lot lamp, spying Mallory lying across the hood. Normally I'd freak, but this is Mallory, my hot girlfriend. I try to calm my body's erection as images of an eighties rock video flash through my head.

With my confident smirk and swagger back in effect, I start walking again, feeling happier than I've felt in years. The sun, moon, and stars have aligned in my world and I owe it all to the girl looking like a sexy pin-up on top of my car—a girl that looks incredible and is waiting there for me. *For me.*

I'm such a lucky bastard.

14

EVAN

I wake up next to Mallory the morning after being fired. We made love twice last night. The first time in the surf shack could actually be considered more of a fucking, but anytime with my girl is loving to me. I grin without an ounce of regret over the firing. The time with her was worth the loss of job. The memories are definitely worth it.

Rolling onto my side to face her, I see she's still asleep with a small smile on her lips. Damn, she's beautiful. I stroke back a section of hair that has fallen across her cheek. As I lay the hair neatly in place, she stirs, but still sleeps. Her expression is content, peaceful. I watch her. I watch her as the sun rises, brightening my world. I watch her as the minutes turn to hours. While watching her, my head clears, and all the pain I had learned to live with in my heart is gone, no trace remaining.

Her eyes finally peek open and she smiles just for me.

I whisper, hoping not to break the serenity of the early hour. "Good morning."

"Good morning."

"You've been smiling for about two hours now. You want

to share what you were dreaming?" I ask, closing the gap and completely invading her space with my knees and hands, my whole body. I want to get as close as I can to her. Fuck it! I want to be inside her.

"My dreams already came true," she replies easily, her tone letting me know she's not moving from this bed anytime soon.

She makes me want to stay here in bed with her—the warmth of her body, the suggestive curves of her breast pressed against me tempt me to stay forever. But I have ideas about her remaining time on the island, not wanting her to miss a thing. Her eyes are bright with possibility, so I say, "You only have two weeks left. I thought we could cram in all the stuff that everyone usually wants to do while visiting the island, starting with that luau Sunny said you really wanted to go to. Would you like to go today since it's your day off?"

"Really?" she asks, crinkling her nose. "You'd do the cheesy tourist thing for me?"

"I would do anything for you, Mallory."

She leans forward and kisses me while her hand weaves into my hair, holding me to her. Her body wiggles even closer and then seductively gyrates against mine letting me know she wants me as much as I want her. "Would you make love to me again?"

"That's not exactly torture you know."

"I'm a simple girl with simple needs, what can I say."

My hand slides against her stomach and upward across her breasts without stopping, skimming back down between her legs. Her eyes grow heavy and I watch as her breathing changes, deepening.

I move on top of her, spreading her legs with my knee, parting her for me. Adjusting my weight on my legs and forearms, I kiss her stomach while rubbing my thumbs across her hipbones, securing her to the mattress. Tilting my head, I lick the apex of her thighs.

"Evan?" she calls, surprised by my quick action.

I don't answer because she'll try to convince me not to do this so we can get to the sex part, but I want to make her feel good. I want to see her writhe under my tongue, to watch and feel her body beg to come then give in to the seduction. And I want to be exactly where I am when that happens.

Mallory has always been responsive to me and she doesn't disappoint now. I learn more about her body and her likes every time we're together. She wriggles when I wiggle my tongue around her clit. She jolts when I flick her lightly and slightly to the right with my tongue. And she melts, relaxing into the mattress when I go deeper. All the time I spent studying her over the last two months is paying off. I can feel her body tightening, coiling, as she grips the sheets in her fists. I continue circling then mixing up my pattern keeping her on edge.

I know she'll orgasm as soon as I touch her with my fingers because I already have her worked into a sexual frenzy. I bring my hand up, sliding it over her thighs to warn her, allowing her to prepare before my fingers find their own warm heaven while continuing to move my tongue as I twist and curl.

Twist, curl, twist, spin, twist, curl.

She tremors under me, squirming around on the bed. "Oh my God, Evan! Get in me now!" She demands, pulling me up by the hair.

I jump up quickly removing my boxer briefs and grabbing a condom. "You want me, baby?"

"I want you, but I need you more," she says, lighting a fire within me.

Knowing I make her feel this way, making her want me so much makes me hard as a fucking rock.

This morning is about love, not fucking I remind myself. After lying back down, hovering over her, I stare into the depths of her eyes.

She frowns, but the lines fade as she softly smiles. Stroking my hair from my forehead, she asks, "What is it?"

I kiss her, really kiss her and she begins to move beneath me as I guide myself inside of her, a physical bond from my soul to hers. My eyes close automatically, the feel of her overwhelming my senses.

Forcing them back open, I watch her face as she wraps her legs around my waist, keeping me close, as close as possible. My chest is against hers and every move is calculated with a slow and deliberate effort. Her eyes are closed and lips parted, her sweet breath inhaled as I breathe her in. I cover her mouth with mine and kiss her again.

An aching begins to build from intense desires. I want to lose control and move faster and harder, for pleasure alone, but I need to make love to her. I need to remember every one of her sighs and gestures, every movement and the whole feel of this experience. I can't treat this casually. It's not, and every time we come together needs to matter and be important.

Her body works against mine, her pull grounding me to her, pushing me to give into her own demanding movements. She breaks away from my mouth, gasping for air, but her eyes are still closed. I pick up my pace and add a hip move I know will feel good to my beautiful girlfriend.

I just didn't count on it feeling so fucking incredible for me when giving her my all. With one deep thrust, I stop, squeezing my eyes shut and take a deep breath desperately trying to stave off my own undoing.

She looks up at me as I open my eyes. Cupping my face, she asks with only a breath between us, "Are you okay?"

Once again, I look beyond the tranquil emerald flecks in the center of her green eyes, and reply, "I love you, Mallory."

"I love you, too."

Dropping my head against her forehead, my emotions get the best of me. "I need all of you. Everything."

"Look at me, Evan." When I do, she says, "You have all of me. I'm yours, completely." She plants a sweet kiss on my lips and then with her heels, encourages me to start moving again.

I do. I start moving and thrusting, letting my mind get washed into its own oblivion of Mallory goodness. And like my mind, my body follows swiftly as I release while buried inside. When comprehension returns, I open my eyes to find her watching me intently as if doing some memorizing herself.

She sighs contentedly and says, "I wish I could capture that face on film."

I drop on top of her, smiling but exhausted, and rest my head snuggled to her neck as it dawns on me what she's talking about. "My come face? You want a picture of my come face?" I chuckle at the notion.

She rubs my back gently, dragging her nails lightly along my skin giving me goose bumps and relaxing me as she explains, "Yes, your come face. You're beautiful all the time, but when you orgasm, you're feral and sexy as hell."

I laugh a little harder, feeling exhaustion starting to kick in. "Maybe one day I'll let you take a pic, but I'm going to need one of you in return."

A satiated smile lifts the corners of her mouth up. "That would be only fair."

She snuggles down, pulling the blankets around us and we fall asleep in a tangle of limbs and mingling breaths, soft words of love, and hearts, minds and bodies satisfied.

I DON'T like waking up alone anymore. It's disconcerting to me.

My arms grapple the vast emptiness of the space beside me and my eyes pop open in response. I look around. "Mallory?" tumbles from my mouth without thought, but on instinct.

Sitting up, I find only silence surrounding me. "Mallory?" Flipping the covers off my body, I swing my legs over the edge and walk into the bathroom, still calling her name. "*Mallory?*"

I don't know why I feel like something is wrong, but when I walk through the house, still naked from our earlier activities, frantic thoughts race through my brain. I open the back door to see if she's out there. "Mallory?" I call loudly, but still don't receive an answer.

Running back in, I grab a pair of shorts from the floor, shoving one leg quickly in and almost tripping to get the other one in as I hurry for the front door. I race by the pool, zipping my pants up, still calling her name.

I rush inside the main house, buttoning the top button of my shorts, out of breath from anxiety, and halt instantly. I hear her. I hear her talking. *I hear her laughing.* I also hear Ms. Chart laughing. Calm overrides all my worries and I exhale, loudly.

Then I call her, softer in tone, more relaxed, and hopeful. "Mallory?"

"Oh, there he is now." I hear her before I see her coming from Ms. Chart's bedroom with a bright smile on her face.

Surprising me, she jumps up on me, wrapping her legs around my waist, and I catch her, holding her by her bottom. I'm liking this new greeting that she's been giving me lately. I squeeze her ass for good measure.

"Good morning, babe," she says, kissing me on the lips.

"I think it's more like afternoon, Mallory," Ms. Chart corrects her playfully then lovingly scolds me, "Evan, you've slept half the day away. You shouldn't keep your guests waiting like that."

"Yes, you shouldn't have kept me waiting because I got into all kinds of trouble while you were sleeping. I was lucky I found such great company to spend time with," Mallory adds, dropping her feet to the floor again.

I smirk. "What kind of trouble would that be, my beautiful girlfriend?" I kiss her on the forehead, wrapping my arm around her shoulders and bringing her to my side.

Mallory looks at Ms. Chart and says, "You're gonna get in so much trouble—"

I can feel the frown form across my face as I look between them sharing secrets like old friends.

"I'll let you tell him. You practically twisted my arm. What was I supposed to do?" Ms. Chart adds, looking at Mallory.

Mallory giggles, looks up at me, and announces, "Don't worry, I love chubby babies."

"What?" *The fuck?*

"You were such a cute little guy," she adds in this baby tone and pinches my cheeks.

I look at Ms. Chart in embarrassment. "You didn't, did you?"

Looking as innocent as a guilty woman can look, she throws her hands in the air. "I couldn't resist. Mallory is very persuasive."

"No," is all I can say, shaking my head.

A huge smile crosses Mallory's face, cocking a challenging eyebrow up at me, she says, "Oh yeah, I saw the goods, ya little chunkers."

"I can't help that they fed me all the time. It's not like I was helping myself in the kitchen." I try to justify my heavy baby build.

"Don't get all defensive. I think you were adorable, like you are now." She reassures me by hugging me tightly and sighs. "I love babies."

Do I want to have a baby conversation right now? *No, not really.* "You love *looking* at babies?" I ask nervous to where this conversation is heading.

"I love babies, looking and holding. I babysat a lot in high school. I love the smell and feel of their soft skin." Her eyes get this far away look in them as she speaks, in a dreamy way. She starts illustrating with her arms in the air. "When they're all cranky and you soothe them and they fall asleep in your arms. Aww..." She places her hand over her heart. "It's just the sweetest thing."

"Seriously, are we talking about babies right now?" I ask, scratching my head.

Resting the palms of her hands on my chest, she asks, "Why are you so nervous? It's not like I'm planning our family or anything. Geez Louise, you need to lighten up, babe. Gail was only showing me—"

"Gail? Why are you calling her that?"

Mallory walks across the kitchen, opens the fridge, and

pulls out two plates, handing them to me. "Can you carry these please? I thought we'd eat lunch by the pool."

I take the plates from her, but still stand there waiting for her to answer. She grabs two cans of soda before walking around me and out the back door. I follow, outpacing her to reach the table first. Setting the plates down, I ask, "Did she ask you to call her that?"

We slowly sit down. She puts her elbows on the table and rests her head in her hands. "Yes, but I can call her Ms. Chart if you prefer. She's really a great lady."

"Yes, I agree. She is. It's—"

Reaching across the table, her hands come to rest on mine. "Do you want to call her Gail, babe?"

Suddenly I feel like I'm five years old in my reasoning. I'm just realizing how controlled my life has been. "I used to... for a few years before the whole Lani thing." My voice gets quieter though it's unintentional. "It was kind of a secret between us, but when my parents came to the island to deal with everything, I slipped up. My mother freaked out. She feels threatened by her and that's her way of making the distinction that she's not family." I pause then add, "I'm being rude. I should put a shirt on for lunch."

I start to stand, but she stops me. "No, I like looking at you, hot stuff. Anyway, it's just us." She lets out a small laugh like she's sort of been caught doing something naughty.

"Come here."

She comes over and settles into my lap, wrapping her arm around my neck and kissing my temple.

Her tone is lilt, happy. "I love being here with you like this."

Squeezing her tighter, I say, "I feel the same way. I don't want you to go, but your college is important. That kind of reminds me of something we need to talk about." I look at her eyes as they meet mine. "You want to go for a walk down on the beach?"

"I'm not sure. You're kind of scaring me right now."

"Don't stress. I just want to share what's on my mind."

I lift up and she stands. Taking her hand, we walk to the steps that lead to the beach. She stops me, pulling back on my hand. "Really, um... we can talk here," she says, obviously thinking it's worse than it is.

"It's not bad, well... it's not going to affect us if that's what you're worried about, well, maybe, but... it won't separate us... hmmm... well... it will—"

She instantly halts. "Stop! You're really freaking me out."

"Calm down. It's good news." I see her breathing deepen from the shallow short breaths she was taking a few seconds before. "My dad offered me a job—"

"In New York?"

"Yes."

"At his company?"

"Yes."

"You said you hated New York?"

"I did... I do." I scrape my hand roughly across my scalp trying to phrase this to her in a way that makes some kind of sense. "Mallory, there are several reasons why I should take this job."

"Okay."

"Well, first of all, it pays well and considering I don't have a job, I kind of need the money, especially if I want to come to Boulder spring semester."

She nods in understanding, but then asks, "Do you really need the money, Evan? I mean look around this place. You have the latest and greatest of everything from TV's to cars, an endless supply of 'fun' money, and no bills from what I can gather. I'm not judging you, but I don't think it's about the money. I think it's about you needing to prove something to your parents."

Thinking about what she said in quiet contemplation for a long minute before I turn, looking at her. "More than my parents, I want to do this for us, for you. You're right, my monthly allowance is more than sufficient to live off of, but I need something to do. I may look like a lazy bastard most of the time, but I like keeping my mind occupied."

"I wasn't calling you lazy," she says, resting her hand on my forearm.

"I know you weren't, but I need to do this for myself as well. This will be extra money that I'll have to help us in Colorado."

"I can support myself at school. I don't want you to take a job because you think you need to support me. I don't live a fancy lifestyle or in a swanky apartment. I have an old box TV, an even older Toyota, but I have a job that pays the bills and I'm happy. So please, if you take this job, do it for you and only you."

"This experience will look good on my resume."

She walks to the edge of the water, letting her feet get covered by the tide. "Work experience is always a bonus on a resume while you're in college. It shows you're motivated and have a good work ethic."

"You sound like my dad."

"I like your dad," she says, chuckling. "So you've made up your mind?"

"I wanted to talk to you about it, but yes, I think I'm pretty solid with this decision."

She wraps her arms around my shoulders. "I'll miss you, but I'd miss you if you were here too." Dropping her head on my right shoulder, she asks, "Can I be honest about something?"

"I hope you're always honest with me."

"The girls," she corrects herself, "the *women* there in New York, they're—"

"They don't compare to you. No one has ever made me feel the way you do. I'm there for a job and to hopefully help my family keep the business in the family. Nothing else, okay, baby?" I kiss her. She responds positively to my answer by intensifying the kiss.

15

EVAN

The afternoon sun is bright, but we're still on a deadline when she finally walks out of the bathroom, dressed and ready to go. "You look great," I say, ogling her hotness. She's all lean legs and tight T-shirt, shorts, and flowing hair tonight. *She's breathtaking.*

While driving to our secret first stop, she states, "You said you hated it when you lived in New York after Yale."

She doesn't say anything else, but I can see where her mind is at. She has those pesky fears of me cheating or falling prey to some Manhattan society chick, but that is not gonna happen. The only way to truly alleviate her fears is to prove it to her, which I will.

I pull into the parking lot of Hilo Hattie, the largest store of Hawaiian shirts in the world. She looks at the store then back at me as if I must have driven to the wrong place. But I smile and waggle my eyebrows. After hopping out, I run around and help her out of the car. She's learned to wait most of the time.

"We're shopping?" she asks, surprised as I knew she would be.

"Yes," I say, "we're shopping." We stop inside the entrance and pose in front of the largest Hawaiian shirt in the world. I hold my phone out in front of us and take a photo.

"What are you up to, Ashford?"

"If we're gonna do this luau touristy thing, we're gonna do it right." Seeing the clothes in the back, we head straight through the knick-knack section and into the women's section. "Pick out whatever you want. My treat."

Her eyes light up. "Really?"

"Really. Now go. We only have thirty minutes before we need to check in."

She spins, eyes scanning the merchandise, and says, "I almost don't know where to start."

"Start wh—"

"Shhh, I'm a girl. That was rhetorical. Stay quiet and try to keep up." She scurries through the racks of clothes.

The sections are divided by design: traditional, modern, muted, and some crazy ones. She goes to the traditional section and pulls out a shirt and some other things. I'm paying attention, but not that closely. I follow her to the dressing room, sit in the provided 'guy' chair, and wait.

When she comes out a few minutes later, she's wearing a blue-based flowery button up shirt. She twirls for me. "How do I look?"

"Um, it doesn't show much skin." That's all I can think to say because I don't think I thought this through thoroughly when I came up with this idea. *Why in the hell would I take her shopping for clothes that cover her up?*

"I like the colors," I say, circling my finger in the air at her shirt.

She turns on her heal, huffing, and goes back into the

dressing room. Two minutes later, she returns wearing a dress in that same pattern. It's fitted to her breasts and has small thin straps. The skirt portion is tied up on her hip and shows off her curves nicely. I stand up and plant a gentle kiss just behind her ear. "You look amazing."

"So, that's a yes then?"

"A definite yes." I'm too busy to say more because I'm still appreciating her soft skin against my lips. "Keep it on. I want you to wear it tonight. I'll meet you up front at the register."

Reaching around, I take the tag off, leaving her to gather her stuff. Then I rush back through grabbing a Hawaiian shirt for me and pulling it on over my head as I walk to the jewelry section. Scanning the cases quickly, I know what I'm looking for because I've seen Kate in a similar pair of earrings, but I'm not looking for earrings. When I spot exactly what I want, I make all my purchases there, hidden from Mallory's sight.

Mallory is on her tiptoes looking for me a few feet away. I hurry to her side not wanting her to wait any longer and ask, "Did you see anything else you'd like to have to remember your trip to Hawaii?"

"I've got you. That's all I need." A huge smirk crosses her face as she pokes me in the chest. "Nice shirt."

"Thanks."

Her finger sways between us several times as she takes in the fabric. Yeah, my shirt matches hers. I went there. "You don't think we're a little matchy-matchy?" she asks.

"I want everyone there to know that I'm the guy lucky enough to get to wear a shirt that matches my incredibly stunning girlfriend's dress. Not too psycho for ya, is it?"

"A little, but I've always been a sucker for your stalker

tendencies." Her finger taps my chin and she walks toward the exit, leaving me there to watch her fine ass.

She's fucking hot.

In the car, she leans over and kisses me on the cheek. "Thank you for the dress. It's really pretty."

"You look beautiful, Mallory."

"I feel beautiful. Thank you."

I throw the bag in the trunk after retrieving her surprise out and shoving it deep into my pocket.

The mood is light and easy on the drive. We finally pull into the large lot on the other side of the tourist buses, and park. We walk to the entrance and down the bamboo corridor that leads us to the greeters. They hand us a Mai Tai, and a girl in a traditional hula outfit welcomes us, "Aloha. Welcome to Luau Paradise, step on up, and we'll take your picture as a souvenir. You have the option to purchase the picture at the end of the evening."

We're shuffled forward by a big burly dude and suddenly a man with some very large parrots is standing very close, warning us. "I'm going to put one on each of your shoulders. Don't make any quick movements, scare, or harm the birds. Mahalo." And that's how I come to find myself standing next to Mallory in a matching Hawaiian shirt, Mai Tai in hand, a very large bird on my shoulder, and posing for a souvenir photo that I'm definitely going to purchase.

Mallory has the biggest grin on her face says, "Cheeeeessssseeeeeyyyy." The flash goes off and she looks up at me. "You weren't looking at the camera." Oops, guess I wasn't, but she can be very distracting, too cute for her own good.

The photographer holds his finger up and says, "One more. Face me and smile." He snaps another shot and we laugh, gently, so we don't scare the birds. The birds are immediately removed from our shoulders and we are shuffled along to make room for the next couple.

Mallory takes my free hand and says, "This is fun. Let's go make a lei."

"Yeah, that sounds fantastic," I reply not hiding my sarcasm.

Thirty minutes later, I managed a bracelet after destroying about a hundred flowers trying to shove that damn needle through their tiny, delicate centers. Mallory, on the other hand, is the proud new owner of a perfect, handmade lei that's already being displayed around her neck. She slips my creation around her ankle and then slips her flip flop back on.

Checking out my girl covered from head to touristy toe, I smile. "I meant to tell you, I'm liking the ensemble tonight. Very hot."

"Hot enough to want to get it on later?" she asks playfully, poking me in the stomach.

"Hot enough to want to get it on now."

With a hit on the chest, she blushes. "You say the nicest things, Mr. Ashford. Are you this nice to everyone?" Walking ahead of me to the old fashioned games area set up on the beach, she turns abruptly before I can answer, and throws her hands around my neck. "Tell me you're not this nice to everyone. I need to hear you say that to me."

She lowers her head in shame, but I lift her chin back up and pull her against my body while gently squeezing her ass. "I love only you. So, those words only come to mind when I'm with you or think of you." I push a section of her hair that the wind has carried across her face back, and say, "I won't ever hurt you. I may disappoint you, but I will never hurt you, Mallory."

She tucks her head under my chin and I can tell she's

satisfied with that answer. With a renewed excitement she pushes off me and says, "Now go spear me a target, sexy."

I turn and suddenly a guy in a Hawaiian loin cloth is handing me a spear and mocking me with a challenging smile. "It's simple, haole. Take the spear in your hand and hit the target. Like this," he says, throwing the spear and hitting the bulls-eye. "See? Simple. Nice shirt, dude."

More mocking. He's getting close to an ass kicking. Glancing at Mallory, I'm rewarded with an encouraging smile. I throw the javelin as hard as I can and miss the target completely. The guy snickers under his breath and says, "Want to humiliate yourself with another try?"

"Yes, he'll try again! Go on, babe. I know you can do it." Mallory stands proud and pushes me forward to the table of spears. My girl's got a competitive streak it seems. She leans over and whispers in my ear, "You hit that target and I'll make the drive home a drive you won't forget."

She definitely knows how to motivate me. Puffing my chest out, I step up for another go. The guy eyes Mallory up and down, lingering on her breasts a bit long for my liking. I grab the spear from his hand and give him a glare that sets him straight. With all my strength and jealousy, I angle the spear back and throw it, focused on my target.

"Yes!" Mallory exclaims, jumping up and down and clapping. She grabs my face and her tongue enters my mouth all possessive and showy, which is totally fucking hot. Just as I slide my hand up to the sides of her breasts, a loud conch shell is blown in the distance, breaking us out of our little world. She wipes the side of her mouth, and announces, "I'm so proud of you. I'm hungry. Let's go eat."

I start to smirk at loincloth guy, but I'm yanked away too fast to show off.

After we're seated at the long banquet tables, the staff starts handing out trays of food. The place is packed and apparently they've done this a few times because they have this service down and they're fast.

Mallory works her way around her divided plate, clockwise, tasting one bite of each thing on her plate until she gets to the Poi. I watch wondering if she'll try it.

She points her plastic fork at it and asks, "What's this?"

"Poi."

"What's Poi?"

"It's made from the Taro root."

"Why is it grey? It looks like glue?"

"Just try it." I roll my eyes.

Coating the ends of her fork, she wipes the tines onto her tongue. She's so sexy, oblivious to what little things like that do to me. Scrunching her nose up and then smiling, she says, "I'm so glad I tried it."

"Really?" I asked shocked.

"No, ya jerk! Why'd you let me put that in my mouth? You knew it was gross and you still let me do it." She huffs.

"Some people love it while others say it's an acquired taste."

"Well, it's not a taste I want to acquire. That's gross!" She takes her napkin and drags it down her tongue.

Oh, fuck me, alright already. I look at my watch, frustration of the sexual kind setting in. Two hours left until I get the sweet release promised to me earlier. I gulp loudly at the thought of her licking... The entertainment starting interrupts my dirty thoughts.

Five hot-looking hula girls start dancing across the stage. Hula dudes come out doing some really loud chanting and stomping behind them and I recognize the one from the spear game earlier. After sending a wink in Mallory's direction, he smiles at her. He fucking winked at my girlfriend right in front of me. He's got some big kehones and damn lucky he's up there dancing right now or I'd pop that winking eye.

Running my fingertips in small circular motions around my temples, I try to calm my irritation, but then, like a bolt of lightning, it hits me. "Shit!" That's how I used to treat women. It didn't matter if they had a boyfriend or not. "Oh Shit!" I say, dropping my head into my hands. Guys don't care that she's my girlfriend! They're going to hit on her anyway. She's mine damn it! Karma is a cold-hearted bitch, so her name is probably Kelly. I feel a snarl rumble through my chest at the thought of her and the shit she told Mallory at the party, hoping to break us up.

Suddenly Mallory's hand is rubbing up and down my spine as she comes closer and whispers in my ear. "Are you alright? What's wrong?"

Looking into her sweet, caring eyes, I can't help but smile. It's small, but a smile all the same. "I just... I've been an asshole for so long," I confide in her. "I love you." Weak, I know, but she knows about my past so it's all I can say that feels justified right now.

"Oh baby, I love you." She turns back to the stage and exclaims, "Look, a fire breather! Cool!"

I turn toward the stage again and settle back into my chair as she rests against me. I move my arm around her shoulders and we watch the show.

Twenty more minutes of hip shaking, foot stompin', fire breathing action and I see the dancers roaming the audience gathering participants. I hate this kind of shit and hope they don't come to our section.

Tap.Tap.Tap.

"Evan! Go!" Mallory says excitedly. "You've been picked. Go, baby, show me your moves."

I look up at the hula girl smiling down at me and then to Mallory. Wiggling my eyebrows, I whisper, "I'd rather show you my moves in private, if you know what I mean."

She doesn't fall for it, so I begrudgingly stand and follow the girl up onto the stage. How can I say no when Mallory looks so incredibly happy right now. Looking at the audience, I realize there are probably five hundred people watching us on stage, and my face heats up.

After a minute of getting adjusted to all eyes on me, I loosen up. I'm here with Mallory, *for Mallory*, and I'm going to enjoy myself. I meet her eyes and smile, knowing she's enjoying this so much.

Trying to follow the girl next to me is hard. I'm apparently doing it all wrong. She puts her hands on my hips and smiles at me. Raising my arms up, I look down trying to make my middle move the way she's showing me. The hula girl pulls and pushes my hips side to side, but it seems of no use and I just start moving, laughing, and having a fun time anyway, throwing in a little 'umph' at the end just for Mallory, which makes her laugh. We're escorted off and the girl who picked and attempted to teach me, whispers, "Hang out after the show and I'll give you a private lesson."

"Thanks, but I have a girlfriend." My tone is light, friendly, and very proud. I love that I'm taken. I would've never thought I'd think that way, but here I am and I'm happy.

Mallory attacks me with kisses when I sit down.

"I'm better with my thrusts," I joke, not really joking.

She laughs, and agrees. "That is for sure. You definitely

have thrusting talent." She then goes on about how cute I was up on stage. She evens mentions that she didn't appreciate that girl's hands all over me, but that she thought it was cool that I went up there.

We finish our meal, the show ends, and we buy our souvenir photo. I should really be more embarrassed over how I look in these photos dressed like this, but I buy it anyway because she wants it.

As we head for the car, we hold hands. Our body language to any passerby could be mistaken for newlyweds. I tighten my hold on her liking the possibility of this thought.

It will take less than an hour to get back home and the first fifteen minutes is filled with an escalating sexual tension, intensifying with each passing minute. I wasn't going to hold her to her offer from the luau, but I can't say that I am going to let her off that easy either. I love her mouth on me and really want to feel and see her doing that to me again.

By the time we get out of Honolulu, Mallory has a devious sparkle in her eyes as she licks her lips—slowly—making a show of it. She reaches over and rubs her palm across the top of my length that's already hard for her, but when she moves closer, I stop her. Quickly closing my eyes, I'm shocked by my own actions.

Since I'm driving, I don't keep my eyes closed for long, needing a second or two to recover.

"Evan? What's wrong?" She sits back in her chair.

Reaching over, I tug at her seatbelt, making sure it's tight and she's safe. "You don't have to do this right now. I want to collect my winnings at home, so I can also pleasure you."

"Doing this for you does give me pleasure," she murmurs into my ear.

Her mouth trails down my neck as one of her hands explores my chest and abs under my shirt. Squirming from anticipation and nervousness, I really shouldn't let her do this to me while I'm driving, especially after being pulled over last time, but she's so fucking hot and persuasive...

She lets me return the favor when we get home.

16

MALLORY

Lying in bed, I'm physically exhausted from Evan dragging me all over the island sightseeing for more than a week. He has his mind set that I *will have* the same full experience as anyone else visiting Hawaii. The difference is—he's my tour guide. My body tingles remembering some of the places we've been making out: in the yellow submarine off of Waikiki Beach where he bought the entire tour's tickets so it could be only the two of us, kissing on the beach instead of snorkeling at Hanauma Bay, and hiding in the maze for well over an hour at the Dole Plantation; I hid and when he found me, he ate pineapple soft serve off my body. That was completely inappropriate with all the families running around, but was fuckin' sexy. We couldn't even make it home that day because we were so hot and bothered, so he pulled over on some dirt road and we finished what we started.

That was last week and my legs are still sore from the hike up Diamond Head two days ago. Well, it might also be from our 'doing it like there's no tomorrow sexcapades, but I would never complain about my Evan lovins.

Throwing back the sheet, I look to my side.

"Oh, good, you're awake," Evan says, bright-eyed, all smiley, showing off his perfect teeth.

I grumble.

He comes over and sits down next to me. "Don't be moody, baby, it's a beautiful day."

I flail my arms in the air as I whine, "Every day is the same here. Beautiful blue skies, the ocean sounds in the distance, birds singing," I let my finger trail down his bare chest, "perfectly tanned, muscular, strong, sexy surfer boys."

He tilts his head down questioningly, "Boys, as in plural?"

"Okay, just one perfectly tanned, muscular, strong, sexy surfer boy."

"Go on."

"Go on?"

"Yeah, I want to hear more."

"*Ahhh*. Well." I continue lightly dragging my nail down his abs. "A surfer who is incredibly smart, has the best blue eyes I've ever seen—"

"You're kind of making my cock jealous of my eyes," he says, batting his lashes playfully at me. He rubs his chest with his hand, spreading his fingers to cover a large portion of it then slides it over his abs, which are looking more defined than usual if that's possible.

I involuntarily swipe my hand across my mouth in case I'm drooling, but stay focused on his hand as it travels downward. I can feel his eyes burning into mine, but I continue watching the show he's all too happy to give me.

He dips his fingers into his pants, slides them up then back down completely disappearing into the fabric of his briefs, and grabs hold of his hard length. "You like watching, baby?"

Gulping, I squeeze my thighs together, my body responding to him.

His hand reappears, and I sigh in disappointment.

"Don't worry," He says. "We'll have plenty of time to watch each other when we're apart. We'll sex-cam."

"Can't you give me a little preview of what to expect? I mean, it won't be the same on the monitor. Wait, what? You want me..." I say, my anxiety showing through my tone. "To touch myself in front of the webcam while you watch?"

He leans down really close, rubbing the tip of his nose along my neck, and exhaling a warm breath. "Yes baby, I want to watch you get yourself off for me like you did that time in the bathroom."

Open mouthed, wet, deep, and intense kisses are exchanged while he slides down on top of me and moves slowly, making me ache for more. My body flows with his as he presses his middle against my pelvis. My mind already lost in feelings and sensations as I start working against him for the friction I need. The cotton of my panties and his boxer briefs are a complete nuisance, but yet provide pleasure as it scrapes against my neediness.

Moaning as I wrap my arms around his broad shoulders, he pulls back, removing his lips from mine, and says in the most sextastic voice, "Does this feel good, baby?"

A mumbled utterance of approval escapes my lips as his hands slide under my tank top and he squeezes my breasts. His moan in return encourages me to grind harder. He kisses across my jaw, dragging his teeth and then sucking gently on my neck.

A tight squeeze on my breasts becomes firmer as his mouth reaches my peaks and teases me with soft licks, delicate touches, and gentle hip presses.

I lift my head to see why the change in speed. He's

looking up at me through dark lashes and half-hooded eyes as I watch his lips kiss my breast and his thumb caresses my other breast's nipple.

Pushing my boobs together, he appreciates them... and then begins talking to them. "I'm going to miss you girls. Remember you're mine and only mine. Don't let anyone else manhandle you, okay?"

Evan releases them and abruptly takes my arms, pushing them above my head, and attacks my neck with kisses while gyrating into me again with passion. I don't know what that stalling was all about, but I'm glad we're back to the action portion of this morning sex.

His lips meet mine again and as we kiss, I wrap my legs around his middle and we grind hard and fast. "Get a condom," I mumble with his tongue in my mouth.

"Let's do it this way," he says, never breaking pace. "I'm already so close."

So am I, which is why I thought we would have sex, but this does feel too fantastic to stop now.

Rubbing down my sides, he glides his hands hard against me on the way up and grabs a hold of my breasts again. Our moaning takes over and he whimpers for a split second before pressing hard against my heat. Pushing back against his shoulders, I reach my orgasm. But we continue moving against each other a few more seconds before he collapses on top of me.

After panting for a moment, he rolls off of me, eyes closed and smirking. "God, I love you."

"Me or my body?" I giggle at his obvious exhausted pleasure.

"Both," he says, turning to face me. He strokes my face with his hand, his expression turning serious. "I love all of you. Everything about you, baby. Especially that beautiful blush that's on your cheeks now." He leans forward, kissing me sweetly on the lips then jumps up off the bed and heads to the bathroom. Before he leaves the room, he stops and looks back at me. "Get that cute ass out of bed. We've got plans today."

I grab the pillow next to me and chuck it at him. "You can't be serious! It's been non-stop, babe. I'm tired. No more hiking or any activities like that. I'm good. I've seen more than my fair share. Can't we just lounge in bed instead?"

"No, we can't," he shouts from the bathroom. "We've got big plans today."

"Uggghh! What do I need to wear and bring?" I give in. Apparently, he has set his mind and there's no changing it.

"Wear what you would normally wear. Or, we can wear our matching Hawaiian clothes," he says and laughs.

"No! Absolutely not! It was cute one time. Twice is too much."

"Okaaayyy, but if you change your mind..." He's wise and doesn't finish that sentence, but he does start the shower.

I get out of bed, disgruntled I might add, and pull off my soaked panties and scrunched up tank top. Tossing them on my growing pile of dirty clothes, I walk naked into the bathroom. He's naked and brushing his teeth, but stops to drink me in with his eyes. With the toothbrush sticking out of his mouth and foamy paste all over his teeth, he releases it and takes my arm, pulling me in front of him. His body is flush against the back of mine as his hands feel me, wrapping around my ribs and stopping on my stomach. Gently rubbing his hands, palms flattened, on my breasts, he cups them. He's been watching me move under his touch until it seems to dawn on him that he's supposed to be brushing his teeth. He lets go of me and starts brushing again.

When I exhale, I realize I'd stopped breathing altogether when he looked at me the way he did. He's touched every inch of my body before—gently and sexually—but something about the moment we just shared reminded me of the way he looked at me the very first day we met.

As I walk under the spray of the shower, I ask, trying to sound casual, "You asked me if I enjoyed myself after the first time we were together. I remember thinking that was thoughtful that you were concerned with how it felt emotionally for me."

He steps in behind me and holds me so were both under the water. Backing up, he grabs the shampoo, squirts some in his hand, and starts washing my hair. "I also washed your hair that first night." He kisses my shoulder. "If you're asking me if I always ask girls that question afterward, the answer is no. I never cared enough about anyone to even think to ask. I really cared if you had a good time." He leans down to my ear and whispers, "I secretly hoped you'd stay with me that first day, but—"

"But I was so pissed that I woke up alone."

"Yeah, you scared me a little," he laughs.

"You made love to me when all I was looking for was a good time." I also laugh, rinsing the shampoo out of my hair.

His hand goes to his chest, ego wounded, and all dramatic. "Oh how your words pierce my very manhood. So, you didn't have a good time then?"

He slides his fingers, conditioner coated, through my hair, carefully spreading it throughout.

I playfully respond, "I didn't say I didn't have a good time, but you made love to me. You didn't fuck me."

"Oh, I see. So Mallory Wray came to the island to get laid? Thank god, I was there to be of service, but my humblest apologies that I left her dissatisfied and in need of a proper fucking. I can only hope that I've made up for it." I see the sparkle in his eyes as he teases.

Shimmying my soapy body against him, I say, "More than made up for it, but if you'd like to keep making up for it, you know where to find me, hot stuff."

He steps out from rinsing his hair and I step under, closing my eyes and letting the water fall down my body. When I open them again, he's staring at me and I recognize the look though it takes me a second to place it, a flashback to our first night together again.

His smile lessens as he looks at me, his other hand rubbing the back of his neck. His gaze drops away for the briefest of seconds, but when it returns there's confusion, his expression mystified again.

He asks, "What am I going to do with you?"

"Just love me. That's all."

"That's easy. I meant what am I going to do when you're gone?"

"You're also leaving."

"But not for a week. You leave in…" A heavy sigh fills in the rest and we finish our shower in silence. Both of us are well aware that I leave in three days and we don't need the reminder.

Within the hour, we're on the road. But when we pull into the airport, I get confused. "What are we doing here?"

"We're doing a day trip to Kauai."

I grab his hand, stopping him as he tries to move forward. "Really?" I can't hide my excitement.

"C'mon or we'll miss our flight."

After the short twenty-minute flight, we rent a convertible and drive along the coast eventually turning inland until we arrive at a place called Wailua River Cruises.

"It's pretty here. Are we going on a boat?" I ask as we walk to the ticket office.

"Yes, we are. This is where parts of that old show "Fantasy Island" and I think some of "Lost" was filmed." He leans forward over the counter, and says, "I have a reservation for two under Ashford."

The girl smiles at him and then starts typing. "Yes, here you are, Mr. Ashford, *aannnndddd...*" She eyes me up and down, but easily disregards me and focuses her attention back to Evan with a flirty smile.

Squeezing Evan's hand, I answer confidently, "Mrs. Ashford." As the words leave my mouth, I go into some minor form of shock. *Why did I do that?* I claimed him because I got jealous. I turn around quickly to walk away, embarrassed for acting so childish and for doing that to Evan. But Evan stops my retreat, gripping my hand tighter in his then bringing it to his lips and placing one sweet, slow kiss on my knuckles. A gentle smile plays on his lips as he takes the tickets without any further acknowledgment of the girl behind the counter.

I don't say anything as we walk hand in hand down the long sidewalk to the pier where the boat is boarding, mainly because I feel a lump forming in my throat. He glances my way several times and I can see the smile that he's trying to hold back. I'm so gonna be teased over that remark.

After finding our seats on the boat, in the back, he can't resist, and asks, "Mrs. Ashford, huh?" His gentle smile gets all smirky —arrogance and satisfaction playing equally.

My face flames with heat. I'm about to go into all the pathetic reasons why I said that back there, but before I can speak, he says, "Stop freaking out. I like the sound of that name. Mallory Ashford has a nice ring to it. Is this something you've thought about before or did the green-eyed monster say that back there?"

I drop my head into my hands, humiliated in my weak jealousy. He's not stupid. He knows I got jealous and I hate that I did. "I'm sorry. Yes I'll admit, I got jealous, but did you see how she was eye-flirting with you. Seeing that set something off inside me."

"I think it's cute that you said that and no, I didn't notice her eye-*flirting* with me."

"That's because you think that's how girls look at everyone, but they don't. They only look at *you* that way and I'm leaving in less than three days and I don't like that girls are going to do that to you and I'm not going to be here to put them in their place and even though I've given you a hard time in the past about territorial pissing on me that's all I want to do is mark you as mine and make sure that every female in a hundred-foot vicinity knows you're mine and only mine!" I word vomit then take a deep breath since my lungs are completely deflated from my rant.

He leans over and kisses me softly. "Welcome to my world, except I don't want guys closer than a hundred yards to you." He laughs, making me smile and a little less crazy for how I acted.

As the boat travels leisurely toward our destination, there's a cool breeze coming off the water. I lean back against Evan, resting my hand on his leg, and appreciate the view.

Earlier on the drive from the airport, I noticed Kauai is less populated and not as built up as Oahu. It really has a peace and calm about its natural beauty.

"So, how do you feel about the name?" Evan asks, breaking into my daydreaming.

"Name? Oh, as in *your* name? I love your name, Evan," I state simply.

He laughs. "My last name, silly?"

"Ashford is a great name. What do you think about Wray?"

"You're being difficult, so I take that as a no to changing your name one day, even for the man that you're madly in love with?" He waggles his eyebrows and drapes his arm across the back of my shoulders as I sit up.

I've given this thought before and always knew I wanted Wray to stay my name. But he's the first one to ever make me think twice about this stance. "I think I'd be willing to change it as long as it wasn't to a more boring name than mine like Smith or Jones."

Sitting up and turning to face me directly, he says, "What about Ashford specifically? Is that more boring than Wray?" He's serious, hopeful, and curious, and wearing his heart on his sleeve for me.

"I like Ashford. I already told you that."

"Do you like it enough to change it if we ever get married?"

I lift my legs and spin so they rest across his lap. "Is that important to you?"

"I don't know. Maybe. I've not thought that much about marriage before, but I do like the thought of my family having one shared name. It feels more like a unit that way."

"A unit?" I ask, raising an eyebrow at him for his choice of word. "Well, I understand that and it definitely makes it easier with kids, but it would be hard to give up a name that you've been called your entire life." He seems to be waiting for the 'right' or different answer. "I think Ashford has a very nice ring to it, but I don't think Mother Ashford would ever allow that to happen and by 'that' I mean us."

"Shit, you're right. You sharing a name with her won't go over well at all. That only leaves us one option."

"What is that?"

"We should elope at once and change your name immediately," he says, laughing.

I laugh because that's funny, but our laughter teeters off as the realization of a real future sinks in, wondering if we even have a chance. We both lean back again and let our minds wander back to the breathtaking scenery along the river.

When we dock, we walk up a long pathway surrounded by the flora of what I'd always imagined for Hawaii. I still can't get over that Hawaii really is this amazing looking, so natural and beautiful, but with this element that feels like you've gone back to the Jurassic era.

Music wafts through the air, and Evan winks at me. "We're here. This is Fern Grotto."

Looking ahead, I see a large open cave structure with ferns hanging from the upper rock covering. "Is this real?"

"Nature made the grotto out of lava rock. It's pretty, huh?"

"Very pretty."

We walk within it and sit on ledges that are used as seats to watch the Hawaiian quartet play their ukulele's and a woman singing in her native language. When she's finishes the song, she announces that the next song is the traditional marriage song, explaining, "In ancient and modern times, couples came to the Grotto to be married. Instead of speaking their vows, this song was played and when it was over they were officially married."

Songs are about feeling and it seems to be joined in matrimony in this place, which is just so romantic to me.

Just as she starts to sing, Evan takes my hands in his, glancing at me, then focusing back on the music.

The song is long, but it's easy to feel the love in it. When it's over, the other tourists start meandering around the Grotto. Evan says, "You know in the Hawaiian culture we're now married." He gets this devious look in his eyes as he smiles all cocky. "May I have a kiss, Mrs. Ashford?"

Taking my hands from his, I slide them around his neck, tug him closer, and seductively whisper, "Is a kiss all you want from your new wife?"

He sighs, arching his eyebrow, and tilting his head to the side. "You're a tease and right. I do want more, but I also don't want to be arrested."

I kiss him before he can say anymore, my tongue moving smoothly past his open lips and melding with mouth. His warm breath envelopes me as his hands slide from around my back to my ribs and his thumbs press purposely against the side of my breasts.

It doesn't matter that we're in public because I have his hands on me and his tongue in my mouth and the rest of the world disappears, like it always does when I'm with him.

Our make-out session is interrupted by an older woman who promptly clears her throat, getting our attention. We both look up, but I notice Evans thumbs are still totally copping a feel of my side boobs.

"It's so lovely to see newlyweds," she says. "You're a very attractive couple and will be blessed with beautiful children. Congratulations."

In a most charming tone, Evan says, "Thank you. I'm a very lucky guy."

I playfully swat at him and correct him, "I'm the lucky one."

We all giggle at the playful banter, and in that moment,

it really feels like we're starting our forever together. Catching his smile as it reaches his eyes, I smile in return.

The woman clutches her bag, as if it gives her strength as she speaks. "I lost my husband of forty-one years three years ago and I still miss him every day. We used to say the same thing about the other because we both thought we were the lucky ones." She laughs to herself. "Cherish each other and every day you have together." She smiles one more time and walks off to join the group tour of the grotto.

We start down the path, but Evan stops me. His smiling eyes have turned serious, desperate even, and he says, "From now on, we're officially married in Hawaii."

He's stating something that legally I know isn't true, but it feels tangible, like something we can hold onto, when here in paradise. We'll always have Hawaii to connect us, to hold us together. He kisses the fourth finger on my left hand then slides a ring onto it.

"Uh!" I gasp loud enough to draw surrounding attention. Cupping my hand over my mouth in surprise, I ask, "What is this?"

"A present for you." His answer seems simple, but there's so much more weighted behind it after what we just shared.

"But babe—"

"Will you accept it?" He watches me with intent, trying to read my emotions through my reaction.

I lean my head against his chest, staring at the rose gold Plumeria flower ring with a diamond in the center that's now on my finger. "Absolutely. It's beautiful, Evan. Thank you."

He rubs my back, tracing his finger down over my spine, then begins drawing circles on my lower back. "I'm glad you like it, and you're welcome."

"I, uh," I start to say, but stop to wipe at my eyes. "I love it. It's perfect and thoughtful and uniquely paradise just like you."

Hope fills my heart as I stare at the ring like it's the forbidden fruit I shouldn't touch.

He spins the ring around on my finger, a peaceful smile playing on his lips. His voice is low enough for only me to hear. "It looks good on your hand."

Touching his cheek with that hand, I say, "Evan, it's stunning."

"Just like you, Mallory."

"It's too much." I shake my head. "You shouldn't be spending—"

"It wasn't expensive and it doesn't matter if it was. It's something I wanted to give you, something to take back to Colorado with you." I kiss him, eyes closed then stop with his lips paused against mine. He takes my face into his hands and a lone tear slides down my right cheek as he whispers, "No tears, okay. We're in this together."

"Okay." Only a one word response, but for now, that seems to be enough.

17

MALLORY

Small talk fills the boat ride back to the dock. As soon as Evan gets into the car, I ask, "Where to next?" I can't help but be giddy. The boy is beyond amazing and romantic. I shouldn't admit this, but I kind of do feel like a newlywed.

"Waimea Canyon and then dinner before we have to catch our flight back." He revs the engine and squeezes my knee. "You ready?"

"So ready," I answer nonchalantly, but really, him revving that engine is the equivalent to him revving my engine and *listen to it purr*. Geez fucking Louise, I might have to attack him while driving again. I try to restrain myself. It's difficult because of the way he's looking today.

The drive is higher up on the island, so I'm thinking we're going to get a bird's eye view of this canyon when we get there. Upon arrival, the view does not disappoint. We stand against the barely there railing and stare out onto the great expanse of the canyon. Looking off to the right is the ocean in the distance and it's spectacular. We take a lot of pictures of the two of us, together and separately. It's fun to take the photos, but I know it's really because we want to capture the moment just in case our memories fade and we never get the chance to make new ones to replace them.

The wind is strong and Evan wraps his arms around me as we watch mountain goats play on the ledges and the random chicken walk by. The colors of the canyon vary from green to brown to rust to orange and I can distinctly smell the salt water in the air.

Walking around the platform several times, we take in the view from all angles before deciding to leave. We're hungry and have just enough time to eat on Kauai before we have to catch our flight back to Oahu.

As we drive back down the winding road, I ask, "You seem to know where you're going. Have you been to Kauai a lot?"

"A few times. Zach, Murphy, and I island hop for surfing when it's breaking from a storm. Kauai has more undeveloped coastline, so the waves get pretty radical. Once Murphy..." My mind briefly wanders from his words to watch his animated movements and expressions. He's so passionate about surfing that I'm still surprised he never pursued it like Noah.

"...total rippage of the skin. It was nasty. His hairy back will cover the scar though. Hey, Mallory? You with me here?"

"Oh, um... yeah, well, no actually. I kind of got lost in my thoughts for a moment. I'm sorry," I apologize while rubbing his leg.

"A hundred for your thoughts."

"A hundred? *A hundred dollars?* The saying is 'A penny for your thoughts.' Not a hundred."

He laughs. "I know, but it's kind of an inside joke between me and Kate."

"I think you might be showing your spoiled side, Mr.

Ashford." I can tease him because he never acts above anyone else although we all know his family is loaded.

"Oh really?" He smiles, grabbing my knee and squeezing playfully, but firmly.

Squirming under his squeeze, I plead between giggles, "No, no, no, stop, Evan. That hurts." I lie because I'm too ticklish to handle it.

"If it hurts so much then why are you laughing so hard?"

He releases as giggle tears fill my eyes. "You're beautiful when you laugh." His tone is serious and he pulls the car onto the side of the two lane road. His hand comes around to the back of my neck and pulls me in for a kiss. Our lips are about to meet when he says, "I love you, Mallory Wray." Leaving no option to return the sentiment, he presses his lips firmly against mine and begins exploring my mouth with his tongue.

Dazed when we part, I open my eyes and see his blues staring deep into mine, I can't help but respond, "I love you, too, Evan Ashford." When I say his name, I realize right then and there that I would take his last name as mine without question. I would want that kind of bond with him. Not with just anybody, but with him I do.

We kiss again and deepen it. He makes me feel needy and wanted and beautiful and I can't stand the thought of being away from him in a few days. My heart lurches into my stomach as our impending separation weighs me down. I keep all that inside as we sit back, a bit breathless, and he starts driving again.

A few miles down the road, he pulls the car into a small paved parking lot, jumps out, and rushes around opening my door before I have a chance. "Right this way, my love."

"Why thank you, kind sir." I hook my arm around his and he leads me down a path lit by tiki torches. As we make our way down the path, an opening is revealed, and I see the hostess stand, but it's not the stand that catches my eye, it's beyond that; the restaurant is on the beach and I can see the tide gently rolling up onto the small private beach.

"I hope you don't mind me bringing you to another place on the beach, but I heard great things about this restaurant and thought it would be nice to try," Evan says, unsure of his choice in establishments.

"It's heaven on earth here."

We're lead to table for two out on the back patio. "It's breathtaking. Private and romantic." As he holds my chair for me, I lean up and kiss him on the cheek. "Thank you for bringing me here, baby."

Sitting back in the chair, I don't worry about ordering or drinks. Evan has great taste and his fancy upbringing shines through at restaurants. I feel safe with him and know he'll take care of me. Since he's driving, he only has one beer to my several glasses of champagne. We enjoy the catch of the day and local vegetables, ending the meal with a homemade upside pineapple cake. I have a physical reaction when eating it, remembering what he has done to me with pineapple. He laughs because he knows my mind is in the gutter. I can't help but savor and moan with each bite I take. It makes me wonder if I'll ever look at a pineapple the way I used to again.

We're walking back to the car when he stops me and kisses me in the moonlight. My body heats from his touches and my insides alight with fire for him as his hands glide down my bottom pulling me tighter to his body.

My hands graze over his length and I feel it harden beneath his shorts. He picks me up abruptly and tosses me quickly over his shoulder, and slaps my ass, hard. After setting me down, I duck into the seat, and when he gets into the car, he leans in next to my ear and says, "Don't think you'll get away with making me hard. You know what they say. 'Revenge is sweet.'"

My head is thrown against the headrest as he peels out of the lot. I watch him carefully as he commands the car and the road while smiling deviously. He definitely has more than the road on his mind.

A sudden turnoff leads us on a dirt road where he parks in the dark between two sugar cane fields. His seatbelt snaps open and mine goes flying and we're all hands and wet lips, moans, and sensations.

"I will never get enough of you, baby, not ever," he moans against my collarbone as he stretches my collar to the side, exposing more skin.

The top is opened as our clothes come off.

We never have to wait for either of us to be in the mood or ready because when it comes to each other, we're always in the mood. So as much as I enjoy foreplay, in times like these, it isn't necessary. Reaching into his pocket, I pull out that familiar little packet and soon after, I'm rocking gently back and forth on top of him. Holding my hips, he closes his eyes as his lips part. His face is pure ecstasy that elicits sexual cravings that were long buried until he coaxed them to the surface. I close my eyes and get lost in the feeling as he balances between falling and bliss, then gives in wholly.

Dropping his forehead against my chest, his breathing is ragged as it races mine unsteadily and we come back to reality, to the here and now.

He finally looks up and says, "We're in a sugar cane field."

I shake my head, laughing with him. "Like pineapple, I'm never gonna look at sugar the same way now."

Companionable silence fills the drive back to the airport.

We're finding ourselves in a serene quietness more often these last few days we have together. I fall asleep in the car as we leave the airport. I vaguely remember him carrying me to bed and sliding in next to me, his warm skin against mine. But I definitely remember his sweet kisses and I hear him as he whispers, "You're my future and my everything."

18

EVAN

"This fucking sucks!" My anger is getting the best of me. Maybe it's grief I'm feeling. I don't know, but I do know this sucks.

"We knew this was coming," she says, much calmer than me.

"I can be pissed if I want. Can you let me be pissed? Wait, you're not? You're just gonna accept this bullshit?"

"Evan..." Her voice instantly soothes me as my name rolls off her tongue like she's said it for years. "I have to leave. I don't *want* to leave, but I have to." She tucks her head against my chest, fists my t-shirt, and loses eye contact with me as she whispers, "Don't make me be the strong one because I can't. I'm not. I need you to be the brave one here. Remember last night..."

I CHASED her down the path. Although, we got caught in another rainstorm, we laugh, both of us a bit delirious from the day. She's about to reach for the door when I catch her.

"Not so fast, pretty girl," I say, feeling the electricity between us.

She smiles and I die inside knowing that I won't get to see her face every day. I've been spoiled by this sweet angel giving me all her days and nights. I possessively take hold of her wrists and like so many fun-loving times before, the air stills as our connection intensifies. I can't help myself when it comes to her and I refuse not to take what I need and give her what she wants.

I kiss her.

Rain pours down harder and I wrap my arms around her, engulfing her body, her love, her soul. I shamelessly take possession of what's mine and claim her once again.

She breaks away from me and giggles, but it's shallow, followed by an anxious laugh, one that borders on fun and heavier emotions. The moment sinks in and she knows where this is going.

"I'm cold, let's go inside," she says, taking my hand. She leads me into the bathroom, our dripping clothes hanging heavy like my heart just looking at her.

Tomorrow... tomorrow... tomorrow.

She doesn't leave until tomorrow. Make the most of today.

She starts the shower then backs up and takes her clothes off, slowly peeling them away from her rain-drenched skin. Tilting her head, she narrows her eyes busting me, sometimes feeling like she knows me better than I know myself. I'm memorizing this moment and everything that's contained within it, needing to remember all of it. These are the memories that I'll hold onto, when we're apart.

"C'mon," she whispers, her breath sending shivers against my cold body as she lifts my shirt up.

Once naked, she pulls me under the warm water and hugs her body to mine. I stroke down her slickened hair, holding my lips pressed firmly to hers, needing to feel her like this.

She lets out the smallest of moans—a moan of pleasure escaping from a smile. She doesn't look up, but says, "Hold me." She sounds confident in what she wants, in what she needs.

I strain to look down, lowering my head so I can see her hidden face. She smiles and I can't help but think aloud. "You look so fucking innocent right now. No makeup, hair all wet, and stuck to your head. Tell me I didn't corrupt you this summer. That this is what you want, baby?"

"You know I went into this with my eyes wide open."

"No, I need to hear the words. Tell me I'm what you want, that I can actually make you happy."

"Don't doubt yourself. You're all I want and I've wanted you since the moment I laid eyes on you." Her eyes look up in thought and she corrects herself, "Okay, maybe not the first time I saw you because we all remember that, but you had me at the restaurant where we really talked for the first time." She looks down. "You knew me even then. You saw beyond all the bullshit. You saw me, the real me. You had me all figured out and though I wouldn't have admitted then, everything you said was true."

I lift her chin up and kiss her sweetly like she deserves. "I want you. I always fucking want you and it scares the shit out of me. I don't want to disappoint you like I have everyone else." My heart is racing with the energy flowing between us and I close my eyes, inhaling her into me. "I want to be all that you need and this separation is really freaking me the fuck out."

My hand gravitates toward my hair for some comfort tugging, but she grabs it and says, "No. You're not going to do this. I can't go there. And I'm begging you, Evan, don't go down that road either. My heart..." She sniffles as her eyes well with tears. "Kiss me and make the world go away just for a little while, babe. Will you do that for me?"

Our eyes meet and we spend a moment looking into the others', reading the fear and the love that mingles within. I move *slowly down and kiss her forehead, her nose, her eyelids, her cheeks, and her chin before I kiss her lips again—soft and gentle, not rushed, but sensual.*

"I want to make love to you tonight." I reach behind her and turn the shower lever off.

Grabbing a towel from the hook, I wrap it around her and then wrap my own towel around myself. As we dry our bodies, our love draws us back together. We kiss, wet hair, dewy skin, high on emotions, we kiss, giving our all.

Silently following her into the bedroom, it's quiet, almost too quiet, but we're not sad, more reflective and grateful for the remaining hours together. We don't want to fill the hours with nonsense or drown in the unknown of what lies ahead, so we stay quiet, settling onto the mattress. My arm goes out, welcoming her into my side. She snuggles and we lay there appreciating what seems to be the last of the calm before the storm of reality that will separate us.

We lay there, eyes open, unmoving, deepened breathing, lost in our own thoughts for hours. Several times I feel a small yawn against my side. Sometimes she smiles, but stays silent, her own thoughts making her react.

But the silence starts messing with my head. I don't want silence. I want Mallory's laughter, her words, her voice, and her breath to swallow me whole, to take me under, and fill my soul as she's done for the last two months.

I roll over, needing the change in scenery, but seeing her face, eyes, lips... I have to kiss her. My more selfish side takes over and I lean forward. I run my thumb across her bottom lip before clearing the way for my own lips.

We've spent the entire day in one long session of foreplay building up to this moment. I push my hips, rolling her onto her back as I position myself between her legs. The look in her eyes is strong, willing, vulnerable, and sincere. I enter her. She's soft and overwhelming, grounding me to her with every breath that she takes.

I struggle for control—one side needing to take her and to own her completely. The other side, never wanting this to end—giving into her, total surrender of heart, mind, and soul.

My mind is in overdrive as I make love to her knowing this will be the last time for a while, maybe forever. It's hard to digest this concept that is starting to override my pleasure. I want to lose myself in her as I've done all summer, but I can't. So I watch her intently as she seems to have the same struggles. For some reason, it's a relief to see her waging her own internal battle.

Even with the warring, that familiar feeling starts spreading from my groin to my stomach and outward to all of my limbs. With barely enough sense remaining in my brain, I move to stroke her. Her battle dissolves before my eyes and under my hand.

Falling as she does, I push her hands tightly against the mattress and both of us vocalizing our release and submission to each other.

"GOODBYE'S ARE BULLSHIT," I mumble, walking out the door and up the path. I throw her suitcase into the trunk and load her carry-on into the backseat. Only ten minutes left until we have to leave.

Ten minutes until she leaves.

Ten minutes.

I walk back into the house and see her anxiously shutting the top drawer of my dresser.

"Hey," I announce, not wanting her to think I was sneaking up on her.

She turns abruptly, pressing her back against the

dresser, clearly guilty of something. "Hey." She walks over to the bed and flops down on it. "I guess that's everything."

Sitting down on the mattress next to her, she pulls me by the elbow and we fall backward. We take a minute to look at each other, really look, deep into each other's eyes. The brilliant emerald flecks in her eyes shine through the worry lines creasing her forehead. Tears fill her eyes as she holds my gaze.

She nods, the words she wants to say so obviously stuck in her throat. Clearing her throat as I catch her tear and gently wipe away its tracks, she says, "We should go or I'm gonna be late."

Like our morning, we don't talk much on the drive to the airport. The reality and accompanying sinking feeling of her departure is all too real to me now. My hand never leaves her leg until I pull into the airport parking area. We get out, slow and unsure of ourselves, awkward even in these final moments.

As we walk into the main terminal, she checks in, and then I follow her to the departures zone outside security. I've been here countless times before, but this is the only time it ever mattered. This is the only time my heart aches and tears fill my eyes.

I don't take my eyes off of her. My gaze doesn't stray or care about who sees me or who I might see or the next group of girls landing for their vacation. I'm focused, desperately committing Mallory's face, body, and smell to memory while I still have her with me. I don't want her to doubt this moment or my feelings for her. But I especially don't want her to be reminded of that first time we saw each other. The first time we made eye contact was over Kelly's shoulder. So I remain, full attention on her, which is easy to do.

I grab her, squeezing her against my body, one last time to appreciate all that is Mallory. This one last time I sense my heart will be whole.

Muffled in my shirt, she says, "So here we are at the scene of the crime."

So much for hoping she doesn't think about how we met. But I have to say, the only reason I'm not ashamed of my behavior that day is that it actually worked and brought me and Mallory together.

I kiss the top of her head, and whisper, "You can trust me, baby. Will you?"

"I already do."

I exhale in relief.

"Evan?"

"Yes," I reply, holding her tightly to me, how she should always be.

She sighs. "You told me to trust you, but don't rely on—"

"You can rely on me."

"I know I can now." She smiles and I see the glorious trust she's given me reflected in her eyes. Glancing over her shoulder at the growing security line, she says, "Guess I should go?" It's more of a question than a statement.

I feel her relax into me again, her arms tightening this time. "This is goodbye."

Closing my eyes, I tilt my head into her hair, holding the inevitable tears back. My voice is weak, so I only nod.

"Flight 2678 to Denver Colorado is now boarding at gate 9."

"That's me," she says, letting her tears fall without care as all her stubborn strength leaves her. She gives in to what we both feel, weakening, her shoulders slumping as she begins to cry.

I quickly take her face in my hands, maybe too aggressively, but I'm panicked and need to try one last time. "Don't leave me. I can't... I need you. I love you, Mallory."

Tears streak her pretty face, coloring her cheeks in red, sadness settling into her eyes. I kiss her. I kiss her for her sake and I kiss her selfishly for my own. My tongue mingles with hers knowing this is it. *Is this, it it? Or is it, just for now it?* I'm so freaked out I don't realize how hard I'm squeezing her, holding her captive to me.

"Baby..." She cries and then as if sounding out each word for herself, she whispers, "I have to leave."

Her wet lids and lashes lift to reveal those eyes that mean the world to me, but are now colored in pain. A small smile crosses her face finally reaching her eyes and she says, "You didn't look away from me once. I saw at least four 'next opportunities' walk by and you didn't even notice them." She giggles as if she just realized how much she means to me, realizing how much I love her.

"Why would I ever look at anyone else when I have you?"

As she holds my hand, she holds my complete attention as well. "I love you. I'll always love you, Evan. Carry that in your heart," she says, tapping her palm on my chest.

I need to say her name so she understands the importance of my words. "I love you, Mallory. You're the only thing in my life worth living for and I will never hurt you."

"Flight 2678 to Denver Colorado is now boarding at gate 9."

She bends down taking her carry-on bag in hand and I take her other hand, walking the last ten feet with her, it feeling much like what I imagine a death row march feels like.

When she turns to go, I jerk her back, hastily dipping her and kiss her hard, for my own selfish needs, for her, and for everyone to see.

Movies, books, daydreams... girls dream of moments like this and I want to give her a moment that she'll remember for the rest of her life. I plan to make many more memories with her, but this is how I want to send her back to Colorado.

I keep my lips on hers as long as I can as my thumb rubs over the new ring I gave her. When I lift her back up, she looks a bit dazed. Bending my head to the side, I give her the smile that was created only for her.

She stares into my eyes, mumbling something incoherently while pointing over her shoulder.

I nod, taking a step back from the security line. She walks backward, and with a small wave of her fingers, she turns and walks away, leaving me standing there alone.

I watch as she goes through security. Once on the other side, she glances back only once. We lock eyes and in that moment, I let her go. I have to, to protect myself. She leaves me there with an empty chest, my heart deciding long ago that it belonged to her, with her, and there it remains leaving with her.

A cold wind blows as I walk to the car, abnormal for this time of year, but the universe understands loss and devastation, and responds accordingly.

Shoving my hands in my pockets, my head lowers, feeling a new burden replacing the one I carried for years. This is the first time I've been worried about anything in a while and it's unsettling the way it has taken hold of me.

Inside my car, her scent surrounds me. I close my eyes and allow myself to enjoy it because I know the scent will fade soon. Remembering that she's wearing my ring on her left hand ring finger makes me smile and I let that feeling tide me over for the time being.

19

EVAN

Mallory landed in Denver three days ago. Her parents picked her up from the airport and she is staying with them this week. Sunny also flew back yesterday to visit her family before the fall semester starts.

Because our girls are gone, this might explain how Zach and I ended up with a box of tissues on the coffee table and "Titanic" on the TV in the middle of the afternoon. I put the bottle of Jack straight to my lips, not worried about etiquette and not caring since I'm not sharing the bottle anyway. I take another shot, thinking this is the third, but it could've been more.

Going through his own form of alcohol therapy since Sunny left, Zach has built a beer can pyramid that I must admit is quite impressive.

"What's up, dudes?" Murphy bellows as he walks in the front door with my sister in tow.

Neither of us bother replying, finding the love story unfolding on the TV before us more interesting.

Kate walks over, smacks the back of my head, and says,

"I've been missing you, baby bro. You still sulking over Mal leaving?" She ruffles my hair, which pisses me off.

I shrug her off and don't bother answering. I take another swig instead, sticking to my *drowning my sorrows away* philosophy.

"Dad wants you back in Manhattan sooner. I've booked your flight. You've got two days until we leave," Kate states.

I sit up, surprised. "I can't! Zach and I already have plans."

"What plans... *Dude! That was totally uncalled for*," Zach says, taking the couch pillow I just threw at his head and tucking it behind him.

"Get over it. It's a fucking pillow, brah. And we've made plans," I say, winking at him, hoping he's onboard with my scheme.

When I glance at Kate, she crosses her arms and arches an eyebrow at me. "You're going. We have a lot to look over before the board meeting and those files are kept at the office." She starts walking away, pulling Murphy behind her. "It's only a few days earlier than you planned, so suck it up. You're going." Her voice trails off as they walk down the hall away from us.

"Your sister scares me sometimes," Zach says, eyes still focused on the TV.

"She scares me too, but I can't let her know or she'll use it to her advantage."

"Two days, Evan. We've got two days... what should we do? It should be something big to end the summer off in the most epic way possible." Zach sits up as if he's plotting the greatest plan ever. His fingers tap against each other and then the light bulb goes off. "Cliff-diving!"

"We've done it before."

"Two words, dude. Spinning. Caves." He jumps to his

feet with a burst of excitement. "We've done the sissy cliffs. We've talked about jumping Spinning Caves for years. We've gotta do it. What better way to send you off into the real world than to get a fucking adrenaline rush like that?"

"Uh, I can think of lots of ways, like sitting my ass right here on this couch and watching this fucking chick flick. I've never seen the ending—"

"No, we're doing this and it's fucking "Titanic." The ship sinks and almost everyone dies." He clicks the TV off. "The fucking end. Now get your ass up and let's do this."

"You suck balls, brah. Ruining a perfectly good movie like that." I sit up, taking this Spinning Caves jump into consideration. "So if we do the jump, we probably shouldn't do it after drinking liquor. A lot can go wrong and it's getting kind of late."

"Where's your sense of adventure? Where has Evan fucking Ashford gone?" He shakes his head in disappointment. "It's now or never, man. And, I vote for right the fuck now!"

"Sense of adventure? Evan fucking Ashford? What the fuck are you talking about, Z? It's suicide to hit it after drinking." I pause in momentary thought, more tempted than I should. Glaring at him, I see a passion in his eyes that I haven't felt for anything other than Mallory in forever. Standing up, I say, "Fuck it, let's go!" I put my hand out and he shakes it, doing the ritual we've done since we were sixteen.

As Zach drives to Spinning Caves, I notice the sun setting in the distance. We have at least ten minutes left in the car and I don't know if we'll make it before dark.

My voice of reason, my more sane side, finally decides to verbalize its presence. "We can't do this in the dark."

"We'll make it, but you can't pussy foot it. We have to go for it. Don't over think this."

We're quiet for the remaining time in the car, lost in our own thoughts. I realize after a minute or two that he shouldn't even be driving much less cliff diving. By the time he's parking the car, all that fades into the background and a different fear starts to make itself known. Zach gets out of the car without hesitation and I follow though I'm hesitant.

He's pumped and turns to look over his shoulder at me trailing behind him. "Don't chicken out."

"I won't. I've got your back."

He nods knowing I won't let him do this by himself. That's not what friends do. I'll go, but it's against my better judgment.

My phone buzzes in my pocket. I take it out and quickly answer when I see the name on the caller ID. "Hey, baby."

"I was thinking about you and wanted to call," Mallory says, making my heart ache at the sound of her voice.

"I've been thinking a lot about you, but Zach and I are about to..." I don't finish telling her because I have a strong feeling she won't be too pleased to hear about the insanity that's about to go down.

"Hello?"

"I'm still here," I say, walking a little bit faster. Zach tosses his shirt and keys to the side. "Mallory, I need to let you go. Zach is about to do something that I probably shouldn't let him do. I'll call you back in a bit, okay?"

"Oh okay," she sounds sad. "I was calling to tell you I've been missing you—"

Unfortunately this is bad timing, her words becoming background to the madness playing out in front of me. With minutes before the sun drops completely below the horizon he takes off running and yells, "It's now or never, E! Cowabunga!"

"Oh shit!" I toss my phone down and take off running after him. He's over the edge in the blink of an eye and hits the water as my feet leave the safety of the earth. Zach is a strong swimmer, but I'm stronger even with alcohol in my system.

As I fly through the air, the sickness of the fall settles at the bottom of my stomach and images of Mallory flood my thoughts. This is the stupidest thing I've done in a long time. Putting everything, my life included, at risk when I have Mallory in my life makes no sense.

I crash into the choppy ocean and water fills my senses, ears and nose, engulfing me whole. I've always found comfort in the water, but right now the jagged cliffs I know are ahead of me become my sole focus. I break the surface and gasp for a large breath just as the water throws me toward a cliff wall. Right when I'm about to hit, the water drags me unwillingly back under as the tide returns me to sea.

My instincts kick in and I fight for my life with each strong stroke I take, hoping Zach is doing the same.

The waves work in my favor, forcing me forward again. A piercing stab to my side wracks my body as I'm pummeled into the jagged coastline. An ache signals I've been cut, a familiar feeling from surfing when I hit the reef, but I can't worry with that. I need to find my way to the shore. Before the ocean drags me out for another round, I grab hold of a lower ledge and secure myself to it.

"Fuck!" I yell at the top of my lungs as I climb up, finding my footing on the rough rocks. When I get to the top, I call out, "Zach?"

"Ev—" I hear a faint response comes echoing in the wind.

The moon has risen high enough in the sky to light the cliffs around us. I spot Zach about thirty feet away, climbing up the side of the lower cliffs edge. He points toward an area that's around the curved wall of rock and just beyond him.

Following Zach's lead, I make my way over to the beach then drop down into the sand spread eagle and exhausted.

"Dude, you made it," he says, crashing down in the sand nearby.

"Fuck you, Zach," I say, raising my hand in the air and flipping the bird. "You're insane."

"C'mon, that was awesome and you know it. You'll thank me tomorrow."

"You suck cock and I'll never thank you for scaring the shit out of me."

"You needed it. That was better than an orgasm."

"You're sleeping with the wrong girl then."

He laughs. "You know that was perfection. Life teetering on the edge like that."

"I hate you." I don't really, but I am pissed as all get out. "Don't talk to me right now."

"Evan, you'll go to New York and conquer the shit out of it because you fucking cliff dived Spinning Caves at night! Now you can do anything."

"So this was a lame lesson to teach me to live life to the fullest?"

He's up and standing over me, with an outstretched hand. I accept his offer then yank him into the sand next to me, and threaten, "Don't pull that shit again, Zach. We could've died out there. And as of late, I've got a lot to live for." I jump to my feet and start walking to the car, which is parked up the hill. Once there, I grab my phone from a small patch of grass, thankful it landed there. It's scratched to hell, but it works.

Running up the hill behind me, he gets his shirt and keys and heads to the car.

When I get in the car, I say, "The next two days better be a lot calmer than this, brah. That's all I'm saying."

"No worries." He laughs, starting the engine. "At least you're not sulking anymore."

Once home, I drop my wet clothes on the bathroom floor and start the shower. I clean up quickly and dry off. With a towel wrapped around my waist, I sit on the edge of the tub and call Mallory.

She sounds like I woke her up, but there's a panic to her tone. "Evan? What happened?"

"Baby," I whisper, lowering my head into my hand. "I did something stupid. I'm sorry—"

"What?" Her panic takes over. "What do you mean?"

"No, no. I meant I'm sorry for hanging up on you," I say.

I hear her exhale. "What happened?"

I'm still pissed at myself and Zach for pulling that stunt. "Let's just say today put a lot of things in perspective." I look myself in the mirror, and say, "I can't wait until I move to Colorado."

20

EVAN

The next morning, I hit the waves early at sunrise, finding peace in the ocean—only me and my board. It was supreme. Alone, setting my mind at ease, and preparing to leave my paradise for the city again.

By lunchtime, I'm home and starting the packing process. I don't have to pack much because I have a wardrobe in Manhattan and walking around Manhattan in board shorts tends to be frowned upon. Ms. Chart folds the few shirts and shorts I can't live without. She's a sentimental, so I know her offer came as a way to spend time together. I'll miss her. We've always been close and I know she's struggling with the impending goodbye. Honestly, I am too.

"I'm only taking one suitcase. I have enough clothes to get me by for some a while and I might get some new suits made anyway."

"I'm sure you'll look very handsome. You always do," she says, concentrating really hard on folding the t-shirt in front of her. "How does Mallory feel about your decision?"

There's something about Ms. Chart that lets me relax. I don't have to put on pretenses or hide my true emotions.

She's a safe place for me and I think I might miss that the most. "I don't think she's happy about it, but she wouldn't come right out and say that. I've shared a few stories before I knew I was going back. Maybe I shouldn't have because now I can tell she's not comfortable with the idea."

I walk to my underwear drawer and pull five or six pairs. As I carry them to the case opened up on the mattress, an envelope drops to the floor at my feet. Bending down, I take the letter in hand, examining it by turning it over, and smile seeing Mallory's handwriting.

"Will going to New York cause problems between you and Mallory?" she asks.

Sitting down on the bed, I hold the letter tighter than I should, but needing that link. "She's knows the deal. We've talked about it. The only thing that Mallory is concerned with when it comes to me being in New York is my mom's inane lack of understanding regarding our relationship. Look at the damage she caused at the party. I'm damn lucky I had the chance to work it out."

"I like Mallory." Ms. Chart stands, hugging me to her. "Don't screw it up. She's a keeper. And remember, if you don't treat her right, someone else will." Walking to the door, she stops, and with her signature kind smile, she says, "Evan, I love you. Be who you are, not who they want you to be." She exits quickly knowing that is probably not what my parents would condone her saying.

I easily return a smile. "Love you."

My attention goes back to the letter. Climbing up on the bed, I sit with my back against the headboard and open the envelope.

The letter has a light scent to it. I recognize it immediately as Mallory's perfume. I would normally rag on a guy for liking something like this. Instead, I hold it to my nose and savor the smell. It's light and pretty like her. After rubbing it on her pillowcase a few times, I open the letter.

Dear Evan,

I miss you already. I know, really poignant and deep, but it's true. I'm not sure I remember life without you anymore and I'm not sure I want to. I tried to be strong and not let our goodbye feel so real, but I know as I ride on that plane back to Colorado it will hit me. You won't be there with me or waiting for me when I land and I have to jump back into my life like I'm not forever changed by meeting you. I am. I have been forever changed by you. You're a beautiful person, Evan, and I'm not only talking about your looks though you are easy on the eyes. Okay, you're very easy on the eyes, but I don't want to inflate that already epic ego of yours. Hehe.

Baby, I want to tell you that I love you. I'm leaving my heart with you and can't wait until we're together again. Thank you for a wonderful summer. Yes, there were a few incidences that I don't care to relive, but it brought us together and made us stronger, so I wouldn't trade those now either.

You go be awesome and I'll be in Colorado waiting for you.

I love you.

Mallory

I FOLD the letter and tuck it into my backpack. This letter will stay with me. I put my passport and the file my mom gave me in the backpack before zipping it closed.

Looking at my watch, it's time to meet the boys at Big Kehones. Fifteen minutes later, I greet Zach and Murphy in the parking lot. We slap our customary handshakes and walk in together.

My gaze lands on Noah's cousins sitting at a corner table. They also see us. With the fight that night at the beach still fresh on everyone's minds, tension fills the space between our groups. We stop, analyzing the situation, but fuck if I'm gonna turn around and leave. I walk to our usual table to prove to them with every step I take that I'm not backing down and if they want more of me, I'll be happy to give them a piece.

Johnny comes over and sets a pitcher down with three cups along with three shots of what appears to be whiskey. "Figured with the girls out of town, you might need this," he says glancing over at the other table.

As Murphy fills our beer cups, Zach sets a shot down in front of us, then holds his up to toast. "To the summer we all met our match—"

"The fight with Kalei and his lackeys?" Murphy asks, glaring at Noah's cousins.

"Nope. Sunny, Kate, and Mallory. Here's to those who wish us well, and as for the rest, they can go to Hell."

I have to chuckle because that toast is definitely fitting for me and Mallory. I down the shot in one gulp, shaking off the throat burn. I slam my glass down on the wood tabletop, turning to Zach. "When are you coming to New York, dude?"

Zach's eyes are glazed like they always gets when he hits the hard liquor. "Maybe Thanksgiving. I owe my parents a visit, but I want to find out what Sunny's plans are first."

"I already promised Kate I'd visit for Thanksgiving," Murphy says, looking more comfortable than I like considering he's cozying up with my sister. "What about you?"

"I haven't talked to Mallory about the holidays. It's too soon for that. Her birthday is coming up... fuck, listen to us," I say, shaking my head again, but for a completely different reason. I want to be disgusted, but the smile that crosses my face when I think of Mallory makes me perfectly content to sit here and hand over my man-card. Yeah, I'm in love. *So fucking what!*

"Hey."

When I look up I see the younger Kalei family member standing there. All three of us immediately stand up, the chairs scraping across the floor.

Murphy crosses his arms and says, "What do you want?"

I don't really know these cousins of Noah because they were young when Noah and I were best friends, so his name escapes me. He shoves his hands in his pockets, giving us a clear indication that he doesn't plan to use them. The other guy comes up behind him and stands with his arms crossed over his chest and a slight scowl that's aimed at Murphy. Guess he's holding a grudge against Murphy for kicking his ass that night. To be expected.

"Yeah, so, we wanted you to know that we didn't know about Lani and the whole heart thing." The younger one pauses and looks back over his shoulder. When his cousin gives him a nod of approval, he turns back. "We only knew what Uncle Kekoa and Noah told us. I mean I can't say we weren't happy that he got some rich haole's money, but—"

"What he's trying to say," the other cousin interrupts, stepping forward. "We're sorry. And for the record, Noah was an asshole about the whole thing, but he hasn't received a dime. That money had some weird stipulation about not touching it for five years or something. So it shouldn't be hard for them to return it."

I fucking hate talking about Lani and all that shit, and I can't help but tense when the con the Kaleis tried to pull is brought up, even in an apology. I take a moment to digest what he's saying before finally wanting this behind me once and for all. I don't want to live in that negative headspace anymore. With a nod of acceptance, I shake both of their hands, not using my words but instead using the grip that bonds us to let them know that I'm not going to harbor any ill will against them.

Right before they turn to leave the restaurant, the older one says, "By the way, Noah lost his first three competitions. One more and he will be out of the tour and dropped by his sponsors."

I've never reveled in someone else's loss or failures before, but somehow Noah being sent packing after the BS he put me through seems fitting.

When I land in bed that night, my thoughts are racing. I can't lie to myself and pretend I'm not a little nervous about New York because I am. But, more than that, Mallory is ever present. Grabbing her pillow, I take in her scent—inhaling deeply—needing to feel her presence to find the calm I need to sleep. Because as soon as I step on that plane tomorrow, my life has a new beginning and now that I'm back in the driver's seat, a new ending.

21

MALLORY

My dreams are lucid, Evan weighing heavy on my heart and mind. *Our connection stretches between us as I enter the security line, leaving Evan back at the entrance to the airport. I try not to look back, but how can I not? It's Evan, and he's always worth a second glance, a third... Fuck! I look back six times, but don't allow myself to cry again. I do smile though, my expression forced upward despite the pain so I don't worry him.*

He remains grounded in the same spot when I round the corner. I quickly sneak a peek, hiding myself from his view, and yet he remains standing as if this isn't happening, as if I'm not leaving him. Maybe forever, which makes my heart ache when I think like that, so I push that feeling down and gather hope in my heart and hope it's just for now.

After returning to my hiding spot on the other side of the wall, I take a deep breath and close my eyes. My eyes pop open as I gasp for air, suddenly unable to breathe. Is this a panic attack? My breath stutters and my throat tugs for air. I grab my throat and squeeze my eyes shut tight, trying to calm myself enough to take another breath. As air slowly fills my lungs again, I look around the corner. Evan is gone, not walking away, but gone—

into thin air. My chest tightens, then snaps, the string bonding our hearts broken.

I'M BOUNCED AWAKE, startled, and like in my dream, I gasp for air.

"Oh my God, Mal. I'm so sorry. Are you okay?" Sunny is sitting on the bed next to me, panic on her face.

Irritated from being woken up like that, I grumble, "Sunny, go away." I pull the covers over my face and feign sleep.

"Get up, chicky, we've got a lot of ground to cover. We're going shopping. I've missed the mall and affordable clothes. Hawaii is too damn expensive on my budget."

"*Pleeeaaaassseee* let me sleep another hour. I'll humor you and go wherever you want if I can just get a little more sleep."

"Mallory, we worked all summer and then I lost you to Evan. I finally get you all to myself and you're getting your ass out of this bed right now," she demands. I don't even have to open my eyes to know she already has her hands on her hips and is tapping her foot. Okay, I can hear her tapping her foot, but I know she does that and didn't need to see it to know she was doing it now.

I sit up and look at her. "Didn't you just catch a redeye home? Shouldn't you be tired?"

She shrugs. "I slept on the flight. Wide awake and ready to hit the stores now."

Protesting will get me nowhere, so I relent and get up.

Within the hour, I'm showered, dressed, stuffed full of eggs, courtesy of my mom, and already standing alone in the middle of a department store. Sunny has abandoned me for the dressing room. I hang up the shirt that I've been holding for twenty minutes and pull out my phone to text Evan.

I KNOW you're not up yet, but wanted to be the first one to tell you good morning. Good Morning, babe.

I DON'T EXPECT to hear from him in the next four hours because it's still early here much less in Hawaii. So I head over to the dressing rooms and take a seat outside Sunny's room.

Lucky for me, she offers to feed me at lunchtime, but only for fifteen minutes because we're off again to hit the back-to-school sales.

My phone buzzes with a text from Evan just after three in the afternoon.

THIS BED IS LONELY without you, baby. My arms are a tad lonely, too.

I QUICKLY TYPE BACK. *Only a tad?*

HE RESPONDS. *Maybe more than a tad. A lot. I miss you, beautiful.*

SUNNY SNEAKS up behind me and surprises me. "Ready to go?"

"Yes, so ready."

. . .

CALL ME LATER. *Shopping with Sunny and going out tonight. I miss you and those arms around me very much. I love you.*

F**IVE SHOPPING BAGS LATER**, she drops me off with the threat of picking me up in exactly one hour to go out.

I have dinner with only my mom since my dad has meetings. We talk about Evan and I show her some pictures on my phone. I also show her the ring, and although I know she wants to say something about which finger I've chosen to wear the ring, she tells me how handsome he is instead and hugs me. It feels good to share this part of my life with her.

Sunny breaks up the bonding moment by letting herself into the house. She insists we have to leave so we're at the club by eight to avoid a cover charge. As I stand from the table, she gives me two thumbs up, approving of my tight jeans and fitted top. It feels weird to be dressing in jeans and heels again since I didn't wear them in Hawaii.

We find a parking spot after a few minutes of cruising and walk to the club down the street. The doorman stamps our hands after we show ID and we go inside. There's a warm glow to the room, loud music, and lots of people considering it's still early in the night. We're waved over by some high school buddies that spot us. Within a few minutes, we've got a beer in hand and kick back in the booth.

It starts feeling like a reunion of sorts in here tonight with all the familiar faces. A few guys I recognize come over and chat me up, telling me how much I've changed since high school and how good I'm looking. The backhanded compliments don't sit well with me since I didn't think I was ugly back in then. It's easy to see their shallow ways now. I wasn't good enough in high school, but now that I've filled out a little more, gotten rid of the braces, and grown into my 'assets', they're all over me.

Uninterested. The feeling identified quickly when you look at the faces of your high school classmates and realize they didn't *really* mean for you to talk about your summer although they asked. It was polite, surface chit chat they were seeking. They lose interest about a minute into that conversation, which makes me inwardly giggle. It's not like we keep in touch... there might be a reason. Several beers into the night, Evan calls and I head outside to hear him instead of the loud bar chatter and music. We don't talk long because he's heading out to meet Zach and Murphy, but it's good to hear his voice.

Tired from the travels and shopping, we don't stay much longer and go home.

Lying in bed, loneliness settles in. I miss Evan and though it's only been two days, it feels like ages. All my fears begin to surface as regret shows up. Maybe I *should* live with him like he suggested? I land on this thought for a moment. Maybe I shot down his idea too quickly? Maybe, I should reconsider it, *really consider it?*

At the time he mentioned living together, I thought it was ridiculous. Not the idea of living with him per se, but more the complications it would bring us at such an early stage in our relationship. Two months is not enough time to make such a big commitment. On top of that, I've already signed a lease with Sarah. I can't leave a lifelong friend high and dry like that. That's not the kind of friend I want to be. Evan got that. He didn't like it, but he got it. Hell, I didn't like it, but it's not like we can't stay with each other if he does move to Colorado.

I give myself a reprieve from that inward argument and try to sleep. It takes more than an hour before I fall asleep, but when I do, I dream of blue eyes and surfboards, sex wax and sunsets. A little after four, I wake up sweating, my insides tight and tingling, a realization that my body misses Evan as much as my mind does.

22

MALLORY

Evan left for New York and today I find myself packing my bags to return back to school in the morning. I have lunch with Sunny before saying our goodbyes since she has to leave to catch her flight back to Oahu.

After dinner with my parents, I return to my room to webcam Evan one last time before I need to pack my laptop. After rebooting my computer twice, I still can't seem to get the camera to come on and a black screen is all that's show-ing. Frustrated, I call him and we end up talking for an hour the old-fashioned way—over the phone.

With every minute that passes, I can feel the change in him, the change the city is causing him. He's been preparing for the board meeting that determines the fate of his family's business and the pressure is starting to affect him. The weight has been placed squarely on his shoulders to carry this burden.

Concern fills me. The main reason is because if the board retires his father Evan will feel like a failure. I try to reassure him that if they don't, he'll be the hero, but it's a lot to ask of anyone much less a twenty-three year old. So I try to be what he needs, someone to listen, but the separation feels like a great wall of divide between us.

When I lay down in bed, I pull the covers up to my chin and roll onto my side, holding the phone close to my ear. When I turn off my lamp, I listen to him breathing almost like he's here next to me in the dark of my room.

"You should go to bed, Evan. It's late there."

"I should, but I don't sleep well."

"Because you miss me?"

"You know I miss you. It's weird here. This used to be my home and now it feels foreign. I think I got used to Hawaii... *and you*."

"I only slept okay the first night because I talked to you. Let's stay on and maybe we'll get tired enough to fall asleep."

"Okay."

His breath deepens, and he rustles around on the other end of the line. I yawn and we settle down into a soft spoken conversation of sappy-ness until I don't remember anything but dreams of him with his arms around me. I feel loved and I hope he feels the same.

MY MOM MAKES the forty-five minute drive with me, her SUV filled to the brim with my crap. My dad is following in my Corolla behind us.

"Are you sure you want to take more stuff up there? You don't have a big closet in that tiny apartment," she says, glancing over at me then back to the road.

"I have room in my dresser. I'm also going to get rid of some stuff I never wear."

With her eyes straight ahead, she tries to sound nonchalant. "Is Evan going to visit you at school?"

"Oh, um. I'm not sure. He said he would, but I don't want to put any added stress on him. He has enough of that as it is."

"It's not stressful to be with the one you love, honey."

I look out the window and exhale a deep sigh. "I don't want him to feel like I'm demanding anything from him. Everyone else is doing that—"

"That's a part of growing up, Mallory. People have expectations and start relying on you. He's going to be working and the business will rely on him. Why are you worried?"

"I'm worried by what this job and Manhattan will do to him. He didn't want to go and I know he feels forced to be there."

"He's not being forced." Her tone is sharp. "He's doing what's needed of him. He's being responsible. I think it shows a lot about the kind of person he is. He's a grown man and can take care of himself. You, my dear daughter need to focus on your studies."

I rest my head against the window, watching as we pass by the landmarks that signal we're getting close. Evan is a grown up. That just seems all wrong in my mind though. Not because I think he's immature. Actually, I feel quite the opposite, but that if he's a grown up and taking care of his responsibilities, what does that make me? Am I all grown up now, too? At what age do you officially 'grow up?'

My heart feels heavy in my chest wondering if Evan will choose New York after having a taste of it again. Maybe he'll choose to run the family business. He won't need a degree to work there. His name is on the company stationary. These thoughts hit me, like a slap across the face, and I realize that there is a distinct possibility that I may never see him again.

I close my eyes and shake my head not wanting to let these twisted thoughts seep in. I knew if they did I would be headed for heartbreak and I'm not willing to go there... yet. I need to believe to get by. I believe in us and our love and will hold as tight as I can to that romantic notion.

My first impression of him echoes inside my head as we continue our drive in silence. *He told me not to rely on him, but to trust him. He told me not to rely on him, but to trust him. He told me not to rely on him, but to trust him.*

But at the airport, he assured me that I can rely on him. Even without him confirming that I could, an epiphany hits me. I already do rely on him, in so many ways.

He changed his modus operandi for me. His whole identity was wrapped up in that spiel he gave me at the diner that first day and yet he didn't use his tactics on me that night or any other night. I know in that moment that I will most definitely see him again even if I have to make it happen somehow.

He was ready for change, and this summer gave him the perfect storm to finally get his ass in gear and fight for what he loves and what he loves seems to be me.

I'm smiling to myself when I feel my mom's hand on my arm.

"Mal, I can really see how in love you are with Evan." She pauses, looking back at the road, returning her hand to the steering wheel. "I hope it works out the way you want."

"I do too."

My mom helps me unload the car and leaves right after hoping to beat rush hour traffic through Denver. Sarah's not home yet, so I start unpacking. I unpack my iPod docking station first and get some music playing. That helps pass the time and distract my thoughts from all the 'what-if's' that seem to be playing out in my head lately.

Two hours on the job and my room is looking the way I want. I stand back to admire, but a knock on the door interrupts me appreciating my work. I know Sarah isn't due to arrive yet, so I stand up and shake out my cramped legs and peek through the peephole. I see a delivery man. Standing there, I'm unsure if I should answer or not until he says, "Delivery for Miss Mallory Wray."

I unlock the door and open it wide. After signing for the package, I scurry back into the living room to open the large cardboard box. It's heavy, but not unmanageable.

Grabbing my car key from the hook I hung up earlier next to the front door, I slice open the taped box. Styrofoam popcorn flies out as I lift the flaps, revealing a brand new laptop. I stare at it a minute, unsure if I should take it out or not. I close the flaps and look at the label again. Yes, it's addressed to me, but it only says the computer company's name as the return address, not who sent it. I lift the flaps open again and more of the packing popcorn comes out, landing on the floor and my lap.

I dig out the packing slip and read the message:

Dear Mallory,

I know you're going to say you can't accept this, but before you call me to say that, you should know that this laptop is more for me than you. I can't go without seeing that beautiful face for too long and since your webcam is broken, I thought it only fitting that I replace it. It just so happens to come with a state of the art laptop attached to said camera.

Accept it, Mallory. It's not a big deal, so stop debating whether you're going to accept it or not and take it.

I love you, baby, and I expect you to webcam me tonight.

Love,

Evan

HE KNOWS ME WELL. I was debating, but how can I deny him this gift. I giggle as I pull the laptop from the box. It's so sleek and new, fancier than I've ever had before. He shouldn't have done this, but he did, and I'm going to appreciate it.

I take it to my room and set it up on my desk. An hour later, the computer is all ready to go. I log onto Skype and type in: Evan Ashford, but he doesn't answer.

He's the first and only person I add into my contacts. Needing an avi picture, I step out of my comfort zone. I wink and lick the corner of my lips—my sad attempt at sexy—and the camera snaps. Checking out the results, I decide that even though it's kind of embarrassing, it's also kind of hot, so I keep it.

It's funny what happens to your sanity when you pretend you're not anxiously waiting for someone to call or email, text, or contact you in any form. I'm trying to play it cool, but it's not working out so well.

Maybe he's working. I rationalize like five hundred times in my head. *Maybe he doesn't Skype from the office. Maybe he's out with his friends or his family. Maybe he's too busy fucking someone else and doesn't realize I pinged him. Maybe I'm losing my mind?* Yes! I'm losing my mind. That is the only logical answer right now.

A knock kicks me out of my crazy thoughts and I'm relieved to be saved by the bell... er, knock. I run to answer the front door and find Sarah, arms full of stuff, standing there.

"Mallory, I'm so glad to see you," she says as I take two bags from her and she walks in.

I set them on the table and turn to face her as she sets her stuff down. We hug each other tight. "I missed you so much," I say, squeezing her tight. Sarah is the polar opposite of Sunny. Where Sunny is outgoing, popular, and ambitious, Sarah is quiet, content, and happy where she is in life. They balance our friendship out nicely. Sarah and I came to the University of Colorado together and Sunny, always the more adventurous, headed for Hawaii.

"I missed you, too. I mean it was nice visiting my Gran in Tennessee, but there's no place like home."

"Where's Josh?" I was surprised Sarah signed another lease with me because Josh, her longtime boyfriend, asked her to move in with him last spring and his apartment is much nicer than ours. She turned him down saying that her parents would kill her if she shacked up with him before marriage.

"He's coming up with some of the heavier stuff from the car." She takes me by the hand and pulls me over to the loveseat that comes with the apartment. "Loved the postcards, but I can't wait for you to tell me all about Hawaii."

"Two words will sum up my summer vacation: Evan. Ashford."

She giggles as she rests her hands on mine all giddy for me. "So you met someone and made it official all in less than three months?"

"We did more than meet..."

"In the bedroom, Sarah? Hey, Mallory, good to see ya," Josh says, walking past us with a large box.

Sarah stands, using my knee to help her up. "Can't wait to hear more, but I guess I should help him out."

"I can help," I offer, walking down the steps of the apartment complex with her.

Two hours later, we're eating pizza and drinking sodas

on the couch. Josh is sitting on the floor and we're all exhausted. The apartment is in pretty good shape and with classes starting in the morning, we thought it best to stop now and finish the rest of the unpacking over this first week back.

When I go to my bedroom and get ready for sleep around nine-thirty, I happen to notice a flashing Skype message is waiting.

SORRY I MISSED your first message on your new laptop today. I was having lunch with my dad and some of his associates. I'm glad you like the present and hope to put it to good use very soon, baby. I love you, Evan.

I JUMP online to see if he's still on, but he's not. I can't help but feel disappointed. I'm so used to having him around all the time, talking about everything and nothing, but we've barely talked since he left for New York.

I pick up my phone and crawl into bed. Before I go to sleep, I send him a text.

I MISS HEARING YOUR VOICE. Sweet dreams.

THE LAMP GETS SWITCHED off as I set my phone on the nightstand. I roll onto my side, away from the phone, hoping it will help me forget about it and the wishful thinking I have that he'll call, but it doesn't. I toss and turn for hours never quite reaching that deep, restful sleep I need.

When sleep finally comes, I'm jolted awake by my phone

ringing. I jump up automatically and answer without my mind fully coherent. "Hello!"

"Hi, baby, did I wake you?" Evan slurs into the phone.

Sitting up, I try to clear my foggy mind. "Evan, what time is it?" In the dark room I look over at my alarm clock. It's after midnight.

"I dunno."

By the loud music and chattering in the background, he's not home and for some reason that irritates me. "Babe, it's late here, which means it's really late there. Don't you have work in the morning?"

"Yeah, I had a tough day." He chuckles, his drunkenness showing. "I'm blowing off steam, but I'm leaving soon. I got your text and you said you wanted to hear my voice. So, here it is, just for you."

Call me crabby from being woken up, but I'm not amused. "I sent that text almost four hours ago. I start my classes at eight in the morning, so I went to bed early to be rested and now—"

"Don't be mad. I'm just hanging with some old friends from—"

"Let me guess, old friends from high school? That's great and I'm glad you're enjoying yourself, but I need sleep." On top of being irritated, now I'm worried about him hanging out with people he always said he didn't care about.

"I miss you." He attempts to whisper, but he's loud as he breathes into the phone. "Will you do me a teeny tiny favor? Please, pretty please?"

I sigh, first of all because I'm tired, secondly because he's drunk and won't remember this conversation tomorrow. And thirdly, because I do want to hear his voice and even drunk it's fantastic. "Okay."

"Touch yourself for me, baby. Touch yourse—"

"I'm hanging up now. Goodbye, Evan."

I push the end button and silence my phone. As I snuggle back under my covers, I convince myself that was the right thing to do. He's drunk. Yes, I did want to hear his voice, but in a conversation with me. I'm in no mood for *'other'* stuff.

My alarm sounds less than six hours later and I begrudgingly pull myself from the warm coziness of my bed.

An hour later, Sarah and I are walking to campus together. It's good to see the familiar scenery, but last night is on my mind, and showing on my face apparently too.

Sarah nudges me with her elbow as she readjusts her backpack. "You said it's good to be back, but I think you're somewhere else. Want to talk about it?"

"Evan's in New York."

"That's good, right?"

"I'm not sure yet."

"What are you worried about?"

"Everything." I laugh, but there's no humor in it. "His mom is evil and hates me."

"No one hates you, especially not parents. They always love you."

"Mrs. Ashford doesn't and has made it more than clear that I'm not good enough for Evan."

"Seriously?"

I nod. "She's going to set him up with women there. I know she is."

"So you're worried he'll meet someone else? That doesn't sound like the guy you told me about."

"This is not really about him, but her. I don't trust his mother."

We round the corner and head toward our first classes.

Sarah sighs. "Well, you can't control anyone else, but yourself. So you have to decide if you can handle a long term relationship or not."

Smiling, I say, "I want this with him and I totally trust him. I mean, the guy can't help that he's fuckhot."

Making me feel better, she laughs. "That he can't."

We see lots of our friends that we haven't seen all summer. I'm smiling because it's good to be back. I loved Hawaii, but this is what I've known for the last three years and it's my comfort zone.

My first class drags with boring first day stuff like lesson plans, project assignments, syllabus, expectations, etc... My mind drifts to Evan and the way we hung up last night. He was the first thing I thought of when I woke up and I checked my phone. He didn't call back after I hung up. He's been on my mind ever since.

The second class on my schedule is called 'English Literature in the Business World.' Sounds interesting and since I'm determined to put my English major into use, I thought this class would give me a nice perspective. It's a bonus that Sarah is also in the class.

We meet in front of the auditorium and go inside, grabbing the last two seats together. We're having a perfectly lovely conversation of gossip mixed with opinions about our first class when someone plops down next to me, slams their notebook on the tiny desk and announces, "Hey, good lookin'. Summer treated you well."

I know that voice without even turning. Sarah tenses, and I close my eyes to calm the anger building inside of me.

Slowly, I turn. "Actually, it was my boyfriend who treated me well this summer, Will."

"Don't get your panties in a twist. You're always so high strung—"

I add that phrase to the list of the most annoying things men say to women, and reply, "Why are you sitting here if you think that of me?" I cross my arms defensively across my chest.

"So you have a boyfriend, huh? When did this happen? Is he back in Denver? Just sayin' cuz I noticed you're quick with the comebacks and judging by how you use that mouth, I would say you've learned a thing or two about pleasing a—"

"Will, how's it going?"

Sarah, myself, and Will all turn to see a tall, handsome man with dark hair and light eyes and a kind smile. I can't tell if his eyes are green or blue from my seat, but I can tell how hot this guy is. He speaks again before any of us have a chance. "I'm sorry for interrupting, but Will is one of the few people I know since I transferred here."

Sarah and I remain silent as he sits down on the other side of Will. Will finally acknowledges him, but is clearly irritated with his timing. "Hey Ryan, this is—"

"Sarah, I'm Sarah," she says with a goofy grin on her face while reaching over me to shake his hand. "And this is Mallory."

I take that as my cue for an intervention. "I'm really sorry you have such bad taste in friends like Will here."

Three of us laugh at the joke, well, kind of a joke…okay, I wasn't kidding at all.

Will huffs and says, "Mallory is a little bitter after the break-up. But she's got one helluva ass on her."

Ryan punches him in the arm as my mouth drops open.

"That's not how you talk about a woman. Got it?"

"Whatever dude," He says, pissed. "She's pretty frigid. I'm only warning you. Don't waste your time on her."

"I think I'm a big boy and can make my own decisions, but thanks, *dude*."

The teacher interrupts their little spat as my eyes fill with tears. Trying to contain the tears Will's words incite, I turn away. Sarah whispers, "Don't let him get to you. He's so not worth it, Mal."

I nod once, unable to speak. I refuse to show my weaknesses to Will again this year. Last year was bad enough. I'm not the same person anymore. I've changed. Hawaii changed me. Evan changed me and I'm stronger because of him.

What happens next is a punishment—a punishment for being happy. I don't think karma can actually live peacefully on my side. She has to come and bite me in the ass to remind me of my place in the universe. As karma sinks her teeth into the flesh of my bottom, the professor declares that the four of us are assigned together for the class project we have due in four months. And, it will determine our final grade. The professor continues by saying there will be no whining or switching teams—the teams are final.

I roll my eyes and exclaim, "Damn it!" My voice carries further than I intend and the professor eyes me as Will laughs.

"Hey, Mallory," Ryan says, whispering, "I look forward to proving this asshole wrong about you." He elbows Will in a friendly manner then focuses back on me, smiles and winks.

I don't know if I should be more worried about having to work on this project with my cheating ex-boyfriend or his very flirtatious and cute friend.

23

EVAN

Walking down the streets of Manhattan, I try to blend into the bustle of the crowded sidewalk, but I don't fit in, every-thing feels off here compared to Hawaii. I need to surf. I need that mental escape hitting the waves gives me. My shoulder is knocked by a passerby, no big deal, it happens in a city of eight million. But then I hear, "Evan Ashford?"

My gaze jerks up and over my shoulder to see a young guy, well-groomed in a black sports coat and red pocket square standing behind me. It takes a second longer for my mind to place him though I should have recognized him immediately. "Oh, wow, Landon Abbott... Hey, I didn't expect to run into anyone. What a surprise. How's it going?" I smile at my old high school buddy.

"Going great," he says, eagerly shaking my hand. "How long are you back in the city for?"

"I've only been back a few days."

He wraps his arm over my shoulders, and says, "Perfect timing. I'm meeting Hamilton and Grant around the corner for some drinks. You should come with me. It'd be good to have the old gang back together."

Pushing back my white sleeve, I look at my silver Omega watch—a watch I wear only when I'm in Manhattan. I figure I have time. It's Sunday and I finally finished working, trying to catch up on the files for the upcoming presentation my dad trusted me with and could really use a beer about now.

What I didn't count on discovering is that 'the gang' still hangs out together. The guys are in their last year of university and fulfilling their internship credits at each other's family's company—cushy gig for sure. They drive in on the weekends from Harvard and Princeton and stay through Tuesdays before returning back for other classes. Being around them again gives me an unexpected perspective. I can suddenly see myself in this world again—working, making loads of money, and living the high life like in the old days with my friends.

Matching them drink for drink, I fit right in, looking the part and slipping right back into my old self.

This group always attracted the ladies and tonight is no different. Through my drunken haze, seeing the short skirts and long legs make me miss Mallory. I want to sneak away, needing to call her so she can ground me back to her and Hawaii. I'm not ready to play this role again, the one I'm expected to play. But being here with the boys, I'm distracted by another round of shots. We end up at Hamilton's apartment. More drinks and several hours later, I finally have an opportunity to call my girl.

She answers in a soft and sleepy voice, "Hello."

"Hi, baby, did I wake you?" I say into the phone, trying not to sound drunk even though I'm starting to spin. My tongue isn't cooperating which is so damn frustrating. I hope she can't tell.

She pauses a moment before asking, "Evan, what time is

it?" There's an edge to her tone that puts me on guard. Maybe calling her wasn't such a good idea, after all.

Looking down at my watch, I have trouble making out the numbers. "I dunno." I hold my hand over the phone, and yell over my shoulder, "Hey, turn down the music." That's when I spot some girls I don't know in the living room. *Where'd they come from?*

"Babe, it's late."

"Uh, yeah, it's late here too, I guess. I just had a tough day..." I chuckle, a joke Abbott told earlier making me laugh again. "...I'm blowing off steam. I'll be going home soon. It's been too long since I saw you. I need to see you, baby. I need to touch you and fuck—"

"Evan! That music is loud. Where are you?"

"Don't be mad. I ran into some buddies."

"I'm not mad," her tone is defensive. "I'm glad you're enjoying yourself, but I need sleep." If she was standing in front of me, I bet she would've been stamping her foot at that last statement. She's such a feisty turn-on.

"I miss you," I whisper, my shoulder dropping as I close my eyes. I should let her sleep, but I'm a selfish bastard and need more. "Will you do me a teeny tiny favor? Please, pretty please?"

There's a long pause, but she responds, soft and open to me, "Okay, what?"

"Touch yourself for me. Touch yourse—"

"I'm hanging up now. Goodbye, Evan. Call me tomorrow," she says, cutting me off before hanging up.

I thought that's what she wanted from me. Fuck! It's what I want from her. I miss her. I miss fucking her. I miss fucking. I miss everything about her and she hung up on me.

"Hey, Ashford, Grant has the clean shit. You in?"

I turn around and see Grant pouring a vile of white powder onto the glass coffee table in front of him. I stare, remembering how much I liked the drug in high school. My shock is evident in my reaction. "You're still doing that shit? Fuck, that's messed up." I run my hand slowly through my hair, the inner devil wanting to come out and play. He takes a seat on my shoulder and whispers, 'Don't you miss the freedom it gave you—no worries, no stress, just fun. We haven't had fun together since you met *her* and became all boring. Let's show the boys how to really party.'

"What? Like you don't use anymore? You've been lounging in the Pacific for well over a year maybe two now. I know you can't be clean," Grant says, an arrogant bite to his tone.

"Actually, I haven't done it since high school. The last time was with you jackholes." I watch as Landon draws it in through his nose and a longing deep inside makes my mouth salivate.

"Hi, we haven't been introduced," a tall, leggy blonde says, sidling up to me with traces of white powder rimming her nose.

Right then! It was right then that I knew it wasn't the drugs, or the drinks, girls, or this city I wanted. Not only would they get me into trouble if I did cave to any of them, but I'd screw up everything with Mallory. It doesn't matter that she hung up on me. I deserved that for being an asshole to her. "I've gotta go. Thanks for the drinks," I announce, grabbing my jacket and rushing out the door and down the hall without looking back.

Behind me, the music returns to full volume, and Hamilton calls, "Ashford, man, come back." He doesn't leave the doorway, letting me escape.

I don't turn around or stop. I don't even hesitate. This

night was wrong on so many levels and I should have kept walking when I heard Abbott say my name on the street. Lesson learned.

Unrolling my sleeves, I button them at the cuff and shove them into my pockets. I walk two blocks before flagging a cab down. One short taxi ride later, I'm back at the place that I'm once again calling home. There is nothing about this place that feels like home to me and I just pissed my real home off with a drunken sex call in the middle of the night.

I'll make amends with her tomorrow, hoping she can get the sleep she needs tonight. The old me would have called her right away, but I want her to rest, so I control myself and go to bed instead.

The next day, I wake with a splitting headache and glazed eyes. Not a good look for the office and especially not a Monday morning. I shower which helps not only the way I look, but my mindset. After dressing, I go across the hall and have breakfast. My parents' chef serves up scrambled eggs, bacon, and pancakes.

While I'm shoveling it all in, I realize I didn't eat last night. That definitely didn't help my state. Those guys were assholes in high school and they're still assholes; assholes with too much money at their disposal, too many women at their disposal, and too much time on their hands. Any of those are bad enough on their own, but mix them together and it's a dangerous combination. I need to stay focused on the reason I'm back in Manhattan and it's not to turn back into one of them again.

I arrive at work twenty minutes late and catch flack from my dad for it, as I should. It's not easy for him to justify his kids having the positions we do without also having to remind me of the company's policies. I apologize to him, to my secretary, and to Kate. I promise it won't happen again and I will take this job seriously.

My dad considers pulling me from the presentation this afternoon. He keeps me on it, but gives me a warning to not screw this up.

Mallory calls me on a short break she has between two classes. I apologize to her as well, but it doesn't seem enough and then she has to go because her class is starting. When the phone goes quiet, I stare out my window, realizing I don't want to live this kind of life and I definitely don't want to live life without her in it. I've got to get my shit together once and for all. If not for me, than for her. Mallory deserves that much.

24

EVAN

Leaning forward, I break into Portuguese, wanting to speak to the clients in their native language. "Os estudos mostram que as Indústrias Pinho são um investimento seguro e uma ótima oportunidade para estabelecermos presença no mercado americano. O diretor financeiro do grupo é brasileiro e possui fortes laços com a comunidade latin e definitivamente agrega valor para possíveis oportunidades futuras. Nós temos os meios necessários para suprir não somente os objetivos financeiros da empresa, como também levá-la a outro patamar de crescimento. Eu realmente espero que você considere estes fatores na tomada de decisão." I take a deep breath *and wait and wait and wait.* The six potential clients sitting before me are an account we have longed to land and my dad has placed his trust in me to bring them over to Ashford Holdings.

Standing at the head of the conference table, I look each of them in the eye, reading them the best I can, but they are a tough bunch. They don't have ticks or signals that give their thoughts away. My dad entwines his fingers together while his elbows rest firmly on the table in front of him. As always, he commands authority. He's completely confident that we'll seal this deal, even if he has to step in and take over the presentation to do it. By the look in his eyes, he's pleased. A Plus, he didn't interrupt, which means I did a good job. The waiting game continues as silence fills the stuffy boardroom and the men look to each other, a conversation occurring through nods and gazes.

Mr. Santos, the President and spokesman for his financial team, stands up opposite from me, looks between my dad and me, and says, "You've got new clients, Mr. Ashford." He walks toward me and I stand quickly, meeting him halfway to shake hands. "Thank you for putting our interests before your own. I have a feeling this is going to be a very rewarding relationship."

"Thank you, Mr. Santos. I look forward to working on the team that will handle your account during this first transaction and getting your company's financials in order for success in the long run," I add.

"I hope you'll be leading that team. I was very impressed by your presentation."

I glance at my father who nods, giving me permission to explain. "We have a great team in place, including my sister Kate, who will head up your account. She had another meeting previously scheduled so she couldn't attend today's presentation, but she is well versed in your corporate structuring and current financials."

"I'll also be on the team, but I thoroughly trust my daughter to be your main point of contact. Please feel free to call me directly if you have any needs or concerns," my dad says, stepping forward.

"I respect a man who makes family a priority. You did a

great job today and I'm sure you'll do a fine job at school. Now, Hugh..." He turns his full attention to my father.

I walk around the room and shake hands with all the men and wait by the door.

My father pats Mr. Santos on the back and they begin casually chatting as he leads the large group down the hall to the elevators. We make polite, but friendly small talk on the way. When they step into the elevator, Mr. Rocha, their CFO, says, "Nós vamos transferir o valor de US$ 6.7 milhões de dólares amanhã pela manha dando continuidade a nossa negociação."

"Muito obrigada pela oportunidade e em nome do todos os funcionários das empresas Ashford Holdings, sejam bem-vindos. Mais uma vez obrigada e tenham uma ótima viagem," I say before the elevator door closes.

"Congratulations, son. I knew you could do it." My dad grabs me into a loose hug and I embrace him, feeling the adrenaline of success kicking in.

"Thanks for trusting me," I say, stepping back.

We walk down the hall toward our offices, but he detours into Kate's office first. "Evan closed Pinho Industries," he announces proudly.

She looks up, her chin dropping, then she asks, "After one presentation?"

"Yep," I answer, "One's all it took."

She pushes away from her desk and runs over to me, pulling me into her arms. "Evan! That's a big account. Congratulations, baby bro. We should celebrate."

"Raincheck?" I throw this out there as I escape out the

door. "It's been a long day and I kind of want to go home and relax."

My dad follows me, offering, "That sounds like a good idea. Stop by if you want to have dinner with us. We eat at—"

"Seven," Kate and I say in unison, and roll our eyes. We've eaten at seven our entire lives. Seriously, does he think he still needs to remind us? I laugh to myself.

"Well, I'm off." I hurry to my office and grab my briefcase. It's past six and I want to get home, wanting to talk to Mallory. Making a dash for the elevator, I slip inside the open doors behind three other employees heading home for the day.

I want to celebrate with my girl. All I want to do is get home and webcam with her. I haven't seen her in four days due to our strange schedules and it's getting to me. Thank God, we've gotten to talk and text, but I'm ready to see her.

The elevator stops and three young women step inside; two of them crowd me into the back corner. There are seven of us in here and room for at least two more, but I seemed to be crammed into the back by them, which makes no sense. One turns around and smiles while the other nonchalantly, but obvious to me, rubs her ass against the knuckles on my left hand. I lift my hand up, feeling uncomfortable in the situation.

I fist that same hand and cough into it followed by a loud clearing of my throat, hoping they'll get the hint and give me some space. One turns around, and says, "Bless you." *Funny, I didn't sneeze.*

I mumble, "Thanks." Just as the doors open, I step forward, but the same two stay in place, making me run into the back of them. "Oh, I'm sorry. Are you not getting off on the first floor?" My eyes dart to the doors, knowing they'll close on us if we don't exit quickly.

They giggle as I wait for them to answer, my patience with this scenario gone. Trying to move without touching them is impossible. The darker haired one of the two says, "Actually, we'd like to get off, but maybe somewhere a little more private?" She takes me by the tie and tightens the knot at my neck.

"Um, I think you misunderstood me—" I start clarifying while attempting to step forward again as I tug my tie from her vice of a grip.

The other girl says, "We understood perfectly, handsome. You're asking if we want to get off and the answer is yes." Her Cheshire cat grin is unflattering as she rubs her fingers through my hair.

"Ladies, excuse me." It's a demand, not a suggestion. I work my way between them and off the elevator, shaking my head confused to how I gave them the wrong impression.

I feel like prey in Manhattan. Everyone on the street is on the hunt for their next dating conquest or looking for someone to conquer them for the night. Keeping my head down, I avoid eye contact, not wanting to engage in the game. I unbutton my suit jacket while making my way to one of the black cars my dad has on stand-by for us to use. Usually I prefer walking, but I'm too tired to make the fifteen block trek today.

After opening my apartment door, I toss my keys on the marble top console table and drop my brief case on the floor. I go straight to my room, past Kate's, and turn on my computer. As it boots up, I strip down to my undershirt and briefs and sit and wait for the program to load.

Bingo! She's online. I click on my girls' avi—a picture that makes my fucking cock ache because she looks so sexy.

"Hi there, stranger," she answers my call. The video loads a second later and there she is in all her beautiful glory.

"Hi there. God, I've missed you, baby," I say, smiling as I stare at her. She's a goddess and I'm not deserving to have someone so perfect anywhere near me, much less as my girlfriend. I swear I did something right in a former life to be given this opportunity with her.

She tilts her head and smiles. "Aww, I've been missing you too, babe. I think about you all the time." She looks over her shoulder and grabs a blanket from her bed before spinning back around on her desk chair and looking at me. As she drapes the blanket over her shoulders, she says, "Sarah keeps this place like an icebox. You sure you're ready to move here and be cold?" She giggles and my heart quadruples in size at the sound of her laughter.

"If it means wrapping myself around you to keep warm, yep, I'm so ready. I'm not missing a hint you're trying to drop, am I?" Anxiety fills my stomach thinking she's over me after being apart for two weeks.

She giggles. "I think you've learned that I'm more the come-right-out-and-say-it kind of girl." She pulls her hair up into a ponytail and I see her ringed finger move across the screen. Fascinated by how much I love seeing her in such a normal setting, being herself, and showing her commitment to me by wearing my ring. A pale pink shades her cheeks, and a smile appears. "What? What are you smiling about, Evan?"

"You and the come-right-now part." I pause to drink in this visual, so I can see her when I close my eyes later.

"Speaking of coming... you're wearing entirely too many clothes for my liking. I couldn't keep you in clothes in Hawaii and now—too many."

My shirt is up and over my head without her having to ask. She raises an eyebrow and smirks, and I swear it's one she learned from me. It looks good on her—sexy and mischievous.

She stands, dropping the blanket. Her nipples are hard through the cotton of her tank top. The top comes off and she sits back down, draping the blanket back over her shoulders, but leaves her chest bare and exposed for me. "I miss your body against mine, babe." Her hand slides up her stomach and oh-so-slowly squeezes her breast. "I miss your hands on me, doing this to me."

I want to watch her body, but her eyes engage me with their soulful depths. Her gaze drops down and I move my hand over to my abs, my body reacting to seeing her. She's quiet, but her mouth is open, her lips barely parted. Lowering my hand, I rub lightly over my hard-on, shutting my eyes briefly as my release starts to build.

Her chest rises and falls with heavier breaths and she slips her hand below the cameras reach. As much as I want to see everything she's doing to herself that's making her head drop back and causing that sexy moan, it's more erotic seeing only her reaction.

Sliding down into my chair, I get more comfortable and tighten my fingers around my dick. Keeping my eyes on her, I watch her—eyes closed and panting as her hand moves, pleasuring herself. I love the sound of her breaths, but I want to hear her voice too. My hand moves up and down my length, hard and fast, and I ask, "What do see when your eyes are closed?"

She fights her reaction to stop and respond, be polite and open her eyes. Instead, she continues, her hand moving faster, her breath picking up, and her sweet moans of pleasure getting louder. "You," she says, as if gasping for air.

"Always you." Her face strains as she squirms, tensing before me. "Evan." And she sinks down into her chair.

My release hits fast, my eyes clamping tight. "Fuck." I have no control over my body when it comes to her. When I look up, a little embarrassed by how fast I came, she's smiling at me—gentle and sweet. There's a light in her eyes that sparkles in the dim light of her room.

"I love you," she whispers.

She knows I love her, but I say the words not only for her, but for me as well. "I love you, too."

"Gimme a sec. I'll be right back," she says, getting up and tightening the blanket around her.

I take the opportunity to clean the mess I made. After I put on a clean pair of boxers, she returns and sits down. Dressed in her tank top again, she's now too hidden in that blanket to see the rest of her body.

Smiling, she says, "Well... that's something I've never done."

"I haven't either, but I liked it."

She blushes, it's apparent even over the webcam. "I liked it, too."

I don't want to embarrass her anymore and decide it might be time to change the subject. "I closed my first deal today."

"You did? That's great! Tell me about it."

I go through the story leaving out all the boring details. I can tell she's sincerely interested in the story and gives me several 'congratulations', 'I'm proud of you', and 'I knew you could do it'. I go on to talk about the dreaded upcoming board meeting.

"I'm confused," she says. "Your parents own the company, yet there's a board of directors who can make him retire?"

"It's complicated, but my parents own majority stock in the company and have final say and the largest vote when it comes to major decisions concerning the business. But, as a public company, they have to listen to a group of advisors who have been brought in to oversee the overall operations of the company as representatives to the stock holders. This is where it gets tricky. There's a clause that says if the board thinks my dad is not making sound decisions they have the right to oust him no matter what he wants." I look at her, watching the monitor, her absorbing the information. "Most boards have representatives from the company on there as well to balance out the decision making process. Sometimes, it's widows who inherit a seat on the board or a trusted outsider. In our case, we inherited a seat on the board when we each turned twenty-two. It's unorthodox to have members our age on there, but not unheard of."

"So if they try to get your dad out, you and Kate have two of the votes for him to stay?"

"Precisely, but we have to have valid reasons and be able to justify those reasons for our votes."

"What if they vote him out?"

"Someone else will take over the company. My parents will still own the majority and would probably take control of our board positions, if accepted by the other members."

"It's a lot of pressure, huh?"

"Yes. We have a lot of information and research, financial statements, and his reputation to back our argument, but I'm still fucking scared to screw this up."

"I love you, Evan. Your parents love you. You can't screw this up if you're prepared and it sounds like you are."

Maybe I shouldn't have laid this all out like I did, but she's the only one I want to share things with. She looks worried because that worry crease is in full effect between her eyes. "Please don't worry about me."

"I don't like you having to deal with so much," she says, glancing down briefly. "I want you to know, whatever happens tomorrow, I still love you. Okay?"

I nod. "Okay."

My eyes find the picture of us on the beach that I use as my phone background, reminding me I want to talk to her about our spat the other night. "Hey Mallory, I'm sorry about calling you when I was drunk *and obnoxious*. I just wanted to hear your voice, so that became my sole focus without thinking about you. I wasn't taking your feelings into consideration and well, I want to apologize for my behavior."

"Evan?"

"Yeah?"

"Thank you. It's hard on me, too. I want to talk to you all the time, but I get your voicemail a lot. I really want to fall asleep in your arms. I struggle at night without you next to me. It feels wrong trying to live life without you in it, but this was the second time you woke me up when you were out partying."

"I know. I'm sorry. But please remember that I'm in your life. I'm just not with you right now. I hope you don't forget what it feels like to wake up next to me. I can't escape the feeling of absence, but some nights, I can feel you so readily against me I would swear you were here. It's like a beautiful torture if that makes any sense at all."

"I understand that perfectly." I hear her hard sigh. "Should I worry about you falling into your old ways?"

"I didn't call those guys. I ran into one of them on the street when I was heading home. He invited me out and I went. It was a mistake. I know that now."

She nods and a yawn slips out. "Sorry, after all that... we did, I might need a nap."

"I need you to believe in us."

"I do. That's what makes the days without you harder to get through."

"But we will. We'll get through them."

"Together."

"Together."

25

EVAN

There's a dress code when you have dinner with my parents, so I choose black slacks and a grey striped button-up shirt. I opt not to wear a tie just to piss them off a little. I can't go changing all of who I am because I'm back in the city. With my hand on the door, I realize I'm being petty and stupid. I want to earn their trust back and exceed their expectations. I don't want to scrape by doing the bare minimum anymore, so I add a thin charcoal grey tie and leave the apartment.

After crossing the hall and covering the distance to their front door in a few strides, I ring the doorbell. I wait only a few seconds before Helga answers, greeting me warmly, "Good evening, Evan. Please come in."

"Good evening to you." We've always been friendly with the staff, but when my mom is home, formality is held in the highest regards.

"Mr. and Mrs. Ashford are in the main living room with your sister."

She starts to lead me, but I stop her. "Helga, I know where it is, remember? I did grow up here. I'm sure you have better things to do than to announce my arrival."

"If you're sure?"

"Positive. Thank you."

I walk through the formal living room and down the hall to the family room. When I enter the large open room, my mom turns from Kate with a big smile on her face. "Darling, I'm so thrilled about the deal. Your father and Kate were just telling me about it."

She stands and comes to me, kissing me on both cheeks as if we're mere acquaintances. But her expression changes and she takes my face in her hands, looking at me for a moment. "Congratulations, Evan. I knew you could do it." She silently appraises my appearance, and then states, "Dinner should be ready. Shall we?"

My dad claps me on the back, bringing me with him as we make our way into the dining room. "Great job today, son. Let's have a drink and celebrate after dinner."

When he moves past me, following my mother, my first thought is I might need more than one drink to survive this meal.

Kate shoulders me. "So, how's Mallory? Did you do a little "Laptop sex" celebration?" She jokes, laughing. Her face turns serious. "Never mind. I really don't want the answer to that."

My loud, guilty laugh grabs everyone's attention.

"Ewwww, gross, Evan." My sister says, scrunching her face. "That ridiculously big smile gives you away and now I must excuse myself from dinner so I can go vomit over that visual."

Shrugging, I make no apologies.

Dinner flows smoothly. I've eaten with my family a couple of times since being back and my mom seems to have eased up on pressuring me about... well, about everything.

After dinner, Kate goes back across the hall to work at home, and my mom and dad take me into the library where the good liquor is kept. I watch as my dad pours three glasses of Remy Martins Louis XIII Cognac. The only significance to this is that I watched my dad drink this cognac on every special occasion and celebration throughout my life, but only once in my honor—when I got accepted into Oxford. I wasn't even allowed a sip because they didn't want to encourage bad behavior by letting me drink since I was only seventeen. Little did they know, I was drinking and doing a lot worse already. I was just really good at hiding it.

It was foolish of them to send me to that elite high school. They were worried about me drinking when they should have been worried about all the drugs I was doing. My mind goes into a sensory memory of how the pot and coke got me through life in the city back then. Hanging with the heirs of famous brand names and celebrities' kids, partying until dawn, that was an average Tuesday for me. I was lucky I was smart. I'd walk into class, completely unprepared, and ace every one of my tests.

"Evan!" My dad says, drawing my attention back to the present. "I think you've earned a taste of the best." He clinks his glass against mine and my mother's and says, "I look forward to many years of working with you and watching as you grow Ashford Holdings."

"I second that," my mother cheers.

Tapping their glasses with a smile, my heart sinks into the pit of my stomach. I want to correct their toast. I want to remind them that I'm only here for four months, but seeing the pride in their eyes, I can't. There's plenty of time to remind them of my plans to move to Colorado. There's plenty of time to remind them that I'm going back to school to get my degree in Psychology. There's plenty of time to remind them of Mallory.

The burn is instant in my throat when I sip the cognac. I can't help but feel that burn is indicative of things to come, so I cough, trying to ease it, trying to ease my fate.

"It's disrespectful to gulp expensive cognac," my dad says lightheartedly. "And probably burns your throat more that way."

With a croaky voice, I say, "Oh, trust me, the cheap shit will do the exact same thing."

"Please don't swear, Evan," my Mother scolds. She sets her glass down and hugs me. "I'm off. I have lots of work to do on the Ashford Gala in December. I'll leave you two gentlemen to discuss business. A reminder, Evan, tomorrow is The Metropolitan Opera House Charity Ball." She stops in the doorway, turning back. "Will you be bringing a date? I need to confirm our reservation."

I watch her carefully as she tries hard to sound like this is an afterthought when in actuality she has probably been thinking about this question for weeks.

"No, no date." I keep my tone flat, not open for discussion.

She clasps her hands together in front of her face in excitement, and says, "Very good. I've already emailed your secretary the details. Black tie and I'll see you there. Oh, and Evan, please don't be late. Thank you, darling."

"I won't be." I swirl the cognac before looking at my dad and asking, "How are you feeling about the board meeting?"

"More importantly," he asks, "how are you feeling?"

"I, uh, I'm a bit anxious. I'm ready for it to be over and to move on."

He chuckles to himself. "Yes, I couldn't agree more."

"Do you really want to talk about it?"

"No."

"Good. It makes me more nervous to talk about it with you." I laugh, but quickly add, "This has been Kate's full focus for two weeks now. She was reading files and stats all summer." I walk to the large window overlooking the city and stare out for a solid minute before I speak again. "She's doing a good job." I turn to face him. He's seated at his desk, looking almost regal. "You know, she'll put in the hours and she has the drive—"

"Kate's already working for the company. Of course, I know she'll do a good job or I wouldn't have her there, daughter or not."

"I'm just saying—"

"I know what you're saying. You want me to consider her for what I have planned for you. Correct?" He sits forward, his posture tense as his eyes lock on mine.

"Yes."

"I saw how good you felt when you closed Pinho, so before you go throwing away opportunities, I want you to give me more than a hundred percent over the next couple months. I think you will find this business even more rewarding than today." He stands, setting his glass down, and walks towards the door. "In many ways, but you have to give it a chance."

He leaves me there with over-priced cognac and a lot to think about. I down the drink to spite his previous warning. Standing, I set the crystal glass on the side table and go back to my apartment across the hall.

When I open the door, Kate is sitting at the dining table with combed wet hair, a robe on, and her glasses. She looks up from a stack of papers lying in front of her, and says, "Hey, how'd it go over there?"

"Fine." I walk past her tugging at my tie to loosen it. "I'm going to bed."

She follows me down the hall to my room. "What's wrong?"

Maybe it's the cognac or feeling like I was under a microscope all night. Or maybe it's all the pressure everyone's putting on me, but I snap. "Shit!" I go inside my room, hearing her trail behind me. "What am I doing here, Kate? This isn't me," I state, disgruntled, as I pull off my tie and throw it on the bed.

"What's not you? The business, the clothes, the city? Evan, it might be time to grow up."

"I don't want another fucking lecture in the form of 'advice' if that's okay with you."

"Try this on for size then. What you're doing here is important. It's important to more than just you. You're a part of something here." She walks to my bed and sits on the edge as I remain standing, arms crossed, and listen. "Hawaii is great. Murphy is great and Mallory is great, but they have chosen their path and you have one that has chosen you. You need to stop thinking about only the here and now, and start thinking about the future. I'm not trying to lecture you, but you really do need to think of the big picture."

"Nice," I start, having trouble keeping the sarcasm at bay. "So you've moved back here with the go-getters and ladder-climbers and you fall in line and forget all about Murphy? Just like that. That easy, huh, Kate? Well, I'm sorry, but I refuse—"

She's looking down at her feet when her head bolts upright. "I'm not forgetting about Murphy! I love him, but he's in school and I'm working. We're trying to make it work the best we can and right now that means we're apart. We're doing what we have to do in the present. Sometimes that's not the easy route, but it's the mature thing to do. What's wrong with that?"

I sit down next to her, looking at the wall straight ahead, my gaze following the lines of the plaster. "There's nothing wrong with that if you have to do it, but don't you miss him?"

"More than anything, but me being in Hawaii doing nothing wouldn't help either of us." I see a half smile cross her face, and with a light laugh, she says, "It would probably tear us apart."

Keeping my voice as low as I can where she can still hear me, I let her know my inner thoughts. "I love her. I love Mallory."

"I know you do, but you still need to live your life. I'm not saying you have to date someone else. I'm just saying that you have to be able to function and work and play and live even when you're not together." She wraps her arm around me and leans her head on my shoulder. "Mallory should be going to parties and class and hanging out with her friends. She deserves to have the full college experience while she can. You don't really want her to miss out on the fun that she should be having because she's at home pining over you."

"I want her to enjoy herself, but I don't want to lose her either. And that's looking very fucking likely if I'm working all the time."

"She loves you. It's time to trust her, Evan. Mallory is pretty damn hot and she's going to get hit on, but you have to trust that the feelings you share for each other are more than a superficial summer thing."

"Being a grown up is *way* over-rated!"

Kate bursts out laughing, "You can say that again."

"Being a grown up...OW!" She pops me in the arm.

"Smartass!" She leaves on that note.

I change into a t-shirt and pajama pants and join Kate at the table. Sitting down, I smile. "Okay, let's do this then."

KATE and I ride into work using the car service together. We get to the office right before 6:30 in the morning, the only ones there this early. The lights flicker on automatically as we walk from the elevator to our offices in the back.

After checking our voicemails and emails, we meet in the conference room and place the handouts in front of each chair at the table. Yes, we have people who can hand the files out to each board member, but the easy task helps to calm my nerves.

At seven, the catering company shows up to set up the breakfast buffet. I'm walking back to my office, to return emails and mentally prepare, when I notice light coming from under my dad's office door. I knock lightly and he responds, "Come in."

The door has a creak when it opens. I walk inside. "Morning, I didn't know you were here."

He looks up from his paperwork spread out on his desk, removes his glasses, and rubs the bridge of his nose. "I've been here for a few hours."

"If I'd known, I would've stopped by sooner."

"I knew you and your sister were busy. I appreciate all the efforts."

I sit down next to him. "Of course, I know this is serious." I look at the photo frames on the shelves behind him and notice that they're all of me and Kate. In one photo, I'm sitting in my father's desk chair when I was two or three. I was happy spinning around. There's another one of me smiling with pride while holding the varsity jacket letters I earned my senior year in high school. There were six for all the activities I participated in. That was taken before Lani's death. I look happy and hopeful despite the hard partying I was doing. I've been trying to get back to that emotional state ever since, but it's been a struggle. I have different goals than I did back then. Now I want to do everything I can to help my dad retain his position in his company. After that, I'll get the hell out of this city to follow my own dreams, which are still somewhat to be determined.

There are other pictures behind him, Kate winning Prom Queen and one of her graduating last May cum laude from NYU. But when my eyes meet his, he asks, "Have you ever seen this picture, Evan?"

He turns an eight by ten silver frame from his desk around for me to see. I nod, recognizing it instantly. It's a picture of my mother holding me, as a newborn, in her arms with Kate on her hip. Kate is kissing or licking my head, I can't be sure, but it makes me smile. My mother looks so young which is amazing because she looks pretty damn young now. She's relaxed and happy. Her hair hangs down all natural, soft waves catching the light from the window. She's beautiful.

"I've always loved this picture of the three of you. It actually motivates me to do my best because it reminds me that I have people relying on me. Have you seen this picture?" My dad hands me a smaller silver framed photo. "That's all of the New York office employees last year at the Gala. It's also a good reminder of my responsibilities to this company."

I look up, meeting his focused gaze and I reassure him, "You're not going anywhere. Kate and I will make sure of it. I know you're not ready to retire. We all do." I stand up, knowing I need to take care of a few things before the meeting starts. Leaning forward, he takes my hand in his and shakes it. His other hand covers the back of mine. He doesn't need to say anything more. He's placed his trust in us and I refuse to let him down. Standing up, I hang onto the company photo. "Can I hold onto this one? I'd like to have it in the meeting."

He nods, puts his glasses back on, and starts flipping through the papers on his desk again.

TWO HOURS LATER

Kate and I welcome the board members to the offices and she leads the discussion. As representatives of the company and our father, she plans to show that he's behind all the success of Ashford Holdings.

FOUR HOURS LATER

We listen to eight of the twelve members and the opinions seem to vary based on that individual's goals for the company or what they want to see happen with the company in the long run.

Lunch is brought in and during that time, we break from the meeting to return emails or call-backs. Kate and I sit on opposite ends of the large conference table and through casual conversation, drive our message home. I glance at the silver frame of the employees throughout the meeting to remind me of the importance of keeping my father in his rightful place, leading this company to further success.

. . .

EIGHT HOURS LATER

I stand behind Kate as she knocks on my fathers' office door. Most of the employees have gone home, but my father calls, "Come in." He's always the last to leave.

"Aren't you supposed to be in a tux and across town in an hour?" Kate asks, sitting down in front of his desk.

"Your mother is going to kill me if we're late to the cocktail party before this ball. As one of the organizers, she is supposed to be there to greet guests, but I had a few things on my mind." He stands and puts on his jacket, preparing to leave. He looks distant and worried.

"Dad, don't you want to know the results of the board vote?" Kate asks, watching him look for his keys.

He doesn't say anything, but stills.

"You're in. It's all okay. You're still in charge, old man," she says.

His head pops up and looks at her in disbelief. "What?" He looks at me and asks, "What?"

I walk toward him and confirm what Kate said. "You're still running this place. You think you can handle it?"

With his confidence back, he grabs us both into a group hug. "I can definitely handle it." His face is buried between us and he whispers, "Thank you. Thank you. Thank you so much." It sounds as if he's on the verge of crying and I hear Kate sniffle. I remain quiet, closing my eyes, and appreciating this moment.

"I love you, kids. Always know I love you."

I know in this moment he's speaking from his heart. He wouldn't have said any different if we would have failed. Kate tells him the same, but I also feel her hand on my back, gripping my shirt to silently let me know she means me too.

"I love you, Dad." I wrap my arm around Kate's waist and squeeze a little. "I love you too, Katie."

After a strong clap to the back, my dad says, "I really have to go before I get my butt kicked by your mother."

We laugh at this relaxed and rare remark from our dad.

"We'll see you there. We have some stuff to do before we go home," Kate says, signaling us to leave.

"Son, you're still coming tonight, right?"

"Yes, I'll be there."

"Good. I don't like to upset the little missus."

Once I'm back at my desk in the privacy of my office, I call Mallory.

"*Hhhhiiiii*, babe," she answers, sounding a bit relaxed herself.

"Hey there. I just got out of the meeting. It lasted all day," I say, kicking my feet up on my desk, leaning back, and enjoying my city view. "Long story short, my dad is still President and won't be retiring anytime soon."

"That sounds like a curse as much as a blessing," she laughs.

"Yeah, to me also. So your first week of classes is under your belt. How do you feel?"

"Fantastic. Sarah is here and we're chatting about it now."

"Well, tell her 'hello' from me."

"I will. I think we're gonna go down to The Sink tonight."

"What's The Sink?"

"Oh," she giggles again. "I forget you don't know about any of the local places here. Um, it's a bar near campus where a lot of our friends hang out." As she's talking, I realize that she has this whole other life that I know nothing about. I look at my shoes, noticing the new scuffs on them and try not to feel bad, when she says, "I get to be the one to introduce all these places to you. Though I have to admit, most of the campus hangouts are pretty dull."

"They wouldn't be with you there."

I smile as her tone turns playful. "Mr. Ashford, you flatter me so."

"And I always will, my love."

She's quiet for a moment then says, "I guess Sarah's ready to go."

I take my feet off my desk and sit up straight, remembering how I need to let her have these experiences. "Oh yeah, you go. I have this event I have to attend tonight anyway."

"An event?" she asks, her voice changing as her curiosity piques.

"Yeah, this ball that raises money for the Met Opera—"

"A ball?"

"Yeah, a stuffy event. It should be a pretty boring meet and greet type thing."

"Why does it suddenly feel like we're living in two different worlds? I'm heading down to The Sink in old leggings and a baggy Colorado sweatshirt." She says exactly what I'm thinking. On the plus side, that outfit she's wearing might be the perfect guy repellant from the sound of it and that makes me smile. "And you're off to a fancy schmancy ball." I hear her swallow loudly. "Are you wearing a tuxedo?"

I smile. "Yes." I appreciate her jealousy.

Another loud swallow. "Send me a picture of you in that tux, okay? I guess I should go. Sarah's standing at the door tapping her foot," she says. "Congratulations to your family and to you, Evan. I'm proud of you."

I'm not ready to hang up, but I will for her. "Have fun tonight."

"You too, babe." She sounds like she's trying to sound happy, but I can tell she's not.

"Yeah, okay."

We hang up on that awkward note and I can't help but feel we're out of sync right now, living in two different worlds.

26

MALLORY

Sarah buys two gin and tonics and returns from the bar with a smile on her face. Sliding onto her stool with a mischievous look in her eye, she says, "Everybody is here tonight, Mal. I'm so glad you finally came out."

"You know you're able to go out without me." My sarcasm is on point tonight. I shift on my stool as I'm elbowed from behind. "And yes, I think you're right. Everybody is out tonight and they are all crammed in here."

"Perk up, girlie!" she says, poking my shoulder. "No bummer talk. I know you miss Evan, but let's have some fun. Can we please do that?"

"I feel bad about how we ended our call earlier though."

"Mallory, I'm sure you were both just distracted. I mean you said he was going out and you were going out." Her words don't soothe my concerns. "Now c'mon, let's enjoy being out. We finished the first full week of classes of our senior year. That deserves a toast!"

We hold up our glasses, tap them together and take a sip. After a few more sips, enough sips to finish my drink, I go to the bar to order the next round. Sarah's right. A lot of our friends are here tonight and it's fun to get off campus. I need to relax, so I order two more gin and tonic's and wait.

Just as the bartender tells me 'ten even', a voice next to me says, "I got it."

Looking to my right, Ryan is standing next to me, handing the bartender cash.

"You don't need to do that. I have money," I say, feeling uneasy about him buying the drinks.

"I'm sure you do," he says, turning to the side to face me, but disregarding my reasoning.

"Well, thank you for the drinks."

"My pleasure." His cocky smirk briefly reminds me of Evan, and our gaze connects a beat longer than I'm comfortable with.

I turn to go, but suddenly I feel guilty for letting him buy our drinks and for walking away, so I stand there awkwardly debating between walking away and staying at the bar.

Ryan laughs and asks, "Do I make you nervous, Mallory?"

"Um." I look up at him, and lie, "No. I should get Sarah her drink though. Thanks again... *for the drinks*."

He raises his beer into the air. "Anytime."

Fortunately, he doesn't follow me back to the table where some unwelcome company has joined us. I hand Sarah her drink and slide back onto the barstool next to her. I ignore *him*. "Ryan bought our drinks," I tell her as if no one else is around.

"*Really?* That certainly was nice of him. I wonder..." she says, tapping her chin playfully "...why?"

"I know what you're doing or should I say *inferring*? I'm not interested in him, Sar. I'm off the market and Evan will be here in four months. I'm sure he'll visit before then."

"I wasn't saying you should date him. I just think he likes

you, is all."

"You're really just going to ignore me, Mallory?"

I hear an annoying asshat saying my name like he still has a right to do so. I sip my drink and continue to ignore Will.

He huffs in frustration, then whines, "Why do you hate me so much?"

That comment gets my insides boiling instantly. "Are you serious? You're fucking serious right now?" I stand, pointing my finger at him.

His head moves back abruptly—a bit meek and a lot worried. "Yes." At least he looks a little afraid.

Just when I'm about to lay into him, Ryan steps between us, and says, "Whoa, whoa, whoa. Why do you let this guy get to you?"

I look up into Ryan's eyes, which are about one foot higher than my own. I don't understand what he's trying to accomplish. He's all mysterious and kind to me, but yet he's friends with *him*. That makes no sense. But my brain finally catches on. This is a set-up. Will is probably trying to pull a trick, a ruse on me. He probably set this whole good cop, bad cop or in Will's case, Stupid cop, act up. Well, I'm not falling for it!

"I know what you two are up to and you can forget about it. I'm two steps ahead of you, which coincidentally looks a little something like this." I walk toward the door while gulping the rest of my drink on the way. I set the glass down on a nearby table and push the door wide open.

The chilly night air blasts me and I shiver, but I still move forward, stepping out onto the sidewalk. I pull my emergency cigarette from my back pocket and bum a light from some guy smoking against the brick building. I've been carrying it around, just in case, this entire past week. I thought I'd kicked the habit when I returned home since I couldn't smoke for the week at my parents' house, but with the stress of Will, and Ryan, and missing Evan, I greedily inhale, enjoying the feel of relief it gives me.

I'm about a block away from The Sink when Ryan runs up from behind and grabs me by the arm. "Hey, Mallory, stop! I think you've got the wrong idea."

Standing there with a hand on my hip and the other one holding my savior stick, I ask, "Really? Well, what's the real deal here?"

"Deal with what?"

"Why are you being so nice to me?"

He looks confused, squinting his eyes until they are almost closed. "What? I can't be nice to you without harboring ulterior motives?"

"Yeah, something like that." I cross my arms and tap my foot for added effect.

His hands go up in surrender. "If you don't want to be friends," he says, but hesitates. "Okay. We won't be friends, but it seems to make sense to me because we're working on this project together and we have some friends in common—"

"Will is no friend of mine. He's an asshole!"

"I stand corrected." When he says stuff like that—a little formal and a little sarcastic—he also reminds me of Evan.

I drop my head, looking down at my phone at the thought of Evan; the picture of us so prominently displayed.

"I didn't expect you to be a smoker." Ryan is quieter, curious.

"I don't. Uh, well, I didn't. Sometimes I smoke, usually when I'm stressed. You don't know me well enough to know things like that about me."

"I was kind of hoping I'd get the chance to know you

better." He points down at my phone and asks, "Who's that? Is that your boyfriend?"

Looking back up, I nod. "Yeah, his name is Evan."

"Where does he go to school?"

With that one question, he built a little trust with me, and that is how my relationship went from basically non-existent to friendly with Ryan.

EVAN

Sitting politely at the table, I wait for my dishes to be cleared before I squirm. I want out of here, but I promised my mother I would stay through the meal, especially a meal that cost fifteen hundred dollars a plate. At least it goes to support the arts, The Metropolitan Opera specifically, so it's all good.

I suffer, listening to two different speakers, and crave a fucking cigarette. I want one so bad that it's becoming painful. I'm antsy and fidgeting with the tablecloth when Kate touches my hands to still them. I thought I kicked the bad habit in Hawaii, Mallory and I both did. Now, here I am with cravings again.

Right before I stand up, I whisper to the other guests seated at the table, "Excuse me, please." I hurry out the double doors in the corner and make my way toward the exit. I walk a block down and buy a box of my old favorites then head back to the hotel where the ball is being held. As soon as I find a protected spot from the wind, I light up.

Closing my eyes, I enjoy the basic sensation of this small pleasure—inhaling deeply— and ignore the burn in my chest that reminds me of how long it has been since I smoked.

"Mind if I bum one off you?" A female voice gets my attention.

Turning to see, a woman is walking closer. She's older than me, maybe ten years or more, but looks fantastic for any age. She's wearing a bright purple dress that fits her curves like a second skin and is wearing heels that not only let you know she's quite confident, but also lets you know exactly what she wants. I can bet money that she wears them to seduce men. I admit the woman is a knock-out.

Leaving the cigarette between my lips, I reach into my pocket to retrieve the pack, but she takes the one from my mouth and brings to her lips. I watch, fascinated, as she takes it between her fingers and blows the smoke to the side of my face. "Thanks," she says, almost purring. "Brrrr!" She shivers. "Do you mind if I borrow your jacket until we're done here?"

"Done? I didn't know we'd started." My eyes are focused on hers, my old confidence kicking in—a hunter and its prey. The only difference between the cliché and my life is the prey doesn't usually invite you to attack, but my prey does. I've always had a hard time saying no, especially to a pretty lady in need of a non-committal good time.

I take my jacket off and place it around her shoulders as she takes another drag. She brings the cigarette back to my mouth, her fingertip brushing against my bottom lip. Something tells me if I take her up on this one seemingly innocent gesture that it might lead to bigger offers and I can't allow myself to be tempted. Not anymore. I respond by saying, "I'm done, are you ready to go back inside?"

"Done?" She asks, "I thought we were just getting started?"

"I need to get back."

"I'll come with you."

Chills shiver down my spine as she tosses the cigarette onto the street and slips her arm around mine, though I hadn't presented it to her. I need to get my jacket back from her anyway and it would be rude to demand it back on the street.

When we enter the reception area of the ball, the event photographer stops us, and quickly snaps a picture.

She removes her arm from mine, and I ask for my jacket back by eyeing it. "I might, um, need that back."

"I was hoping you'd want it back in the morning, maybe say after a night at my place?"

In the past, my body would have definitely reacted, but my brain knows that's wrong, knowing I'll lose Mallory if my body wins this battle.

Just the thought of her name brings her face into focus in my mind—Mallory smiling, Mallory laughing, Mallory coming undone beneath me.

"My apologies, but I'll have to pass, though I appreciate the offer." I don't appreciate it. She doesn't hesitate handing my jacket back to me either. She doesn't even seem upset by the rejection, but I still feel awkward.

I pull my jacket back on and Kate appears with her perfect timing. "I've been looking for you, baby bro."

We both look at the lady from outside, and Kate gives the complete head to toe onceover before saying, "Mother wants a family photo taken."

Relieved by the excuse to leave, I add sarcastically, "Oh, yes, we must get a family photo." I look back to the lady in purple, and politely make my exit. "You'll excuse me..." It should be a question, but I don't want that option out there.

"Stop by and see me before you leave. I'd love to formally introduce myself, Mr. Ashford, maybe for some future business."

I smile and nod politely, tucking my hands in my pockets and follow Kate across the room.

We make it to the hall that leads to the restrooms before she turns on her heel and asks, "What the fuck was that and how does she know who you are?"

I roll my eyes and take her by the arm. "It was nothing. And I have no idea how she knew my name, but she needed a cigarette and then got—"

"That *cougar* was looking for more than a cigarette, Evan. That photo is gonna hit the Met's website before this party is even over." She stands on her tiptoes to look for my parents. When she spots them, she says, "Listen, you don't have to fall into the old trappings of this place. Do what you have to do for the business, but don't lose focus of your heart either."

I shake my head in understanding. *Stay focused. Stay focused. Stay focused.* I've been so wound up the last two weeks that I really need to relieve some stress when I get back to the apartment, but I usually relieve stress with sex. Before my sexcam time with Mallory, I hadn't masturbated in a long time, maybe even years. I hadn't had a need to, but I'm thinking I'm going to become very friendly with my right hand again.

Looking down at my phone, I want so badly to press the button that brings me my salvation, but I shouldn't. Kate is right. Mallory needs to enjoy her time in college and a night out with her friends.

I tuck my phone back into my pocket and join my sister and parents across the room, posing for the fake happy family photos we're so used to imitating.

MALLORY

"You want to grab some coffee?" Ryan asks, pointing at the all-night coffee shop we're currently standing in front of. "You can tell me all about your boyfriend. Trust me. I only want to be your friend, Mallory."

My dad always says, 'Never trust anyone who says trust me.' But like many things in life, sometimes you have to go off instinct. I think Ryan is being genuine and I'm willing to trust him because I don't want to be one of those cynical girls who thinks every guy is only trying to have sex with them. He's asking about Evan, for God's sake. "All right."

Inside the cozy shop, I order a decaf caramel latte and he orders coffee, black. I note another thing he has in common with Evan. After getting our mugs, we find two leather chairs in the corner window and settle into them.

We start with the usual talk about our majors and why he transferred his senior year. Ryan took two semester course loads this past summer. That's where he met Will, and has a very full year scheduled to make up for lost credits. By transferring now, he'll get preferential treatment when he applies for the Masters program here. He's very driven, which is something I admire in a person.

I tell him about growing up in Colorado and he asks me how I ended up in Hawaii this past summer. This conversation leads to Sunny, ending up on Evan. Through another cup of coffee, I tell Ryan about Evan working in New York for his family and how he's coming here for the spring semester. His face doesn't seem to give way to anything but sincerity. This relieves me because I've really enjoyed chatting with him. It's been easy, which is something that seems opposite of what I've been through lately.

He leans toward me, resting his forearms on his thighs, and asks, "So, it's pretty serious with this surfer?"

"Yes, and he's more than just a surfer."

He sits back, crossing his ankle over his other knee. "That's cool. I was in a serious relationship that ended last spring."

"What happened?"

"The standard 'It's complicated' applies here, but simplified. She had her own thing going on and I was moving here. It seemed like the best thing to do especially with the distance between us."

This makes me think of me and Evan. *How can it not?* I look down at my cup and swirl the coffee aimlessly around wondering how *the ball* is going. I've never been to a ball and I wonder if we have differences that might be more insurmountable than initially thought.

"You know, I didn't mean to imply anything about your relationship," Ryan says. "I'm sure you and Evan will make it. I was telling you what happened to me, nothing more."

"Oh, I know. Evan and I are solid," I say, backing what I want to believe is true.

Ryan stands, offering me his hand and help up from the well worn leather chair. "We should probably get going. Believe it or not, I have to work on a paper tonight."

Now this surprises me. "You're going to do homework after drinking?"

"I only had one beer and that was hours ago. It's just past midnight. Still early."

"Time flew." I accept his assistance and take him by the hand.

"Because we were having fun." He pulls me up, putting us face to face, our bodies close.

His hand still holds mine. Finally, something tangible that isn't similar to Evan—no intensity, or tingles, no feeling, but friendship. Evan and I share a spark that can't be replicated.

I drop his hand and say, "Yeah, I guess we did." I cradle my arms across my chest as a breeze blows down the street.

"I'll walk you home...*for safety and all*," he says, chuckling.

We talk about his paper and a little about the project due for our class.

Outside my apartment, I turn to face him, and say, "This is me." I pause, recognizing this situation as eerily close to the end of a first date. Guilt washes over me as I unlock my door, ready for the awkwardness to be over. "Thanks. I had a good time. Good luck with that paper and I'll see you on Monday." I hurry inside.

I'm about to close the door when I hear him say, "Goodnight, Mal—" I shut the door and stand on my tiptoes to peek out the peephole. His face is scrunched in confusion, but then he smiles directly at me, giving me a little wave before walking away.

The embarrassment would normally send me sliding down the door into a pool of humiliation for being busted peeking, but I'm on a mission, so after locking the door, I rush to my room. I fire up my laptop and change into my night clothes. As soon as the programs load, I press the chat icon to see if Evan's online, but he's not. *Should I call him?* It's late there, almost three in the morning. *What if he's sleeping?* I don't want to wake him. I huff and rest my head in my hands and stare at the blank text screen.

I really want to talk or see him, to hear how his night was, and to tell him about mine. I make an on the spot decision—a decision that I shouldn't follow through with and that will probably haunt me the rest of the semester. I do something I have never done to someone I know. I do an online search for Evan Ashford. Seemed innocent enough when I came up with the idea, but when page after page of results appear on the screen about him and his family, I can't help feeling like I've opened Pandora's Box.

Despite my regrets, the top link catches my immediate attention. I click on the image and there's a picture of Evan from tonight in his tuxedo with some woman draped on his arm like she belongs there. My heart sinks as I stare at the photo, analyzing every detail of it—the way she's wearing his tux jacket and how her arm is interlaced with his. Her head is angled toward him and the look in her eyes is like they just shared something private.

I can use the anger, the hurt, and the pain that's invading my body to help protect my heart and attempt to be strong, but there is no logic to be found in the moment, so I cry instead.

Through my tears, I see his face staring back at mine, frozen on the screen. I can't read his expression and that makes me feel worse. And though I know I shouldn't, I call him anyway. My heart hurts and I miss him so much. This photo sends me over the edge. I need to hear his voice and right now have lost all respect for the late hour.

Taking my phone in hand, I push his number, waiting for him to answer while I slip under my covers, burrowing in for protection from the outside world.

"Hi, baby," he whispers.

I attempt to stop the tears, but fail. "Evan, I miss you so fucking much."

"What's wrong?" His voice is louder this time and he sounds worried.

"So much is wrong. I don't know if I'm strong enough—"

"Strong enough for what, Mallory? You're freaking me out."

"I need to be with you. I need you here."

I hear his breath intake, loud and deep. "I want to be with you, too."

"This isn't a *want* situation, babe. It's a need. This is all wrong. Everything is wrong without you. I thought being back to my routine here in Colorado would make things easier, but when I was talking to Ryan, he said him and his girlfriend broke up because—"

"*Who's Ryan?*" He asks as a question, but I could swear it more of an exclamation.

"Who was the slut on your arm tonight?" *Shit! That didn't come out right.*

Silence.

Silence.

"Mallory, I think we should talk in the morning."

Completely freaked out by that last comment, I snap, "No, that's bullshit! We should talk about this now. I have nothing to hide. Ryan is a classmate and a friend. I spent *my* night talking about you. How'd you spend your night, Evan?"

His tone is louder and abrupt. "I spent *my* night being miserable and missing the fuck out of you, so where does that get us?" He pauses, but then says, "She was some woman who bummed a cigarette off me and was cold, so I loaned her my jacket. Listen, I didn't do anything wrong. I didn't even get her name. I could care less about her. I was being polite and that's when the photographer took a picture. She's no one, Mallory." I can't hide the fact that I'm still sniffling from crying, but I attempt to anyway, wanting us to be together and all better, wanting the ache in my heart to ease up. "Baby, let's not do this. It's been two weeks and it already feels like years since I've been with you. I want this to work more than you know."

I saw that picture and it took me by surprise, but hearing

him say all that makes me happy, but also scares me equally. "I do, too. I keep thinking I trust you, but I see some random picture of you and I fall apart. I feel helpless not knowing what's going on or—"

He surprisingly demands, "Get online."

I moan, worn out and cozy. "I'm in bed. Let's just—"

"Turn the laptop on and get the fuck online, Mallory!"

Shocked by how he's speaking to me, I crawl like a zombie out of bed and bring up the video program. I sit at the desk and call him. As soon as I see his face, I smile, just a little, but I do. I try to be annoyed with how he's talking to me, but I can't because I'm too happy to finally see him. He's struggling to contain his own smile when he sees me too.

He leans forward, smile gone as he moves closer to the camera, and asks, "You're feeling helpless, what does that mean for us? Do you still want to be with me?"

"Of course, I want to be with you. When I said I feel helpless, I don't mean I don't want to be with you. I meant that sometimes I have to give into the bad emotions that being separated from you brings." I sit up straighter as I explain, "I want you more than anything, Evan. I love you with all my heart. I don't think I could leave you anyway. Hell, I couldn't even leave you this past summer when everything was turned upside down."

"Mallory, *slooow down*. I believe you. I just needed to see your face when you said it." His fingers run across the screen, stroking it. "Please don't cry. I wish as much as you do that we could be together, and we will. I promise."

Seeing him on the screen changes everything, his eyes reflecting the same emotions I'm feeling. "Evan, I didn't think you'd done anything with that woman. It just hurt to see a photo like that when I wasn't expecting it. You were in your element in that tux with all those fancy people in the background. Made me feel insecure and small town in comparison. We live in such different worlds and I can't promise you balls and limos. I don't even own a fancy dress and yet you probably own your tux."

"It's custom made," he says, laughing softly, which lightens the mood.

I laugh. "Of course, it is. I wouldn't expect anything less." I roll my eyes, teasing him.

"What you don't seem to understand is that I don't need all this. It's not what I want. I want you and I don't know, whatever you want, baby, I want that too." He adjusts in his seat and then suggests, "I've got an idea. We both need to go to bed. Go climb in."

"But—"

"I think we should fall asleep together sometimes. We can leave the camera on. If you wake up, you'll know that I'm still here with you. In the morning, when you wake up, just turn it off."

His sweet idea makes me smile and my heart swoon. "Okay," I answer, and extend the sleep timer on my computer before climbing back into bed. I pull the covers up to my chin, but lift my head up to watch him slide into his own bed. "Evan?"

"Yeah?"

"Can we do this more often? Maybe even *most days*?"

"Even if I only get you for a minute, I need you more than you know." I watch him drop his head onto his pillow, so I rest mine. "I love you. Sweet dreams."

"I love you, too. Sweet dreams, baby."

I look up every once in a while and see his body lying there calmly and it reminds me of the times I would watch him sleep in Hawaii. I feel whole, feeling one with him again and fall asleep.

27

MALLORY

This first full weekend back in Boulder, Sarah and I finish organizing our apartment. She ends up staying at Josh's both nights though, leaving me to enjoy our place alone. With all the me time I've been having, I find myself reaching for a cigarette to comfort, but because of the woman at the ball, Evan has decided to quit and I agree to give up the bad habit as well. I have no idea how the ball or the lady in purple relates to quitting smoking, but I'll take it. We both need to get healthier.

The next week and a half flies by with classes, school commitments, and study groups. I have my first exams in three of my classes and start preparing for my other two tests on the upcoming Monday.

"Evan and I are better. It's been a month and I think we've finally hit our stride. We make the time for each other and chat online and call every day," I tell Sarah casually over lunch one day. I never doubted that I was committed to him, but for all we've been through, I truly trust him. Even when our schedules are crazy, I know he loves me and I'm determined to live in that happy place.

I'll be twenty-three this coming Friday. Sarah tells me there's a party over at one of the frat houses that she thinks will be fun. I only agree to go because it seems like everyone I know is also going. Not my ideal way to spend my birthday, but it will have to do since I can't be with Evan.

He also told me that he's sending me a surprise and to be on the lookout for it. Although I beg to know what it is... a lot, he doesn't budge. I give up trying to figure it out and wait in excited anticipation all week.

Thursday turns into Friday. At midnight on the dot—my laptop pings and my phone buzzes. I run to check online first and see Evan's smiling face looking back at me. "Happy birthday, Mallory."

"Thank you."

I look down at my phone and check a text message. It's from my parents.

HAPPY BIRTHDAY. Can't wait to see you this weekend. Love you. Mom & Dad

I SMILE because of the message.

"I wanted to let you know I'm gonna be working late this evening, but I promise we'll see each other. I'm not sure when, so make sure to be online tonight if you can."

I kiss the screen because I miss him and because I want to. He chuckles then kisses the screen back.

"You kissed the monitor for me. You're too sweet, spoiling me rotten on my birthday," I playfully joke.

"I'd rather be kissing your lips, but I guess a cold, unfeeling monitor will have to do for now."

I laugh. "But only for now. I expect the real deal sooner rather than later. Just sayin', sexy. So what's this business about a surprise?"

"You surviving the unknown? You're not good with surprises."

"I'm good when they're from you," I say, waggling my eyebrows.

"Do you have a birthday wish, my love?" he asks, giving me his full attention.

"I have everything I could ever want. My only wish would be to spend my birthday with you and that can't happen so, I have no wish this year." I laugh at how sad that sounds. "Geez, depressing enough?"

He smiles, and says, "Wish away, babycakes, but you know what they say? Be careful what you wish for because you just might get it."

"*In that case.*" I close my eyes, cross my fingers, and wish that Evan could hold me in his arms for my birthday.

"You're so fucking cute. I should let you go though. I know you have early classes. Happy birthday again, sexy girl."

"Thank you for... for everything, babe."

I climb into bed, pulling the covers up to my neck. It doesn't take long to fall asleep with no worries weighing me down.

SARAH and I walk into our English class and pick seats near the upper section aisle. Will starts working his way toward us, but he diverts and sits down by two giggling girls. A few minutes into class, Ryan rushes into the room, looks around for a seat, dashes up the stairs, and smiles at me as he passes.

I feel someone tap me on the shoulder and turn to see a pretty yellow rose. Following it from bloom to stem to the hand holding it and further up, I see Ryan sitting behind me.

When I arch an eyebrow up at him, he leans closer and whispers, "It's yellow. Yellow means friendship."

I laugh because that is true. "Thank you." I take the rose and turn back to listen to the professor.

Sarah whispers, "I used to think you had an admirer in Ryan. Now, I know you do."

"It's yellow," I whisper, justifying.

"Keep telling yourself that, Wray. Keep telling yourself that," she teases.

I stare at the rose most of the class questioning once again if he's playing me or if he really is being up front with me.

When we leave class, I spy Ryan behind us, quietly apart from our group, but biding his time in our shadow.

Sarah heads off to her next class and I start walking across campus. I know Ryan's still behind me. "You know, you're going to get people gossiping if you keep doing such nice things for your friends," I say loud enough so he can hear while holding up the rose to back my words.

"Let them gossip," he says, his voice closer than I expected, but he's still trailing behind me.

"What if I'm not comfortable with these kinds of gestures?" I ask without looking and keep walking.

"You shouldn't be skeptical of nice gestures. You obviously don't have enough nice people in your life."

I stop, feeling defensive. "My boyfriend does a lot of nice things for me."

"Happy birthday, Mallory," he says confidently, ignoring my last statement. "Have you had a good day?"

Walking over to the grass, I sit down, enjoying the sunshine and open my backpack. Just as I suspected he would, he sits down next to me, lounging back on the grass.

"It's been good and had a great start at midnight."

"Have you received lots of gifts and a cake? Everyone deserves a cake on their birthday," he states matter of fact.

"Sarah gave me a scarf and glove set this morning—"

"And the boyfriend? What'd the boyfriend send you?"

"He's sending me a surprise. I just haven't received it yet. I've been in classes all morning."

"What if nothing shows—"

"Stop!" I give him a pointed look. "I don't know what you're trying to gain by upsetting me, but stop."

"Are you upset about something?"

"No, uh, well, yeah, no. Listen, Evan doesn't have to give me anything at all and I'd be happy because I have him."

"You *have* him?"

"You know what I mean? Anyway, he gave me a laptop as an early present in August. That was too generous, so I don't expect anything. But if there's one thing I can rely on, it's Evan. So if he says I'm getting a surprise today then I'll get one. It's as simple as that."

"*Ahhh*, I see," he says, all knowing.

I shove my book back into my bag, and stand up, looking back only once before I leave. "Ryan, thank you for the rose. It was very... unnecessary."

"Gifts aren't about necessity."

"I've got to go," I say before walking away, annoyed, and leaving him there in the grass.

Walking into the cafeteria, the smell instantly reminds me why I don't eat in here and haven't in years. I walk to the line and grab a small salad. After purchasing it, I sit at a corner table and pull out my phone.

I call Evan, my calls go straight to voicemail, but hearing his voice on his recorded message makes me feel better. I remember he said he has a long day ahead of him, so I leave a message and try not stress.

Will sits down next to me. Reflexively, I turn my back to him.

"Mallory, can we please stop playing this game. I'm sorry. I'm sorry I cheated on you. I'm sorry for calling you names and I'm sorry for hurting you. Honestly, I didn't know you liked me that much."

I spin on my chair, hitting him with my best glare. "We dated long enough to be called a couple and I thought couples talked to each other. I expected that you would talk to me if you were unhappy with something, but you didn't. You went off and had sex with someone else then blamed me for it."

"I wanted a little sexual adventure and you wanted marriage—"

"Bullshit! I didn't want marriage. *Not then anyway*. I'll admit I thought you broke my heart, but I've learned I wasn't in love with you. I only thought I was. You aren't the love of my life, Will. So it's easy to put our relationship in perspective now." All this anger toward him feels like wasted energy, remembering that Will cheating on me technically led me to Evan. I stand up, tossing my bag onto my back. "Actually, I'd like to thank you."

"What? *Why?*" His voice raises an awkward octave higher.

"Because if you hadn't cheated on me, treating me like you did, I wouldn't have gone to Hawaii and I wouldn't have met the person I *am* going to marry. So, I'd like to say thank you, Will," I say this, meaning every word. "We might even have to invite you to the wedding now." I laugh and leave him dumbstruck at the table and finish my school day with a smile on my face, forgiveness inside, and love in my heart.

JUST BEFORE SEVEN THAT EVENING, Sarah barges into my bedroom as I'm straightening my hair. She turns down my birthday playlist she created for the occasion and stands there grinning at me. Pulling a robe on over my bra and panties, I wait for her to say whatever she came in here to say because I can tell she has something on her mind.

She finally breaks into a squeal, then says, "You've got to come into the living and see this right now, Mallory!"

Picking the iron back up, I reply, "I'm almost done. Let me finish my hair."

She takes the straightening iron from my hand, sets it down, and says, "Now!" Grabbing my hand, she starts pulling me through my bedroom door into the living room, but stops to ask, "Are you wearing that?"

"I haven't figured out what I'm wearing to the party yet. I was gonna try on a few things and let you choose. Anyway, what do you care, if this is such an emergency?"

"Fine. Don't say I didn't warn you."

"Warn me?" The warning makes me nervous. I round the corner into the living room and see a delivery guy with a huge bouquet of tropical flowers—flowers I remember seeing in Hawaii. The bouquet is so big it actually takes my breath away.

It's so huge it completely hides the delivery guy until he lowers the flowers, and says, "Happy birthday, baby."

To be continued in book 3 of the Playboy in Paradise Series,
Loving the Playboy.
For a preview, keep reading.

LOVING THE PLAYBOY

I don't know what I expected. Maybe I thought this would make sense to her as it would to anyone else in the world... anyone with a heart. But I forgot, Evan's mother doesn't have a heart.

"Oh," she says, her tone remains emotionless. "I didn't know it was your birthday. I would normally send my best wishes, but alas, this is not a social call, so we won't waste time with petty occurrences in your life." I stay silent, forgetting that I have the ability to hang up as she continues her verbal assault. "I'm going to be frank with you, Mallory. I want my son living in New York. He can finish his degree here and continue in the family business. Three generations have worked hard to make Ashford Holdings the success it is, and Evan will one day lead it to greater success." She sighs as if she's bored with this conversation. But her words are stern, and I can tell she means every one of them. "With that success, Evan should marry an equal worthy of the Ashford name. Wray is sweet, but pedestrian. It's entirely unnecessary for him to attach himself to someone that can't uphold our family ideals. You live in a different world with different traditions and values. Your Mile High City charms won't work here. I don't know what he was thinking back in Hawaii, but he's returned to New York, a place where Evan Theodore Monroe Ashford is revered and respected. He's a catch not only amongst the best families in Manhattan, but across Europe as well. If you care for him at all, you will cut ties with him and let him live up to his potential. Don't ruin his destiny. He can own this city if he chooses. He's *that* talented."

"Mrs. Ashford—"

"This isn't a discussion or a request, Miss Wray."

Loving the Playboy is now available.

PORTUGUESE TRANSLATIONS

Studies show that the Pine Industries is a safe investment and a great opportunity to establish presence in the American market. The CFO of the group is Brazilian and has strong ties with the community and latin definitely adds value for potential future opportunities. We have the means to not only meet the financial goals of the company, as well as take it to the next level of growth. I really hope you will consider these factors in decision making.

We will be doing the transfer of 6.7 million in the morning to start the ball rolling.

Very good and thanks again for this opportunity. On behalf of our entire staff, welcome to Ashford Holdings.

ALSO BY S.L. SCOTT

To keep up to date with her writing and more, visit her website:
www.slscottauthor.com

To receive the Scott Scoop about all of her publishing adventures, free books, giveaways, steals and more, sign up here: http://bit.ly/2TheScoop

Join S.L.'s Facebook group here: S.L. Scott Books

Audiobooks on Audible - CLICK HERE

Playboy in Paradise Series

Falling for the Playboy

Redeeming the Playboy

Loving the Playboy

Playboy in Paradise Box Set

The Crow Brothers (Stand-Alones)

Spark

Tulsa

Rivers

Ridge

The Crow Brothers Box Set

Hard to Resist Series (Stand-Alones)

The Resistance

The Reckoning

The Redemption

The Revolution

The Rebellion

The Revelation

The Everest Brothers (Stand-Alones)

Everest - Ethan Everest

Bad Reputation - Hutton Everest

Force of Nature - Bennett Everest

The Everest Brothers Box Set

The Kingwood Series

SAVAGE

SAVIOR

SACRED

SOLACE - Stand-Alone

The Kingwood Series Box Set

Talk to Me Duet (Stand-Alones)

Sweet Talk

Dirty Talk

From the Inside Out Series

Scorned

Jealousy

Dylan

Austin

From the Inside Out Compilation

Stand-Alone Books

Missing Grace

Until I Met You

Drunk on Love

Naturally, Charlie

A Prior Engagement

Lost in Translation

Sleeping with Mr. Sexy

Morning Glory

ABOUT THE AUTHOR

To keep up to date with her writing and more, her website is www.slscottauthor.com to receive her newsletter with all of her publishing adventures and giveaways, sign up for her newsletter: http://bit.ly/2TheScoop

Instagram: S.L.Scott

To receive a free book now, TEXT "slscott" to 77948

For more information, please visit
www.slscottauthor.com

www.ingramcontent.com/pod-product-compliance
Lightning Source LLC
Chambersburg PA
CBHW020301200626
46814CB00006BA/2025